Love, Anatomy and Coconut Chutney

PRIYA MARY JACOB
& SAJNA V M KUTTY

Srishti
PUBLISHERS & DISTRIBUTORS

Srishti Publishers & Distributors
A unit of AJR Publishing LLP
212A, Peacock Lane
Shahpur Jat, New Delhi – 110 049

editorial@srishtipublishers.com

First Published by Srishti Publishers & Distributors in 2026

10 9 8 7 6 5 4 3 2 1

Printed and bound in India.

For Appachen
(Mr. K. U. Eipe)
who gave me my love of reading.
–Priya Mary Jacob

For Uncle Thomas, who shone the light on the path I was to take, and for Nihal, the brightest light in my life.
–Sajna V M Kutty

ACKNOWLEDGMENTS

Our batchmates from the 40th and 41st batches of Calicut Medical College have been an integral part of this journey; many of the stories in this book are woven from our shared experiences. We would especially like to thank Thomas, Bindiya, Gayathri, Sandhya, Sonia, George, Anoop from the 41st, the Pugilists 41st group; the Glam Girls 41st group; Tony, Anjana, Vandana, Sajith from the 40th; the Girls of 40th group, Jairam from 38th; Dalia and Padmaja from the 42nd; Swathi from 59th; Anagha from 61st; and Sreya from 57th.

We are grateful to our beta readers — Viz, Suma, Ivan Aaradey, Anees, Grishma, and Anand from Facebook, and Anisha, Anna, Chachu, Sachin, and Rahel from our families — for their thoughtful feedback. Our thanks also to Rajiv and Rebekah, from family, for their valuable suggestions on the book cover design. Rakhi, Priya's childhood friend, for helping us out with the book title.

We remember with gratitude, Priya's uncle, the late Mr. John Kurrien, for his guidance. Authors Joshua Mathew, Prof. Dr. MR Rajagopal, Prof. Vinaya Kumar and Rohini Rajagopal for their advice. Anuradha Menon and Mary Joseph for editing our drafts at different stages.

We are deeply grateful to Mr. Anish Chandy of Labyrinth Literary Agency for agreeing to represent two debut writers, and to Mr. Arup Bose and the team at Srishti Publishers for being an absolute joy to work with.

Most importantly, we thank our families, whose patience and support made this book possible.

GLOSSARY

This novel is about medical students in a fictional medical college in Kerala.

Trust us, you *will* need to refer to this page.

- *Aanungalodu kalichaal ingane irikkum:* (ah-noon-gah-loh-doo kah-litch-chaal in-gah-nay i-rik-koom)*:* This is what happens when you mess around with boys. (A judgemental phrase often used to shame girls for stepping outside traditional gender norms).
- *BuJi* (boo-jee): Intellectual; short form of *buddhi jeevi*
- *Chakkarae* (chah-kah-ray): Sweetheart/Darling
- *Chammanthi podi* (chum-man-thee po-dee): Dry chutney powder
- *Chumma* (choom-ma): Simply
- *Eshoye* (ay-sho-yay): Oh Jesus!
- *Gundu* (goon-doo): Cooked-up story
- *Ishta (ish-tah):* Friend/Yaar
- *Janavirudha nyayangal* (ja-na-vi-roo-dha nya-yan-gal): Policies that are against public interests
- *Kafir* (ka-fir): A Muslim who does not believe in God as per Islam or rejects the tenets of Islam
- *Kittiya kitti, poya poyi (KKPP)* (kit-tee-ya kit-tee, poi-ya poi): If you're lucky, you win, or you could lose it all
- *Kozhi*: (koh-rhi-with the Malayalam 'zh' sound, not found in English): Literally means chicken. In colloquial usage, it refers to a man who is lecherous and ogles women. Often used mockingly in campus slang. (e.g., 'avan oru *kozhi* aanu' – 'he's such a creep').
- *Kuli scene* (koo-lee): A term for a bathing scene watched by a voyeur.
- *Kundi kandein* (koon-dee kan-dayn): 'I saw the butt' (A slip of the tongue in Malayalam can have disastrous consequences).
- *Line*: Boyfriend/Girlfriend
- *Maakri* (maa-kree): Frog

- *Makku/Mandoos* (muck-koo / man-doos): Ignoramus/Fool
- *Mukku! Mukku!* (mook-koo!): Push! Push!
- *Ninte ammayide mol aano?* (nin-tay am-my-i-day mole aa-no): 'Is she your aunt's daughter?' (Usually asked when you show undue interest in someone unrelated.)
- *Njarambu rogi* (nja-ram-boo ro-gee): Pervert (used in common parlance; context-specific)
- *Padipist* (pud-ee-pist): An extremely studious person
- *Paavam* (paa-vum): You poor helpless thing
- *Poda!* (poda): (rhymes with *soda*, but with a retroflex 'd') 'Get lost!' – usually said to a boy or man. It's informal and often used playfully among friends, though the tone can make it sound rude or dismissive.
- *Thendi* (then-dee): Asshole (context-specific); literally means beggar
- *Thendikal* (then-dee-kal): Plural of *thendi*

1. Zara, 2016

Heathrow Airport
8th March, 2016

There was a time when I thought he genuinely didn't give a damn. Not about people.
Certainly not about women.
And definitely not about some barely-remembered med school batchmates with names he probably mispronounced then, and forgot entirely now.

So, when his name popped up on my Facebook feed, with a flurry of notifications, I did what any self-respecting woman would do.

I scrolled.

Hovered over the 'Add Friend' button like it was a detonator.

Because nostalgia is seductive, but it's also a liar.

And the past – especially the med-school variety – has a way of crawling back like an old crush with a God complex: smug, inconvenient, and convinced it still matters.

I flipped out my phone and read the post, trying to make sense of it.

On this International Women's Day, I cannot help but think of all my female batchmates and juniors at Calicut Institute of Medicine who have turned out to be accomplished doctors and wonderful human beings despite the lowly way in which they were treated by some of their male counterparts, yours truly included. I deeply regret being among those who delighted in name-calling, body shaming, and casting aspersions on any girl who dared to have a fallout with a guy, all with the intention of showing girls their proper place. But I consider myself lucky that good sense finally prevailed upon me, unlike several others who I am sure will show up in the comments section to put me in my proper place!

I realized a while ago that a post like this was inevitable if I wanted to make peace, not only with those I tormented but also with myself. But for many years, I was a coward. It's only now, close to my forties, that I've found the courage to do the right thing.

I know I cannot take back all I have said or repair the damage I have done; I can only ask you all to accept this as my personal apology for past misdeeds born out of the ignorance and arrogance of an entitled young man.'

– Vaibhav Reghuthaman

I stared at the screen.

Was this some kind of ploy to boost his female follower count? Classic.

Social media was the new opiate – cheap, addictive, and dressed up as a connection.

People would post anything for a hit of digital validation.

A form of virtue signalling. There was a word for it – something annoyingly academic.

I started to Google it, but the word strutted in uninvited before the page even loaded.

Peacocking.

The evolutionary art of being louder, flashier, needier than the next guy – all in the hope of being seen, remembered, and, if the algorithm was kind, adored.

The comments had started trickling in – applause, appreciation, surprise, confusion.

I scrolled through, looking for names.

Had Mohini weighed in yet? Daisy?

Nothing.

Mohini would have something to say. She never spared the punches.

It was only just past eight in the morning in India. Too early for most people to be online. A smattering of strangers and sycophants, and that one girl from the junior batch who'd always been a little *too* supportive.

Mohini's call, in fact, was the reason I was on this flight back home. Vivian had called first, demanding I attend my nephew's baptism. I'd made excuse after excuse, dreading the onslaught of nosy relatives just waiting to pounce on me for the crime of staying unmarried – and surviving it.

But then she called. And everything changed. I booked my ticket on impulse. Mapped out a route that included short visits to old friends before heading home. And now here I was, boarding pass in hand, already scanning WhatsApp. The LIKA group (Liverpool Keralites Association) had gone quiet lately, barring the occasional forward. But I scrolled back to last September, to the flurry of photos and videos from our Onam celebrations at the Fernsby Leisure Centre. I opened the same video again – for the umpteenth time – froze the frame, and zoomed in on the dancers performing on stage.

Could it really be her?

Maybe Mohini was mistaken. Maybe this would all turn out to be a wild goose chase.

A shuffle of feet snapped me out of the loop. Passengers around me were standing, reaching for their bags. I hoisted my backpack and walked towards the gate.

Wild goose chase or not, I was on the damn flight.

2. Sheetal, 2016

9th March 2016,
New Delhi

I knew she'd come.

Even if we hadn't spoken in years.

Zara always had a way of showing up when it mattered.

The doorbell rang just as I was adjusting the knot of my headscarf. I opened the door, and there she was – Zara Ann Mathew. A little older, a little thinner, but still unmistakably Zara. Short hair now. She looked like she'd just walked out of a travel documentary. Sun-kissed, linen-clad, effortlessly worldly.

But when our eyes met, hers welled up.

"I'm so glad you came," I said, pulling her into a hug. I felt the tremble in her body. And something inside me, tired, worn out, but still stubborn, clenched tight. I wouldn't let this illness reduce me to just a diagnosis in her eyes.

"Why didn't you tell me?" she asked, wiping her tears.

I gave a shrug that I hoped came off stronger than I felt. "It's not exactly news I enjoy broadcasting. And anyway, Daisy's still the BBC of our batch, isn't she?"

Zara gave a choked laugh. "True."

I raised a hand before she could spiral into more emotion. "No more talk about the C-word. I'm sick of people tiptoeing around me like I'm already dead." I tilted my head, forcing a smile. "Now tell me about *you*. Is there any place on earth you haven't been to? And look at you! The girl with the plait and maroon bindi I roomed with – what happened to her?"

Before she could respond, lunch was announced. Thank God. I wasn't sure how much more of that intensity I could handle.

We ate dal, jeera rice, and a simple sabzi – stuff I could stomach on my better days. I let her do most of the talking. It was easier that way. Safer.

After lunch, I showed her around the house. It wasn't big or flashy, but it was mine. Every corner held something I'd chosen, something I'd created. My refuge. My rebellion.

Zara paused in the hallway, drawn to a cluster of canvases hung with deliberate asymmetry. Her gaze settled on one – soft blues and greys, a woman walking away from a door that had just swung shut behind her. The latch still mid-fall, the figure mid-step. You couldn't tell if she was relieved or devastated.

"I started painting again," I said quietly. "Used to love it in school. Stopped when college took over. But now, on the bad days – when chemo feels like it's burrowing into my bones – it's the one thing that helps."

She moved closer, scanning the other canvases. More doors. Some ajar, some sealed tight. One with claw marks near the frame. Another with light leaking through the crack at the bottom.

She didn't say anything for a long moment.

I could feel her reading them – not just with her eyes, but with some deeper intuition.

"You've got a thing for closed doors," she finally murmured.

I shrugged. "Maybe. Maybe I'm just trying to figure out which ones I walked away from. And which ones were slammed in my face?"

She looked at me then – in a way a mirror looks back at its reflection, like she was seeing more than I intended her to.

More than I was ready to admit.

We sat in the drawing room after that, drifting into batchmate gossip.

"You saw Vaibhav's Facebook post, right?" I asked.

She nodded. "I'm hardly on Facebook," she said, "but that one… hard to miss."

"Brave of him, don't you think?"

Zara shrugged. "Maybe. Knowing him, sincerity wasn't exactly his strong point."

I looked straight at her. "People change. I have. But I don't think I could ever make a public apology like that."

Her eyes didn't waver. "Is that why you never joined the batch WhatsApp group?"

Partly. Mostly. Not just that. But I nodded. "Some wounds don't heal with time, Zara. Sometimes healing needs names. And real apologies. In person."

She looked away. "I haven't spoken to him in years."

"What about the others? Daisy? Mala? Kenza?"

"I'm with Daisy for a bit. Planning to meet Mala. And guess what – Kenza just cracked the entrance exam. Post grad at 37."

That made me smile. "She was always razor-sharp. Remember how she handled dissection in the first year?"

We both laughed.

"Daisy emailed me," I added. "Said she's writing some memoir."

"Ya, she's being secretive. Only a few guys sent stuff – Madhu Mohan, Luqman… and Sunny."

I stiffened. "Sunny?"

"She said he wrote something about research during undergrad. Apparently, he's in the UK now."

I glanced at the photo on the wall. My family. My carefully arranged, fiercely protected, often dysfunctional family. My husband, our boy, our girls. We looked so complete in that frame. And for a while, maybe we were.

"He's in Blackburn," Zara said, noticing the photo. "I bumped into him at a conference once. He was with his wife, a paediatrician."

"Oh." I kept my voice even.

"And no word on Nayana?" she asked.

I shook my head.

The silence between us thickened.

"I miss everyone," I said finally. "Whenever there's talk of a reunion, I tell myself I'll go. But I never do. I still carry too much shame, Zara. I've got dues to pay, before I run out of time."

She looked stricken. I hated doing that to her. But I had to say it.

"It's strange," I added, my voice trembling, "how clear everything becomes at stage three."

We hugged at the gate. Longer than necessary. But maybe not long enough.

Just as she turned to call her cab, I called out. "Zara… I have a confession to make. Back in college, I lied. I was a scopegoat too."

She smiled. "I figured. Your paintings told me."

That night, I sat by the window in my bedroom, scrolling through Facebook. Vaibhav's post was trending. Some praised his honesty. Others tore into him.

I closed the app and looked around at my quiet home.

My son's cricket bat leaned against the shoe rack, worn smooth by use. My daughters' schoolbags stood like sentinels on either side of the hallway, still as shadows.

But in my mind, I was far away. Back in our hostel room. Walls covered in Salman Khan posters, some curling at the corners from the humidity. The scent of coconut hair oil and Maggi. The rhythmic clatter of table fans.

Our first fight had been about *Khamoshi*. We'd argued late into the night—did Salman Khan actually get Manisha Koirala pregnant during the *Baahon Ke Darmiyan* song?

It felt like such a monumental question at the time. Love seemed grand and uncomplicated. Betrayal was black-and-white. Two decades and too many scandals later, Salman was no longer anyone's poster boy. And those walls – those fragile, gossip-stained, confessional hostel walls – were long gone.

Now all I could see were doors.

Doors half-open, doors shutting quietly, doors that had never been fully closed but had never really opened either.

We used to think love was a doorway – something you simply walked through, hand in hand.

And that betrayal was the slam of wood and brass, loud and final.

We were wrong.

Sometimes, love closes slowly.

Sometimes, betrayal is just the soft click of a door you didn't notice had shut behind you.

3. 1st Year, 1996-97

"You're saying you never wanted to be a doctor?"

22nd October, 1996
Calicut

Dear Pappachen,
It seems like yesterday that I joined MBBS, and more than a month has already gone by! I've settled into hostel life, and frankly, the reality of it is a far cry from what I had imagined. The Ladies Hostel is old – like, creaky-stairs-and-haunted-vibes old. I share a room the size of your Kottayam storeroom, with three girls: Nayana Krishnakumar (who sleepwalks at night), Sheetal Tyagi (who, from the looks of it, has already memorized Grey's Anatomy), and Daisy Chacko (who owns a portable heater and shares scrumptious Maggi noodles in exchange for hot gossip). We had a fourth roommate, Mala Diwakaran, but she wisely fled to a paying guest setup in town before the walls started closing in.
Fun fact: no ceiling fans. Apparently, there were… incidents. (Yes, the hanging kind.) So, everyone has to buy their own table fan. The bathroom situation is… avant-garde. Some bathrooms have no doors, just a curtain flapping like it's auditioning for Phantom of the Opera. The toilets have doors, but the latches are ceremonial. You just have to trust that no one's in the mood to see you in the buff that day. And last week, when it rained, it rained inside.
College is exhausting. Lectures start at 8 a.m., followed by practical labs and Anatomy dissection up to 4 pm. On most days, we reach the hostel only after six, thanks to our seniors, who treat ragging like it's a family heirloom passed down lovingly through generations.
And like I've told you before, I'm still not sure if I made the right decision by pursuing medicine. But if you're happy, then so am I.

Oops, no more space in this inland, but I promise to write more next week, assuming the rats don't chew through my pen.
Your affectionate granddaughter,
Zara

At a quarter to eight, Zara and Sheetal, who had letters to post, set out from the Ladies Hostel for the college building, a short walk away. The early morning sun dappled the narrow tree-lined road and bounced off the window panes on the clock tower that rose from the terrace of the three-storeyed college building. They dropped their letters into the mailbox on the portico and made their way to the amphitheatre lecture hall on the ground floor. Zara refused to sit in the first row, so Sheetal reluctantly followed her to the back. No sooner had they sat down than Zara began to titter, pointing to some words inked into the desk:

SEMEN ANALYSIS OF THE DJANGOES:
Katta – 500 million sperms and counting.
Pambu – Partly motile sperms wandering aimlessly in the fallopian tubes.
Chandupottu – Motile ova confused with sperm.
Panchara – Only sugar, no sperms.

"What's so funny?" asked Sheetal, who was from Delhi and understood very little Malayalam.

"*Katta* means block or brick and is what you call someone who's muscular; *pambu* means snake and is slang for a boozer because, you know, they sway after getting drunk; *chandupottu* is a derogatory term for someone who is effeminate; and *panchara,* or sugar, refers to the sweet talk of a flirt," Zara rattled off.

Sheetal rubbed her glasses with a soft piece of cloth and sniffed disapprovingly. "Well, they certainly are eloquent, the foes of these …" she peered at the name, "these Djangoes, whoever they are."

"It's the name of an informal club in the Men's Hostel," Zara started to say and then trailed off, for at that moment one of the Djangoes was climbing up the steps towards where they sat.

"Hi Zara!" said Vaibhav Reghuthaman, "Just come outside with me for a minute, will you?"

She followed his long strides outside the lecture hall.

"Where are you taking me?"

"My friends from the hostel want to meet you."

"Which friends…" she stopped abruptly, seeing the three senior boys waiting in the portico.

Vaibhav greeted them with high-fives. "Hey guys, this is Zara, the friend I've told you about."

Zara swallowed nervously. Vaibhav was forever telling her tales about this trio, notorious for ragging and causing bedlam during college functions. They were 'chronics,' meaning they were several batches senior to the current one, but still in college, having repeatedly failed exams over the years.

The largest of the trio, a dark and fearsome giant called 'King-Kong' Kamaraj, was perched on a Kawasaki bike and picking his nicotine-stained teeth with a key. Leaning against the same bike was James, lanky and long-haired. The third was Charles, tall with saucer-shaped ears and a pleasant face. Zara remembered Pappachen saying that a certain Charles Varghese Palakunnu, a distant relation, was studying MBBS at Calicut. But this certainly wasn't the right time to ask him.

"She *is* Christian, isn't she?" James asked Vaibhav, who looked taken aback by the question, but nodded. "Okay, your work is over. Push off!"

"But, but you said…" Vaibhav stammered, looking confused.

"*Poda! Poda!*" King-Kong shooed Vaibhav back to the lecture hall, with Zara giving him murderous looks. She couldn't believe he had unwittingly led her straight into a ragging session!

"Relax, we only want to get acquainted with you," James drawled, "What's your name, sweetie?"

She held her head high in a show of bravado even though her insides were quaking.

"Zara Ann Mathew."

"You're in luck, sweetie – I'm Christian too! Don't you want to know my name?"

She didn't reply.

"Be a sport! I'll give you a clue – I'm named after one of the apostles of Christ." He turned to his buddies. "If she guesses correctly, I will consider it a sign from heaven." King-Kong looked up suspiciously at the sky.

"Well, guessed my name yet?"

In her most innocent voice, Zara said, "Judas?" Charles and King-Kong burst out laughing as James's mouth fell open.

"Well played, Zara," said Charles, wiping his eyes, "so tell us – why did you join MBBS?"

Desperate to be rid of them, Zara blurted out the first thing that popped into her head, "Because my parents told me there is a lot of scope in medicine."

The three of them broke into loud guffaws.

"So you're a scopegoat!"

"Why am I a scapegoat?"

"Not scapegoat, SCOPEgoat." Charles cleared his throat and recited in a sonorous voice: "And Aaron shall place lots upon the two he goats, one lot for the Lord and the other lot for Azazel, for absolute removal."

Zara wondered if he was unbalanced.

"Shut up with the Bible verses, man!" groaned James.

Ignoring him, Charles continued, "The concept of a scapegoat comes from Leviticus 16:8, where one marked goat is cast into the desert with the sins of the community. Now the scopegoat is a parallel to the scapegoat – it gets cast into the jungle with the *hopes* of the family. You see, many parents urge their kids to join MBBS because they believe there is a lot of scope in medicine. And guess what – they are absolutely right! There's the stetho-scope, the micro-scope, the colono-scope, the laryngo-scope, the broncho-scope …" he enumerated, holding up his fingers one by one.

Zara's ears grew hot with embarrassment.

"The poor scopegoat struggles through six years of undergraduation, followed by three years of postgraduation (and another three years of super specialization if he is masochistic), all the while convinced he is the Chosen One. In between, he gets married and struggles to keep his family afloat on a lousy student stipend. While the scopegoat's sibling who opted to study engineering has started earning a fat salary after a mere five years!

"When the scopegoat's career finally takes off in his late thirties, he realizes that his sibling has enjoyed his youth, travelled half the world and is financially secure enough to contemplate a retirement home at some hill station. The bottom line is," he concluded, "both the scapegoat and the scopegoat are royally screwed by the people around them!"

Charles opened his mouth to further expound on his philosophy, but just then the Vice-Principal came around the corner.

"Why aren't you in your classes?" he barked, giving them suspicious looks.

"Nothing, Sir, nothing!"

The trio took off instantly on King-Kong's bike, and Zara darted back to the lecture hall.

***

Sheetal sat cross-legged on her bed, cradling a voluminous textbook and trying to ignore the scratching noises coming from the desk near the window. At length, she looked up and asked, "Why don't you read Guyton with me instead of colouring alphabets like a five-year-old?"

"It's a poster for our door," Zara replied. "There, done!" She walked over to the open door and stuck the paper on it with cellotape.

"The Scopegoats? What does that even mean?" asked Sheetal, her brow furrowed.

There was a shuffle of feet in the corridor outside as Nayana and Daisy entered the room. Seeing the poster, Daisy groaned, "Oh God, Zara! Are you still thinking about that idiot chronic's drivel after all these days?"

"The poster's very pretty," Nayana said encouragingly, opening her high ponytail with a flick of her hand, "but is there such a word?"

"Course not!" snorted Daisy as she plopped her portly frame onto the bed, "They made it up. Don't tell anyone this, but rumour has it that when the boys of our batch came to join the hostel, they found their rooms empty. And this trio was in the hostel car parking area selling 'second-hand' furniture. Only much later did our boys realize that this furniture was what had originally been in their rooms, removed the night before they arrived!"

Nayana's face bore a mixture of amusement and horror. "Why didn't they complain to the Warden?"

"That's even more unbelievable," said Daisy, rolling her eyes, "The boys said they preferred losing their money rather than proclaiming that they had been royally fooled!"

Sheetal raised one hand in the air, her face flushed. "Excuse me, I seem to be the only one here who doesn't know what 'Scopegoats' means."

Zara slapped her forehead with her palm. "After class that day, you came back to the hostel while the three of us headed to the Coffee House and discussed the whole Scopegoats event. While returning, we got caught by some senior girls, and then by the Warden for being late… and by then I had totally forgotten about it. But I'll tell you now!"

She plonked down next to the disgruntled Sheetal. "So, although the name 'Scopegoats' sounds a bit fantastic, if you think about it, it's a perfect description of us and our situations," she concluded.

"You're saying you never wanted to be a doctor?" Sheetal asked incredulously.

Zara shook her head. "I just fulfilled my grandfather's dearest wish so that he can brag about his favourite granddaughter to his cronies at the local club. I actually wanted to be a sports writer like Ayaz Memom."

"I wanted to be a pastry chef," Daisy said, "but would my parents allow it when I had such a great rank in the medical entrance exam? No way!"

"I wanted to be a professional dancer; I studied Bharatanatyam. Or, maybe a Kathakali artist like my father," Nayana said dreamily.

Sheetal gave the three girls a pitying look. "Well, I never wanted to be anything else, though my doc parents put absolutely no pressure on me to become one."

"Er, yeah, maybe," Zara said uncomfortably while Daisy rolled her eyes behind Sheetal's back.

"Phone call for Nayana, first year!" someone shouted from the corridor.

"Coming!" She dashed outside.

***

While Zara and Daisy contemplated whether to add 'Except Sheetal' to the poster on their door, Sheetal went back to her textbook. Sheetal's parents expected her to be a topper and maybe bag a few gold medals, but her marks in the first average exams had been next to deplorable. Truth be told, all her roommates had much better medical entrance ranks, and they had done quite well in the average exams, making her feel mediocre and unworthy by comparison.

Nayana returned to their room looking, Sheetal thought, a little unsettled. But then again, Nayana always looked disturbed, lost in her own world, prone to weep for no apparent reason, and the worst of all were her sleepwalking spells. Sheetal shivered slightly, recalling the night during their first week in the hostel when she woke up hearing a noise, only to be petrified by the ghostly sight of Nayana in a billowing nightgown, sleepwalking down the corridor. After that, they started padlocking the door at night. Sheetal was almost certain Nayana had some psychiatric problem. And yet, despite all her inner turmoil, Nayana had topped Anatomy in the exam! It was incredible. Sheetal didn't dare spill her suspicions about Nayana's state of mind to the others lest they accuse her of insensitivity. She was the only North Indian in a room full of Malayalees, and as much as she liked them, there were times she regretted her decision not to share a room with the other Northie girls.

Zara had been the reason behind that decision. Several months earlier, at the MBBS counselling session in Delhi, Sheetal Tyagi had been disappointed to find that her marks were not enough for her to opt for a medical college in her hometown or any of the neighbouring states. While fretting over the remaining choices, she bumped into a girl with a long, thick braid, a Malayalee raised in Bombay (newly christened Mumbai), settling for a medical college in Calicut, a small town hitherto unknown to Sheetal. Spurred on by the vivacious Zara (and feeling she had an ally in her), Sheetal opted for the same college, and the two girls arrived together at the Ladies Hostel 10 days prior to the start of their classes.

Those had been good times, talking about everything under the sun, consoling each other when homesickness struck, avoiding the senior girls as much as they could, shopping for their textbooks at the nearby store RamCo, and wondering about their upcoming classes.

Then the other girls arrived.

Daisy Chacko, the plump and outspoken one, almost instantly enquired whether Sheetal wouldn't be more comfortable sharing a room with the North Indian girls. The same thought was echoed by Mohini Deshpande, the most vocal amongst the Northies.

But Zara argued it was Sheetal's decision to make – a decision that had not gone down well with Mohini and that now put Sheetal in a difficult spot.

After a reshuffling of rooms by the Warden, Mala Diwakaran and Nayana Krishnakumar joined them. Mala suffered their dingy, congested room only for as long as it took her NRI parents to arrange paying guest accommodation in town, and she left by the end of the month. By then (much to Sheetal's great disappointment) Nayana and Zara had become thick as thieves, especially over their shared love for jigsaw puzzles.

Sheetal peeked over her book at the duo as they sat on the spare cot that had been Mala's, rummaging through a puzzle box of 6,000 pieces. "My uncle in the Gulf gave this to me on my birthday. It's a famous painting called *The Allegory of Sight and Smell* by Jan Brueghel," Nayana said, pointing to the cover that showed many famous paintings within a painting. "See this woman sitting at the round table, looking at the mirror? She represents sight, along with the magnifying glass, telescope and stacks of famous paintings. The woman receiving the bouquet represents the sense of smell, as does the civet cat, which represents unpleasant odour and the dog for a fine sense of smell."

"Have you got all the 6,000 pieces with you here?" asked Zara.

"No, after doing the borders, I separated the rest of the pieces by colour. This box has the brick red carpet pieces. I'll bring the next box from home after the Christmas holidays. By the way, that doesn't fit there," Nayana said as she leaned over and placed the piece in its correct slot.

Zara sighed. "I'm not in the mood for this right now. Let me see what Daisy is up to. You coming, Nayana?"

"Sure." Nayana put away the box and followed her out of the door.

Sheetal went back to her textbook, trying not to mind being ignored by Zara. But tears blurred her vision.

***

Let conversation cease, let laughter flee.
This is the place where death delights to help the living.

The engraved stone stated on the wall inside the colossal Anatomy dissection hall on the third floor of the college building. On any other day, hushed conversations and muffled laughter were a constant, with reverberating humming emanating from the 10 stainless-steel tables where the students tackled their cadavers with scalpels, forceps and Cunningham's Manual of Practical Anatomy, the hum dying momentarily whenever a faculty member decided to check on the students' progress. But today, the air was thick with the tension of the second average practical exams, and students revising feverishly as they paced the corridors outside the hall, awaiting their turn. A Tutor appeared with a clipboard in his hand and announced: Kenza Abubacker, Latheef KP, Luqman Harris, Madhu Mohan, Mala Diwakaran, Mohini Deshpande.

The six of them hastily put away their books and followed the Tutor, who motioned for them to wait. The 10 stainless-steel tables with the cadavers they had been dissecting till yesterday, 20 students to a table, had been pushed to the far end of the hall to make seating space for the five examiners who were questioning the students in front of them with an assortment of limbs and organs from the trays on their tables.

The acrid smell of formalin wafted up to Kenza, making her

cough, and she quickly covered her nose with the loose end of her *mafta*. From her very first day in the dissection hall, the sight of the cadaver hadn't distressed her as much as the fumes that came along with it. Several months on, she still struggled while her 'bodymates' joked that formalin was the bonus flavour on the birthday treats secretly passed around under the dissection table. Kenza squeezed her sweaty hands together as she watched the proceedings.

Sunny Kuruvilla answered confidently while Tarachand Sinha mumbled his answers and irritated the examiner. Zara looked pitiable as she hunted miserably for the Median nerve on the disarticulated forearm, the dark circles under her bloodshot eyes bad enough to scare a cadaver or two. Waheeda Musthafa was confidently explaining the origin and insertion of biceps to the expressionless examiner, all the while holding up triceps. Vaibhav's answers had his examiner's eyebrows raised so high that they were in danger of fusing with her hairline.

Finally, it was her turn. Kenza swallowed nervously and moved to the examiner indicated by the Tutor. An hour later, she was relieved to escape the hall without mortal wounds.

"I have absolutely no luck," wailed the small built and stocky Mala, who had been grilled on one of the most difficult topics – the sole of the foot.

"At least you didn't identify the Hyoid bone as the developing Mandible of a fetus," Latheef said with a wince, sending everyone into peals of laughter.

"Don't worry, you guys," Luqman consoled them, "the more difficult the topic, the better you score. That's the dictum."

Mala started pulling off her white lab coat, but Kenza stopped her. "Don't! There's a large ladder on the side of your top," she whispered.

"Thanks!" Blushing intensely, Mala put the coat back on.

"If you come to the hostel, I'll lend you a *kurta*," offered Mohini.

Mala declined. "It's okay, I'll go home wearing the coat."

The three girls parted ways at the college portico. Kenza walked towards RamCo near the Ladies Hostel – a ramshackle general store that stocked everything from thumb tacks to OHP sheets and hard-boiled candy to stethoscopes. While the store owner rummaged for unruled notebooks, Kenza looked at the precariously balanced textbooks in the overhead shelves and wondered if his epitaph would read *Death By Medical Books*. She paid for her books and stepped outside.

She had barely taken a few steps when a truck raced by, and she heard a popping sound and a sharp yelp. She whirled around to see the truck disappearing around the bend and a large dog lying motionless in the middle of the road. The poor animal was whining piteously; one hind leg twisted at an odd angle. Unsure of what to do, but certain that the next vehicle would run over and kill it, Kenza cautiously approached the dog and tried to pull it by the shoulders. The dog gave a sharp yelp, and she let go.

From behind her came the sound of a motorcycle skidding to a stop. A young man in a helmet knelt down by her side. "What happened?"

"It was hit by a truck."

"Hmm… looks bad. Here, I'll grab the shoulders, and you support the rear."

Together, they carried the howling dog to the side of the road. The man flagged down a passing autorickshaw and, after arguing with the driver for a bit, he bounded over to Kenza. "He's agreed to take us to the veterinary centre in town. Come on!"

The alarm must have shown in Kenza's eyes, for he quickly added, "Don't worry, I'm a first-year General Medicine postgrad." He flashed his college ID tag at her. "I can't do this by myself; you'll have to come."

A few minutes later, they were on their way, the whimpering dog in their lap, and the reluctant autorickshaw driver grumbling all the way till they reached the hospital. When two attenders from Casualty carried the dog away on a stretcher, the young man turned to Kenza. "You can leave now. Thanks for all your help."

"But I didn't do anything."

The man looked at her for a moment, his eyes resting on her *mafta*. "I don't know of a Muslim who cares this much about an injured dog when it is *haram*."

Kenza bristled at the insinuation. "Dogs are *haram*, but to help one that is hurt is not forbidden."

She turned on her heel and walked to the bus stop just outside the gates. As she boarded the bus, she saw the man give her one last look before walking off.

When Kenza reached home, her younger brother, who was playing in the living room, looked up at her and ran a finger across his throat.

"Why?" she whispered. Before he could reply, their father appeared and slapped her face. "It's seven-thirty! Where have you been?"

Their mother hurried over to hold him back before he struck her again. "You've already brought shame to this family once!" he thundered.

"I… I was dis… discussing the exam with the girls at the hostel," Kenza lied.

"I'll put a stop to your studies once and for all!" he bellowed, "Do you know how long they waited for you here?"

Kenza had no clue who or what he was talking about. Her mother motioned for her to go upstairs. Her younger sister followed Kenza inside the bedroom they shared and shut the door.

"A marriage broker came unexpectedly around 4 p.m. with the groom and his family. The guy is an engineer in the Gulf. He's a divorcee too, but has a kid who lives with his ex-wife. Uppa and Umma kept saying you would come soon, but they got annoyed and left."

"Thanks." Kenza stepped inside the bathroom. She gripped the sides of the wash basin, shaking with anger, and hot tears streaming down her face. From her kurta pocket, she pulled out a balled-up handkerchief that held some sand. According to their faith, she had to bathe six times with water and once with sand after touching a dog. Kenza dumped the sand in the toilet and pressed the flush. Then she washed her face, changed into a nightgown and went straight to bed.

***

The Christmas holidays left the Ladies' Hostel quiet. The only voices to be heard were those of seniors who had chosen to stay behind owing to upcoming exams. A few weeks after college reopened, batch tour for the first-year students was announced. Destination Ooty, the Queen of Hill Stations. They would leave on Friday evening and return on Sunday night, chaperoned by two faculty members.

By the end of the short trip – with sunny skies and a chilly breeze, winding roads through the lush greenery of tea plantations, the scent of wild roses and the smoky blue haze of the tall eucalyptus trees – a few 'lines' had formed. On Monday morning, the hangover from the tour had still not cleared for the first-year students. Zara, Vaibhav and Tarachand sat close together in the Anatomy dissection hall, pretending to read Cunningham's dissection manual while actually dissecting the events of the trip. Zara was upset they hadn't been able to visit the Human Biologicals Institute (HBI), which manufactured the rabies vaccine. Visits required prior approval.

"That was a great loss, Zara," agreed Tarachand, "You missed an opportunity to be rid of your rabid look with a few injections."

Vaibhav chuckled. Giving him a nasty look, Zara said, "I heard your great plan to 'propose' to Arundhati during the trip sank like a soggy biscuit in masala tea."

"Well, it's *her* loss that she opted not to experience some Vaibhav Reghuthaman charm."

Indeed, several boys had made total fools of themselves chasing the gorgeous Arundhati Sahadevan. But at the end of the tour, victory had gone to the underdog – a bodymate called Anand whose existence was realized only when his name came up on the roll call. *Arundhati could have done better,* was the general consensus.

"It's true that opposites attract," Vaibhav said with a sigh.

"Shh! Clavicle Sir is coming," Sunny muttered with a nudge to Vaibhav. The Tutor with the unfortunate nickname (because he walked around holding a clavicle bone in his hand) stopped at their table for a few minutes, taking in the two students dissecting the cadaver and the others who sat hunched over their Cunningham's.

As soon as he left, Zara resumed, "And what about Bibinraj?

Did he hook up with anyone as planned?"

"Didn't work out," replied Vaibhav. "In any case, he was only looking for a fling, that's why he was after the Northie girls."

"What's that supposed to mean?"

"Well, everyone knows that Northie girls are more *forward* than Malayali girls. They are always available for no-strings-attached relationships. Malayali girls expect relationships to end with a string around their neck" – he imitated tying a *taali* – "which is equivalent to a thicker string around the guy's neck." He imitated a noose.

"Is that the general opinion about Northie girls?" Zara asked, surprised.

"Not among all boys," muttered Sunny. He gave a quick glance at Sheetal, who was dissecting the cadaver.

"Well then," continued Zara, "shall I ask Mohini what *she* has to say about it?" Vaibhav and Tarachand gave horrified gasps and shook their heads.

In the days soon after their admission to college, Mohini, the feisty leader of the Northie girls, was subjected to lewd comments from some senior boys for 'daring' to walk around campus without a *dupatta.* To which Mohini replied, "Take a moment to pray that your mothers and sisters aren't hearing such filth when they step out of the house."

"How dare you insult my mother and sister!" one of them bellowed, charging at her while the others pulled him back.

Later that day, Mohini requested the help of their hostel Warden to inform the Principal, who, in turn, threatened the culprits with suspension unless Mohini voluntarily agreed to withdraw the complaint. Soon, it was hot news all over the campus that a fresher had brought some foul-mouthed seniors to their knees. Although the senior boys had besmirched her name throughout the campus in retaliation, her own batchmates now handled Mohini with kid gloves.

"I was only repeating what Bibinraj said; that wasn't my personal opinion," Vaibhav said quickly.

"Ditto," said Tarachand and pleaded, "Zara, please don't tell Mohini. She might rip out our tongues."

"You three, stand up!"

Whirling around, they saw Clavicle Sir glaring at them. They jumped to their feet. "What were you discussing so eagerly?"

"Ah… Sir… brachial plexus," stammered Tarachand.

"Is that so? Name the components of the brachial plexus!"

"Er, roots, trunks, cords," they blurted out haphazardly.

"Imposition! Twenty times!" declared Clavicle Sir and walked off.

***

"Phone call for Zara Mathew, first year!"

Zara rushed into the visitors' room and picked up the handset. "That was fast!" exclaimed her mother. "How are you awake so early on a Sunday morning?"

"The whole hostel is wide awake, Mama," Zara replied, yawning. "Didn't you see the newspaper? Princess Diana is dead."

"Really? We're just back from church; I haven't seen the newspaper. Oh, your father just shouted out the news to me. So young, so tragic, but it's a good reminder that women who consort with people disapproved by their family will meet a sticky end."

Zara rolled her eyes.

They talked for a while about home and college before Zara said, "Mama, there's something I need to tell you. Umm… I've met someone I really like."

There was a sudden silence at the other end.

"Mama, are you there?"

"Of course I am here!" her mother snapped. "What nonsense, Zara!"

"But this just sort of happened," she said, toying with the end of her long, thick plait.

Her mother sighed heavily. "Is he an Orthodox Syrian Christian like us?"

"Yes, Mama. From a family of reputed ancestry."

"Really?" The suspicion in her mother's voice was almost tangible. "What's his name?"

"Arthur."

"Oh! That's uncommon. What's his family name?"

"Guyton."

"Eh? Arthur Guyton? What kind of name is that?"

Zara crumpled a piece of paper in her other hand over the mouthpiece of the phone. *Tzz, tzzz.* "Hello Mama? Hello?" *Tzzz, tzzz.* "Can't hear you, too much static."

Replacing the receiver in the cradle with a cheeky grin, she patted the textbook of Medical Physiology by Arthur Guyton and David Hall that someone had abandoned on the teapoy. She stepped out of the visitors' room and collided with an anguished Daisy.

"Some seniors say the funeral will be broadcast next Sunday. We *must* see it," she wailed, following Zara into their room.

"Forget it, Daisy," said Zara. "You know the seniors' rules – no TV or newspapers for the first year is a part of hostel ragging."

But Daisy couldn't forget it, and the following Sunday she sneaked behind the TV room and peered through the window. Through the crowded room, past the craning heads, she could see a bit of the TV screen showing the huge crowds at Kensington Palace and Westminster Abbey waiting for the funeral cortege. Daisy watched enthralled, forgetting she was trespassing, until she heard a silky voice behind her, "Looks like we caught a rule breaker!"

Turning around, she broke into cold sweat seeing three second-year girls grinning at her.

"What's your name, first year?" asked a girl whom Daisy recognized as Mubashira Gafoor, the student magazine editor.

"D… Daisy Chacko."

"And why are you sneaking around the TV room?"

"I just want… wanted to know what happened to Princess Diana."

"Why? *Ninte ammayide mol aano*? We would've saved you a front seat."

The other two girls giggled.

"So, are you the cat that curiosity killed?"

She gulped. "I hope not, *Chechi*."

Mubashira lost her smile. "Let's find out, shall we? Come to my room at 5 p.m. And if you don't…" She glared at Daisy and marched off.

"I told you not to. I *told* you," Zara said angrily when she heard.

"No point in berating her, Zara. What's done is done," said Nayana. "Anyway, whatever they are planning can't be that bad."

Seeing her so miserable, Zara softened. "Nayana's right. Come on, let's go for lunch."

As soon as they were out of the door, Sheetal gave a snort. "How stupid can you be? Getting yourself caught by the seniors, and all for what – to see the funeral of a British Princess!"

Nayana looked up from putting her puzzle pieces away. Sheetal was lying on her belly, nose buried in Guyton's textbook and mumbling with her eyes screwed shut, trying to memorize from it. Nayana hesitated for a moment and then said, "Sheetal, I've been meaning to ask – if you'd like some help, we could do group study."

Sheetal gave a start like she'd been poked in the bottom with a sharp pin. "Well, I *do* mind you inferring that I'm a halfwit!"

Nayana gasped. "I didn't mean to… I would never," she fumbled for words. "It's just that you never have *any* fun. You never come to chat with the other girls, you never attend any of the college functions, you're always studying."

"But I never get as good marks as any of you!" finished Sheetal, flying into a rage. "Isn't that what you were going to say?"

Nayana's eyes welled up. "You know how you can help?" continued Sheetal. "By not distracting Zara with your stupid puzzle or idiotic prattle whenever she's reading with me. Being a topper doesn't grant you the right to distract others as you please." With that, she got off her bed and marched out of the room.

At 5, an ashen-faced Daisy knocked on Mubashira's door. She was ushered to a stool, and two senior girls worked on her with a makeup kit. They draped a skirt made of jackfruit leaves around her waist, fastened leaf bracelets and anklets, and clipped a hibiscus flower behind each ear. Daisy's heart sank – this was going to be a dance performance, she just knew it. And she had two left feet.

"Sit tight till we return," said the girls, shutting the door behind them. Feeling jittery, Daisy got up and went over to the window. She could see into the visitor's room where Nayana was talking on the phone. Suddenly, she slammed the receiver down, walked out into the garden and sat weeping on the edge of the broken fountain.

Some problem at home, Daisy surmised.

The door opened. "Come on, it's time for your act."

Daisy's knees nearly failed her when she entered the common room and saw the entire hostel seated there. There were giggles and whispers, and among the expectant faces she saw Zara, who gave her a thumbs-up sign.

Mubashira addressed the crowd, "Good evening, girls! Daisy Chacko, first year, has decided to entertain us all this evening. She dedicates this performance to her *ammayide mol*, the late Princess Diana."

Amidst giggles, the trembling Daisy heard the click of a tape recorder button, and a song started. *Tu cheez badi hai mast mast, tu cheez badi hai mast…* Daisy stood frozen until Mubashira looked daggers at her. She swayed awkwardly, wiggled her hips and flapped her arms around. The silence in the hall gave way to loud guffaws and boos. A few minutes later, the song changed.

Pennale pennale karimeen kannale kannale… She did a clumsy hopping sort of step and tripped over. The entire room shrieked with laughter, and a few senior girls tossed coins at her. Daisy saw red; she was trying her best to dance daintily, but if this was the response, well then, she might as well go all out. When the next song started – a racy Tamil *dappankoothu* – she hitched up her skirt and pulled open her ponytail.

For the next half hour, through a medley of songs, with the common hall erupting into howls of laughter, wild applause and hearty boos, Zara stared open-mouthed as Daisy gave the performance of a lifetime.

***

The lecture hall filled up slowly with many students sauntering in well after 8 a.m. The Associate Professor from Biochemistry was already on the podium, droning on and on about fat-soluble and water-soluble vitamins, unmindful of who listened or who didn't. Consequently, everyone was happy. The front benchers took notes like champion stenographers while the back benchers idled in a world of their own. Between these extremes were the middle benchers, like Kenza, who was usually inclined to listen except on rare occasions like today, when she could clearly overhear Daisy discussing hostel gossip in the row just in front. The salient points were that Nayana sleepwalked inside their room, and this annoyed Daisy, who was a light sleeper. Nayana surely had mental health issues, because she was forever weeping in the garden. Sheetal was jealous of Nayana's friendship with Zara, who, as always, was totally oblivious to the drama unfolding around her. She was either daydreaming about Vaibhav or cribbing about Tarachand, who was besotted with her.

It seemed ironic to Kenza that Daisy started each statement with 'Don't tell anyone this, ok' as she continued spilling secrets to everyone!

Kenza looked around furtively – sure enough, Zara and Vaibhav were chatting away in one of the back rows with Tarachand glancing at them every few seconds from the row across; Sheetal and Nayana were in the front bench (but not together), listening with rapt attention to the soporific lecture.

Nayana was Kenza's bodymate, and even though she was a bit introverted, Kenza found her friendly and agreeable, just like Mala, who was now fast asleep next to her, with arms crossed on the table and cradling her head. The side of Mala's kurta was patched up with a clumsily stitched yellow panel. Kenza realized that it was the same top she'd been wearing during their Anatomy practical exam.

Maybe it's her favourite top, thought Kenza, for surely her NRI parents could afford to buy her a new kurta, unlike her parents, who never seemed to have any money to spare. As if underlining this point, Waheeda Musthafa suddenly landed in the empty seat on her other side.

"Hey, since we don't have practicals this afternoon, could you please, please explain this chapter? I can't make head or tail of it."

Seeing as she couldn't escape, Kenza reluctantly agreed. Waheeda was her father's second cousin's daughter. She was younger than Kenza but tended to be a bit bossy because her family was quite well off.

Waheeda's home was at Thalassery, a two-hour drive north

of Calicut. When both girls got admission to Calicut Institute of Medicine, Waheeda's father had suggested she stay at Kenza's house instead of in the hostel. But Kenza's father had candidly explained that his home was too small and his finances too meagre. Consequently, Waheeda had been rather cold to her initially but warmed up on realizing Kenza was much better academically.

Post lunch, Kenza was finally rid of Waheeda as they were at separate tables for dissection. Today, they were to dissect the brain. The crania of all 10 cadavers had already been sawed open by a technician, and faculty members came around to briefly explain the procedure they were to follow. No sooner had they left than squabbles broke out at every table between table-bullies over who would do the dissection. These were the aggressively studious ones who read their Cunninghams beforehand and battled every day for the opportunity to dissect. While arms and legs and several organs came in pairs, the cadaver had only one brain.

This is going to be a fight to the finish, thought Kenza, watching Luqman turn blue in the face from arguing with Mohini. The obstinate table-bully in the otherwise good-natured Luqman fascinated her immensely. Finally, the two contenders agreed to take turns with Luqman going first, and everyone else crowding around him, with textbooks open.

Kenza watched Luqman place precise cuts with the scalpel he held tenderly in his long, slender fingers. His fair face was flushed, and his cheeks dimpled as he bit his lower lip in concentration. Beads of sweat escaped from his curly mop of hair onto his long eyelashes and slid slowly down the bridge of his pointed nose. A dreamy expression crossed Kenza's face.

I might be older than him, but so was the first wife of Prophet Muhammad, peace be upon him, she thought with a smile. Then she snapped back to reality. Chastising herself, she brought her eyes back to her textbook.

***

Passers-by on the road outside the Ladies Hostel stared curiously at the din emanating from within. Inside the common room, pandemonium reigned as groups of girls jostled for space to practice their dance routines for the upcoming Batch Day. Amidst the cacophony, someone yelled, "Phone call for Nayana, first year," and Nayana dashed away.

Fifteen minutes later, Mohini's patience was exhausted. "What's taking her so long? We're wasting time!"

"She's forever getting phone calls," Daisy said, yawning, "Have some patience."

"Easy for you to say! You're the *devi* statue in the centre; you don't have to memorize any dance steps!" fumed Mohini.

Daisy looked offended. "Well, feel free to get yourself another *devi*. Let's see if you can find anyone to match my graceful face or figure." The other girls in the group giggled, but Zara managed a straight face; she didn't want Mohini more annoyed than she already was.

Nayana returned looking a little flushed. "That was Madhu Mohan on the phone. The boys are dancing to *Sheher ki ladki,* and they want me to do a cameo in it. Should I do it?"

Zara's heart sank. She knew Vaibhav was also in that dance; why hadn't he thought of asking her?

"I think you should," Mohini said excitedly. "It'll be realistic and fun."

Forcing a smile, Zara nodded in agreement.

The following evening, she accompanied Nayana to the college auditorium for the practice session. The boys were already on stage; Madhu Mohan and Vaibhav clambered down to greet them.

"You don't need to dance," explained Madhu Mohan, "just catwalk the length of the stage like Raveena Tandon does in the song, and maybe pout a bit as she does. Come, let's try it out."

While the boys danced, Nayana sashayed effortlessly from one end of the stage to the other, striking a few poses in between. Zara felt a stab of envy.

"Hey, why didn't you ask me instead of her? You know I would've said yes," she hissed to Vaibhav.

"It was Madhu Mohan who insisted on Nayana; they're bodymates, no? And since Madhu Mohan is Sunil Shetty in this dance..." Vaibhav shrugged. "Besides, the song is about *sheher ki ladki*, not *gaon ki ladki*!" He fell over laughing.

On the way back to the hostel, Zara was in low spirits. Apart from Mohini's semi-folk dance, Zara was in another group dancing to *Kannai Kattikolathey* from the Tamil blockbuster *Iruvar*. Three girls would be dressed as males because an actual dance with the boys was out of the question. It would be frowned upon by the faculty, and the whole campus would be rife with gossip. At the moment, however, the image of Nayana sashaying with the boys made her group dance look quite ridiculous by comparison.

Finally, the great day arrived. At 5 p.m., the girls set out in a group, all decked in colourful silk saris and ornate, tinkling jewellery. Zara tottered on high heels in her mother's light pink and silver sari, her long hair swaying freely to her waist. At the auditorium entrance, she ran into Vaibhav, who did a double-take on seeing her. He silently mouthed 'Wow'.

Several seniors, postgrads and faculty members had already occupied the front rows. The girls settled down, and at 6 p.m., the programme commenced with the lamp-lighting ceremony, followed by speeches from the Principal, the faculty coordinator for Fine Arts and the batch representative. It was common knowledge that faculty members would leave around 7 p.m., hence the first hour was dedicated to solemn performances, including a Kathakali performance by Nayana. By half past seven, the last faculty member had left, and the seniors and chronics ambled in to fill the front rows. Backstage, Zara nervously smoothed her bottle-green and blood-red dance costume, wondering if the ensemble made her resemble an oversized parrot. The compere boomed, "Before the next performance, we will have our first song dedication for the evening. It's for Zara Ann Mathew from Tarachand Sinha!"

Zara froze. The speaker crackled, and a Bryan Adams song came on.

… T-shirt when it's wet...

…shower when you sweat…

"Oh God, I'll KILL that idiot Tarachand!" she fumed.

I wanna be your high heel, when you kick it…

She groaned and covered her face as the last line of the chorus played out.

I wanna be… your underwear.

Mohini walked up to her, arms akimbo. "I hope your Bihari beau has not given you a reason to back out. Our dance is next."

"Not my beau and not backing out," Zara croaked.

As the curtain went up, the deafening whistles nearly drowned the music, but nevertheless, the girls managed. Zara spotted King-Kong Kamaraj, Charles and James prancing around in front of the stage. Each time Zara passed close to James, he blew kisses at her, and she, in turn, stuck out her tongue at him. The audience fell over laughing. The dance concluded to thunderous applause, but Mohini was beyond angry.

"This was supposed to be a dance glorifying the *devi,* but thanks to you and that buffoon James, we're a laughing stock!" She stormed off before Zara could apologize.

Twenty minutes later, when Zara and the other participants of the fashion show returned backstage, the audience seemed to have become wilder. She peeked at the brouhaha from behind the curtain and saw inebriated boys dancing on chairs and kicking what seemed to be small sausage-shaped balloons.

The fashion show was announced, and the models strutted one by one onto the stage in time to the catchy music. When Zara reached the edge of the ramp, she realized to her great shock that the 'balloons' rolling around on the floor were actually inflated condoms. Just as she turned to walk back, a red blur whizzed past the side of her head, followed by a loud curse – the boy coming up the ramp behind her had been hit squarely in the chest by a large tomato, his face turning as red as the stain spreading over his pristine white *jubba.* The next second, he hurled the smashed tomato (and a stream of expletives) back at the perpetrator with the skill of a fast bowler.

Almost instantly, several tomatoes began flying left, right and centre amidst screams from the audience and participants alike. Zara made a hasty escape to the changing rooms, swearing and dislodging bits of tomato from her hair.

"Our Batch Day couldn't get any worse than this!" wailed a girl whose dress was totally ruined.

"It would be best if we cancelled the rest of the programme," suggested one of the boys.

But half an hour later, tempers were restored, a truce declared, and the pulpy mess cleared away sufficiently to continue the programme. Zara and her roommates sat as close to the stage as possible for a better view of the *Sheher ki Ladki* dance.

The curtains went up, and six boys started dancing, followed a few minutes later by Nayana, who sashayed in front of the dancers' striking poses, pouting and looking every bit a professional model in her heavy make up, ruffled top and fish-cut skirt. The rumbustious crowd at the front of the stage broke into loud cheers while King-Kong and company whistled themselves into asphyxiation. Zara felt extremely uncomfortable – not just the unruly crowd, but the dancers also seemed to be getting carried away, and their dance movements were now overtly suggestive, quite unlike the mood of their practice sessions. Then, out of the blue, Vaibhav gestured to the boys in the front to join them for the final chorus. Ten to twelve boys leapt onto the stage, dancing and singing *Sheher ki ladki* at the top of their lungs. A horrified Nayana shrieked and elbowed her way out of the crowd. She jumped down from the stage, broke the heel of her shoe and twisted her ankle. The girls rushed to her side and supported her back to the changing rooms, where she dissolved into tears.

"What in the world… atrocious behaviour... idiots!" spat Daisy, too furious to form coherent sentences.

"I say we just leave," declared Mohini. "Let the boys play with their 'balloons'!"

The girls gathered their belongings and left the changing rooms. As they neared the staircase, they saw several students leaving the auditorium, looking disgusted and embarrassed; the reason became clear all too soon. The rowdy boys at the front of the stage were hollering along to a dedication song but with new words: *Nayana O Nayana, Aisi Vagina, Har Koi Chahe Thujse, Milna Akela!*

Nayana burst into fresh tears as they made their way down the staircase and to the hostel. All the girls felt insulted and betrayed.

An emergency meeting was held in the common room after dinner. The condom balloons, the tomatoes, the disgraceful way in which the dancers had played to the gallery, Nayana's humiliation – it was unbelievable how the Batch Day had been hijacked by a bunch of drunken and vulgar boys. Finally, the girls unanimously agreed that they would ignore the boys completely for one week as a sign of protest.

On their way to college the following morning, Daisy suddenly appeared at Zara's side and linked arms with her.

Zara tittered. "Why so lovey-dovey this morning?"

"My foot!" said Daisy. "I'm just keeping an eye on you. Despite all your indignation last night, you'll just turn soppy when you see Vaibhav and go running to him."

"I will not!"

"Well, we'll see, won't we?"

When they entered the lecture hall, Zara spotted Vaibhav waving to her from the back row. "Do not smile. Do not make eye contact. Do not back out of our decision," Daisy chanted in Zara's ear, manoeuvring her into a seat near the front row.

"If I could just explain to him why I'm not speaking…" she trailed off, seeing Daisy's murderous expression.

Zara managed to ignore him the whole day, mostly because she knew she was under Daisy's scrutiny. But as they were washing up after the Anatomy dissection, Vaibhav cornered her near the row of sinks at the back of the hall. "What's going on?"

"I'm so sorry, but I have to honour the oath the girls took yesterday."

Vaibhav was livid. "I thought you were my friend! When the boys heard about the boycott, I told everyone that Zara was different, not like the other girls. But I see I was wrong; you're just like them."

"What you boys did on and off the stage yesterday was inexcusable! You made a mockery of us girls."

Vaibhav gave a short laugh. "That's all a part of college life, Zara. How old are you, 10? Grow up!"

"If growing up means acting like a hooligan, I'd rather remain 10. Throwing condom balloons and tomatoes at the girls in your batch doesn't qualify as maturity."

"That was King-Kong and co, not us," Vaibhav said quickly.

"And that vulgar song about Nayana?"

"I can't remember. Charles, maybe? Look, Zara, I agree we were a bit reckless, but we honestly didn't mean anyone any harm; it was just guys being guys, you know. But what did you girls do? Instead of talking things out, you all just ganged up and gave us the silent treatment. I thought at least *you* would have some sense."

Zara opened her mouth to answer, but Vaibhav held up his hand. "Whatever the excuse, I don't care. In the golden test of friendship, you have failed!" He walked away, leaving Zara heartbroken and confused.

Later that evening, Nayana sought her out while she was reading in the common room. "You talked to Vaibhav, didn't you?"

"How did you know?" Zara was surprised.

"I've been your friend long enough to know."

Zara lowered her eyes miserably. "I'm sorry, but both of you are my best friends. I don't want to lose either of you."

Nayana sat down next to her. "Be truthful. Had it been you instead of me on that stage, would you have talked to Vaibhav ever again?"

"I don't know," Zara mumbled.

"You're not being truthful."

"But look, couldn't we have asked them for an explanation instead of ignoring them completely? That's what Vaibhav asked me."

Nayana gave a sharp stare. "You're saying it's not a matter of what *they* did, but how *we* chose to react, that's the problem? Does it not occur to you that this mess would never have happened if the boys had behaved decently?"

Zara lowered her eyes again.

"You're a smart girl, dear," Nayana said, her voice soft and sad. "Don't lay your heart at Vaibhav's feet. He'll trample it to a pulp and make you feel like a loser. I honestly don't know what you see in someone as shallow as him."

"Vaibhav *did* say they didn't mean anyone any harm," Zara tried again.

"But did he apologize?"

Zara thought hard and realized he hadn't.

***

In the blink of an eye, days and weeks flew by, and dates were announced for the first-year MBBS University Exam. Tensions escalated with each passing day. The thought on every mind was that those who failed the finals would not only have to attempt the exam six months later but also become a separate 'additional batch' with different timings. These 'additionals' could not rejoin the main batch for the remainder of the MBBS course, and *that* was the unbearable part.

Not surprisingly, the study holidays saw much drama with nervous breakdowns, tears of frustration, thoughts of hopelessness, and several students wondering gloomily whether their decision to join MBBS was the right one.

"I'm a little scopegoat round and stout, here is my frown and here is my pout," sang Zara from the bed, a notebook covering her face.

"If you're taking a break, please do it somewhere else," Sheetal said crossly. She covered her ears, reading loudly and repeating every line three to four times. Zara got up and went in search of Nayana. Instead, she found Daisy sitting with a textbook at a window in the common room.

"Are we having biryani for dinner?" asked Zara.

Daisy turned around quickly. "What?"

"You were mumbling something about chicken biryani."

"Oh that!" Daisy gave a nervous giggle, "It's my code for the division of the brachial plexus: Roots-Trunks-Divisions-Cords-Branches. Raveena-Tandon-Dislikes-Chicken-Biryani."

Zara laughed. "That's brilliant! But now you've made me hungry. I think I'll go to the mess hall for tea. Coming?"

"Only after I finish this chapter."

As soon as Zara was gone, Daisy returned to the window. Just outside the hostel gates, Mala was trying to get rid of a shabbily dressed woman who looked like a manual labourer. Mala would be staying in their room for the study holidays. Daisy couldn't hear them, but she wondered why Mala was arguing with her instead of telling her to push off. The woman left shortly, and Mala stomped around the garden in a huff, hardly glancing at her notes.

Very fishy, thought Daisy, but then she returned to her textbook.

All of a sudden, the first exam was upon them. At 8.50 a.m., the first years filled the seats in the auditorium according to their roll numbers, and 10 minutes later the bell sounded. Kenza's heart was in her mouth as she scanned the Physiology question paper. There were six short notes for 10 marks each and a single essay question worth 40 marks for a total of 100 marks. She felt it was very unfair that they didn't have a choice of an essay. If you hadn't studied that one topic, you were done for. The logic behind this lack of choice was that if a patient came with pain in the left leg, you couldn't tell him, *I'm sorry, but I've studied only about the right leg.* As a doctor, you had to know everything! Luckily for her, the essay was on the blood supply and action of the heart, which she was thorough with. Fishing out her coloured pencils, Kenza started drawing diagrams.

An hour into the exam, Zara found herself stuck on the fourth short note – Zollinger-Ellison syndrome. She simply couldn't recall anything about it, no matter how much she taxed her grey matter. She looked around discreetly, and her eyes made contact with Tarachand's. With a quick glance at the invigilators, she held up four fingers.

Tarachand gave a shy smile and whispered, "Go on a date with me."

"Go hang yourself," she whispered back. Just then, a sheet of paper on Zollinger-Ellison syndrome landed in her lap. She looked the other way to see Vaibhav flash a smile. But it certainly wasn't his handwriting! *Oh, who cares whose paper it is,* she thought, copying the answer hastily.

Several rows away, Daisy was having a panic attack. In a fit of generosity, she had lent her beautifully written answer sheet on Zollinger-Ellison syndrome to the boy who sat just in front of her. In the same spirit of generosity, he had passed it to the person in front of him. By the time Daisy was wise to the situation, her answer paper had travelled halfway down the hall. To make matters worse, Clavicle Sir was stalking their row. Leaning forward, she gave the poor boy an earful and ordered him to retrieve her answer sheet immediately.

Meanwhile, Sheetal was regretting the missed opportunity to peek at Daisy's answer sheet as it made its way past her. Feeling frustrated, she sat with one hand to her head and the other one tap-tapping her ballpen on the desk while she tackled short note number five. Sensing someone stop by her side, she looked up and saw Clavicle Sir making an ugly face.

"No Morse-coding friends for help!" he whispered.

"I wasn't," she whispered back and bent over her paper. She thought Clavicle Sir would leave, but he kept staring at her answer sheets. He bent slightly towards her, whispered for a few seconds and then floated away. Sheetal stared after him in shock; Clavicle Sir had just given her answer tips to short note five!

Just then, there was a loud thud like a gunny sack full of coconuts had dropped onto the concrete floor. All eyes turned towards the sound, only to see Tarachand lying flat on his back. The rotund Tarachand had leaned a little too far back in his chair, trying to peek into his neighbour's answer sheets and lost his balance. Daisy took advantage of the commotion to make a final, frantic appeal for the lost sheet, but to no avail. Gnashing her teeth at the boy in front, she made haste to reproduce the short note in what little time was left.

Clavicle Sir helped Tarachand up, his gaze moving between the boy's portly frame and the rickety plastic chair he had been seated on. Then he motioned for him to sit on one of the solid wooden chairs on the auditorium stage, from where he was perfectly visible to *every* invigilator in the hall! Titters erupted at Tarachand's desolate expression, but soon died down, and for the remaining 15 minutes all that was heard was the scratching noise of two hundred pens writing.

***

June arrived, signalling the end of the first year of MBBS and the start of a month-long vacation. The students temporarily abandoned their worries about the University exam results and packed their bags to head home.

Daisy, Nayana and Waheeda left together for the railway station early in the morning. They were seated on a wooden bench on the crowded platform, waiting for their respective trains, when they spotted Sunny standing a few metres away. Waheeda, his bodymate, waved to him, but he pretended not to notice.

"Don't bother, Waheeda. He's trying to avoid me," remarked Daisy without looking up from the book she was reading.

"Oh why's that?"

"Because he thinks I'm a nosy blabbermouth."

Nayana and Waheeda exchanged glances. Daisy had not earned the nickname 'BBC of the '96 batch' by being discreet.

"Besides, our families are connected by marriage, and he lived in my neighbourhood in Ernakulam once upon a time. We were thrown together in school, in Bible class, at the tuition centre and now in college. I guess he's just fed up seeing me."

What Daisy stopped short of mentioning was that her parents saw in him a suitor worthy of their daughter. In fact, if Sunny could see what Daisy was reading, he would have had a heart attack – *'Linda Goodman's Love Signs, A New Approach to the Human Heart'*. The chapter she was currently poring over dealt with the compatibility of the Aries woman (Daisy's sun sign) with the Virgo man (Sunny's sun sign). It was plotting and planning on a celestial scale.

"Any special plans for the vacation, Waheeda?" asked Nayana.

Waheeda wrung her hands in agitation. "I don't have any, but my parents have. A marriage proposal has popped up, and I've a gut feeling this is the one that's going to seal my fate."

"But you always say you don't mind marrying whoever your parents choose for you."

"I don't, but it's just so sudden, and my parents seem really happy about this proposal. He's a first-year postgrad in General Medicine; that means he's quite a catch. And yet his family hasn't asked for much dowry – they want only a hundred *pavan* of gold and a Maruti Zen."

Nayana's eyes bulged. "You're being sarcastic, right?"

Waheeda shook her head. "My parents think it's reasonable. The last proposal they rejected was from an orthopaedician who demanded one crore in cash, two hundred *pavan* of gold and a Mitsubishi Lancer. He was from a famous *Tharavadu* and a highly educated family, but there was no way my parents could afford him. Besides, this guy insists on a doctor bride, and his family says they will consider letting me work if circumstances are favourable. My *Uppa* made some discreet enquiries at his college, and everyone from the tea-stall owner to his Warden gave good reviews."

"Oh well, best wishes to you then," Nayana said, still reeling with shock.

Waheeda's train to Thalassery arrived, and she left. Twenty minutes later, Nayana and Daisy boarded their train. Nayana's stop was Thrissur, while Daisy was headed to Ernakulam. There was no sign of Sunny, and the girls assumed he was in some other compartment.

They stowed their luggage under their seats and settled down in the crowded compartment. A pantry waiter carrying a steel container and a stack of paper cups passed by, bleating 'Copee, Copee' with a nasal twang. Daisy bought two coffees from him, and they sipped the weak but piping hot liquid, trying not to spill any while swaying along with the rattling train.

"Sometimes, I wish I were a day scholar like Kenza or Mala," said Nayana. "Then I wouldn't have to wait for holidays to go home."

Daisy gave a nasty grin. "Now that you mention Mala – what did she tell us when she left hostel accommodation after two months?"

"That she's staying as a paying guest."

"Well, she was lying. Her family is not NRI, and she is not a paying guest."

Nayana stared in disbelief. "How do you know?"

Balancing her coffee cup on the windowsill, Daisy sat cross-legged on the berth. "During our study holidays, I was reading by the window in the common room when I saw Mala arguing with a haggard and shabby woman at the hostel gate. She looked like a beggar or a manual labourer. But there was this, call it suspicious body language, between the two of them. I'm really good at picking up subtle clues like that."

Nayana nodded with a straight face.

"On the evening before our last practical exam, I saw Mala arguing with this woman again. Finally, the woman started sobbing, and Mala stormed inside. I waited a few minutes, sneaked outside and confronted the woman just as she neared the main junction. When she refused to talk, I threatened to call the police. That's when she said she was Mala's mother!"

Nayana almost spilled her coffee. "Really!"

Daisy nodded. "They're terribly poor. Mala's father runs a *beedi* shop, and she nearly discontinued the course because they couldn't afford it. Then a wealthy businessman in Calicut hired both mother and daughter as housemaids, gave them accommodation and agreed to fund Mala's studies. But Mala now resents her background and has forbidden her mother from setting foot on campus." She sighed dramatically. "While the poor woman toils day and night, Mala goes around lying through her teeth. It's downright shameful."

Nayana looked suspiciously at Daisy. "Umm, how many others know of this?"

"I told Zara and Sheetal, of course. Then I told Mohini, but I can't be sure if she has told anyone or if someone overheard our conversation. There were several girls milling around."

"That's quite a lot of people," Nayana said in a tone of disappointment that Daisy was quick to notice.

"I too liked Mala, you know that," she said defensively, "But she was making fools of us with stories of her NRI family."

A thought struck Nayana. "Do you think Madhu Mohan will come to know?"

There were rumours in their batch that Mala and Madhu

Mohan were now a 'line'. They had often been spotted chatting in one or another lonely corner of the college campus. Daisy had not thought of this consequence, but she stuck to her defensive tone. "Well, he deserves to know the truth, doesn't he?"

Back at the hostel, it was a quarter past three when Sheetal zipped up her suitcase with a triumphant grunt. She was already dreaming of her soft bed in Delhi and her mother's hot *aloo parathas* slathered in butter. Didi and Jeeju had just flown in from Dubai with gifts and gossip, and there was even talk of a family trip to Shimla.

Strapping on her overstuffed backpack, she dragged her suitcase out of the room. In the corridor, Zara was slouched against her own bag, rereading a letter she had got that morning. It was from Rishab Manchandani, her tall, floppy-haired schoolmate and neighbour from Mumbai. He was urging her to ditch the boring life and come with him and a few others on a wild weekend road trip to Goa.

Yeah, try explaining that to my parents, Zara thought, snorting.

Apparently, they were planning to drive down in his Maruti 800. Space was tight, so Rishab had generously offered to shove her in the trunk. The itinerary read like a public service warning: Feni, weed, and skinny-dipping.

Zara frowned. *Skinny-dipping? Must be the street name for a new drug,* she decided, shaking her head.

With a wistful sigh, she folded the letter and tucked it away. She would have loved to go. Rishab was hands-down the coolest person she knew. They'd grown up playing gully cricket in the sweaty Mumbai evenings, and he was the only boy who hadn't once tried to teach her how to bat.

"Ready?" asked Sheetal. They bade goodbye to the few who were yet to leave, left their key on the board in the Warden's room and hailed a passing autorickshaw to take them to the railway station.

Towards the middle of June, the bomb of the First MBBS University Exam results exploded. The casualties were 20 per cent of their batch of two hundred students. The day scholars had been entrusted with conveying the results to those who were away, and they immediately got down to the job.

On hearing she had passed, Zara let out a whoop and grabbed her younger brother Vivian in a victory dance, much to his annoyance. Waheeda was being 'interviewed' by her husband-to-be and swooned at the news, only to be promptly caught by the young man in true *filmi-ishtyle*. Sheetal was relieved to have scraped through in the Biochemistry exam, which she had found exceptionally tough.

"And do you know," said Mala's voice over the phone, "Nayana is our Anatomy gold medallist!"

"Let me know when she *doesn't* top something, and I'll act surprised," said Sheetal acidly. "By the way, how many casualties are there? Mala? Hello?" But Mala had disconnected. She couldn't bring herself to say that *she* had failed.

4. Zara, 2016

11th March, 2016
Calicut

"*Kooooooiiiii! Ayala, mathi, koonthal, karimeen!*"

I jolted awake, heart pounding, not quite sure where I was. For a second, I thought I was dreaming, but then the blaring fish vendor's call cut through my grogginess. Where was I?

Not a hospital tent in South Sudan.

The Spiderman bedspread, the framed family photo, and the Avengers wall clock blinking 11:30 a.m. brought it all back. I was in Daisy's house. Calicut.

Still half-asleep, I shuffled to the bathroom. A long shower later, I padded down the stairs, pausing on the landing to admire the massive aquarium. Goldfish swirled in hypnotic loops. I grinned. Still obsessed with goldfish.

"Hubby darling hasn't stopped collecting them, huh?" I teased as I stepped into the kitchen. "Do they have names now?"

Daisy turned from the stove, eyebrows raised. "Good afternoon, sleeping beauty! You picked a great time to show up last night and an even better one to wake up."

I yawned, stretching lazily. "You sound just like Mama when I was in college."

She rolled her eyes. "Well, I've got two boys on the cusp of teenhood, so I've earned the right."

She poured hot water into a rice pot with the confidence of someone who has truly made peace with carbs. "Achachan's away at a conference in New York, thankfully. Or he'd have had a heart attack seeing you land at 2 a.m. with suitcase and all."

I raised an eyebrow. "He still thinks I'm a bad influence, doesn't he?"

Daisy gave a sheepish shrug. "What can I say? Fourteen years later, and he's still salty about you convincing me to strip on stage."

I snorted. "It was *not* a striptease."

"You're still single, globe-trotting, footloose... All the things he's allergic to. Anyway—forget him."

She handed me a mug of black coffee. No sugar. Because we were adults now. Supposedly.

"Speaking of drama," Daisy said, "Did you see what Mohini posted on Vaibhav's thread?"

That got my attention. I took a sip of the lukewarm Nescafé. Mohini had gone full throttle:

Wow, Vaibhav. Didn't think you, of all people, would even go near the elephant in the room. Congrats! Truly. I still remember the charming Malayalam pet names I was gifted in my first year — all because some sexually frustrated seniors asked for my bra and panty size, and I suggested they go and ask their mother hers instead. That's when it started. The 'image'. The legend of the Girl Who Talked Back. I dressed provocatively, I talked provocatively, I laughed provocatively – and hence I deserved all the gaalis coming my way.

There was plenty of sexism on our campus, ranging from outright to subtle, with every degree in between. It was like an epidemic – boys who entered the campus uninfected or with subclinical infections soon manifested to full-blown disease thanks to overwhelming peer pressure. The immune minority who didn't were labelled weak, or secretly gay.

And the professors? Oh, some of them moonlighted as sociologists. "Girls waste taxpayer money," they'd say. "They'll just quit medicine once they pop out a couple of kids." This was said casually. Except it landed like a slap across the face. You see the irony, right? Society programmes girls to prioritize marriage over ambition – and then mocks them for it.

On our campus, boys were born stars. Macho figures, djangoes. Girls? We could shine too — as long as we did it in the boys' reflected glow. Speak up? You're difficult. Disagree? You're arrogant. Say no? You're frigid. Say yes? You're easy. The goal was to be desirable — but not too desirable. Friendly – but not too friendly. You had to land perfectly in that tiny sweet spot between 'available' and 'wife material'. Otherwise? You'd pay.

Take Batch Day, for example. The horrible attack on Nayana. Even the ones who clucked in sympathy added a footnote that maybe she deserved it for being 'sexy' on stage.
Why did she agree to perform with the boys anyway?
Good girls would never behave like that on stage.
Boys will be boys, girls need to be careful.
Let me clarify something – I don't mean to discredit every single boy on campus. Most were decent. But the great disappointment lay in the realization that the bad and the ugly also existed in those who were good. It lay beneath the surface, bubbling up through small fissures every now and then. When you think about it, this shouldn't be surprising considering that our campus was, after all, a microcosm of the world outside. If a person chooses to define women who dress or behave in a particular manner as 'loose', then they are definitely going to pass on this prejudice to their kids.
And now I see these former chest-beating misogynists on Facebook posting woke things like "Gender roles are a scam' and 'Respect women' memes with emojis. Reformed or rebranded? I don't know. But then you, Vaibhav, go and post a full-blown confession. Out loud. In public.
So yes, I applaud the effort. But I have to ask — is an FB post really enough of an apology?

I looked up from the screen. The room was quiet.

The floodgates had opened, and it wasn't just Mohini. There were dozens of comments—raw, angry, unfiltered – unpacking years of silent pain which we had brushed under the carpet.

Later that evening, while Daisy's kids were out playing cricket, we circled the park on the jogging track, the topic still heavy between us.

"Do you really have to leave tomorrow?" she asked. "You're on leave for three weeks."

"I don't want to impose—"

"Oh, shut up," she cut me off. "Save the politeness for your Brit friends. You're staying. End of discussion."

I laughed. "Can you manage time off work at such short notice?"

"You're staying. I'll call in sick. I'll say I have chikungunya."

We walked in companionable silence for a bit. Then she asked, "How's Sheetal doing?"

"She's holding on. Weak, but she's staying positive. But tell me, how did you find out?"

"Through my colleague's brother's friend... long story. Surgeon at the same hospital as Sheetal's husband."

"I called her immediately," Daisy said. "She was surprised I knew."

Of course, she was.

"She misses everyone," I murmured.

"But doesn't want to see anyone?" Daisy raised a sardonic brow. "Why am I not surprised?"

"Come on, Daisy. Show a little compassion."

"I *do* feel for her," she said. "But that doesn't erase what she's done… to Nayana, to Mala... and how she dumped Sunny when a shinier prospect came along."

I sighed. Daisy never did forgive easily, especially not Sheetal. And it was true –Sheetal hadn't done much to challenge Daisy's harsh views about the North Indian girls in our class.

"Maybe she should take a leaf out of Vaibhav's book," Daisy muttered. Then her eyes brightened. "Speaking of books, you haven't asked about *my* book yet!"

I blinked. "Wait, you're writing a book?!"

She laughed. "You know I have a YouTube cookery channel, right?"

"Yeah, but I can't recall the name."

"*Daisy's Delicacies.* One of my recipes – *CMT curry, Chakka Maanga Thenga* – went viral. Guess who shared it?"

"No idea."

"Ancy Titus!"

"Who?"

She gasped. "Are you living under a rock? The hottest Malayalam actress right now?"

I shook my head, sheepishly. Daisy continued with flair. "She loved my recipe, shared the link, and boom – over a lakh subscribers in a week! I was on TV, in newspapers, and even asked to judge cookery contests. You seriously missed all of this?"

I grinned. "I've been off the grid a little."

"Clearly. Anyway, Curry Leaf Publications reached out. I pitched a cookbook with personal stories from our med school days. They loved it."

I burst out laughing. "Please tell me you're including the frying pan incident with Tarachand!"

We doubled over, giggling like schoolgirls.

"I *have* to," she said, wiping her eyes. "No way Taru's included that in his pompous '*Bihar se Baltimore Tak*' autobiography."

"Oh God, remember his FB posts? 'Haven't heard of my American supermodel wife? Go Google her!'"

"'Haven't heard of my groundbreaking research? Go Google it!'"

We were hysterical. "He was such a *makku*," I said. "Remember our prank on April Fool's Day? We called him up on the hostel landline and told him we were from the electricity board and asked him to count the tube lights in his corridor. When he said four, we said, 'It's five – you're the fifth!'"

Daisy laughed till she wheezed. "And the seniors tricked him into going to RamCo to buy a Buffy Coat and an Anatomical Snuff Box!"

"Unbelievable that he's now a hotshot cardiologist with a private jet."

"I *have* to put the frying pan story in the book," she declared. "Taru would kill me. Or maybe just sue me."

That night, once everyone was asleep, I stayed up scrolling through the endless comments under Vaibhav's post. The discussion had evolved into something much bigger – stories of harassment, sexism, regrets, and apologies. Then a comment from Madhu Mohan caught my eye:

For many of us boys, ignorance and foolishness came with our age. We were young, cocky, and hell-bent on proving our superiority to… well, pretty much everyone. Especially the girls.

I grew up in a family where politics was more than dinner table conversation – it was oxygen. Uncles in the panchayat, cousins quoting Marx at parties. So naturally, I thought I knew better. Especially compared to the girls in our batch, who, in my not-so-humble opinion at the time, voted based on who smiled at them last. It infuriated me – this lack of ideological purity. This… casualness.

Back then, I was an ASU loyalist. All Students United. Fierce. Vocal. Permanently in campaign mode. I was also, let's face it, frequently accused of backing a thuggish party. Fair criticism, honestly. I turned a blind eye to a lot of things – the sloganeering, the veiled threats, the occasional elbow thrown too hard. I shrugged off complaints. I played along. For the greater good, of course.

But looking back… I was complicit. Not in a dramatic, blood-on-my-hands way. More in the quiet, everyday way. I knew things were off. I stayed anyway.

I stopped reading.

Was he talking about Mala?

A flash of something – not quite shame, not quite fear – burned at the edge of my memory.

And then the question I didn't want to ask myself:

Did he regret it… or just finally learn to name it?

5. Second Year, 1997-98

"Why were you clambering up a wall in the middle of the night?"

6th July, 1997
Calicut

Dear Pappachen,

The second year starts today. And what an auspicious beginning! A good old-fashioned state-wide bandh –this time to protest the janaviruddha nayangal of the ruling party. (Translation: someone in power did something awful, again.)

The silver lining? At least this one came with a heads-up. Not like last year's surprise bandh, when I got off the train in Calicut at 7 a.m., suitcase in hand, full of post-Christmas optimism… only to discover that nothing was moving – not buses, not autos, not even the chaiwala's eyebrows.

This year, the bandh was announced much in advance, so Sheetal and I played it smart and arrived yesterday. Which means we are among the select few who get to enjoy the full, uncensored glory of Day One of Clinics. Lucky us.

Zara folded the half-written letter, shoved it into a drawer, and began the daily wrestling match with her hair. She jammed hairpins into her stubborn braid, trying to force it into a vaguely medical-looking bun, the kind that said: *trust me, I know where your liver is.*

As she worked, her mind wandered – *janaviruddha nayangal.* What did that even mean, really? Was it about the fuel prices again? Or the unfinished flyover that seemed to grow scaffolding but never an actual road?

Zara felt a familiar twinge of ignorance. It crept up whenever someone talked about current affairs or, God forbid, started quoting headlines. She hadn't touched a newspaper in years. In school, even glancing at one was considered academic treason. The only acceptable literature was whatever helped crack the entrance exam.

Now here she was, technically an adult, halfway to becoming

a doctor, and still not entirely sure who the Chief Minister was. Outside her Anatomy textbooks, the world had become a blurry, half-remembered place. Ministers changed, governments fell, policies passed or failed. But none of it ever seemed to affect her directly. Her days were neatly carved out: lectures, labs, the occasional existential crisis.

The rest of the world? Background noise.

Not all her batchmates were as ignorant or indifferent. She glanced at Mala, who sat reading at the table, preparing for her second round of exams. Mala had a rather good idea about current affairs and was an avid supporter of the ASU, more so because of her closeness to Madhu Mohan. As if sensing that Zara was thinking about her, Mala looked up from her book. "Hey, can I ask you something? Are you and Vaibhav a 'line'?"

Zara nearly drove the hairpin through her skull. "Wha... Who..." she spluttered.

Mala looked embarrassed. "Sorry. I asked because I've been hearing rumours. Just forget it."

Zara didn't know whether to feel elated or agitated. Mama's customary reminder in every other phone conversation popped into her head, "If you're adamant about finding a match from college, make sure he is from an Orthodox Syrian Christian family of ancient lineage."

"Yes, Mama, the moment any guy proposes to me, I'll run the checklist – Orthodox. Syrrian Christian. Ancient family."

Zara's mother was a firm believer in genetics. Particularly when it came to *caste-adjacent* things like 'good breeding' and 'Syrian Christian values'. It wasn't so much snobbery as it was... eugenics.

This ideology was inherited, of course, like a family Bible or an ancestral curse. Her grandfather, Pappachen, used to say with great solemnity: "The only way to become a Syrian Christian is to be *born* one. It's a privilege of blood and birth and ancient, inherited convictions." Which sounded very holy, until you realized it was just a fancy way of saying, *No converts allowed.* While it wasn't legally forbidden, in practice, it would need the approval of the local church, which was seldom given.

When Zara was in school, all her holidays were spent at Pappachen's old house in Kottayam; an elegant, crumbling place that always smelled faintly of rosewood, wet soil, and coconut oil. Every evening, like clockwork, the electricity would vanish—*load shedding*, as inevitable as rain. And during that hour, they'd all huddle around a kerosene lamp, while Pappachen spun epic tales about their divine lineage.

It always started the same way.

"St Thomas—yes, *that* Thomas, the disciple, landed at Muziris (present day Kodungallur in Thrissur district) in AD 52. Converted seven Namboodiri Brahmin families. That's how the Nasranis, or Syrian Christians, came to be."

According to Pappachen, the Roman Catholics were basically colonizers with fancier robes. The Syrian Christians, on the other hand, were the *originals* with ties to Antioch in present-day Turkey, bishops who spoke in tongues, and Sunday Masses delivered partly in Syriac.

"Other factions broke off—Marthomites, Jacobites, all the usual suspects. But *we*," he would say, leaning in meaningfully, "we are the *originals*."

Zara, spellbound and impressionable, absorbed all this like doctrine. Her sense of self became so inflated that on her eighth birthday, she was genuinely confused as to why the morning newspaper didn't run a feature about her.

At the medical college, however, the ground realities were more sobering. The only other Syrian Christian in her batch was a boy named Sunny. Zara decided she would rather take the vows at a convent than marry a stick-in-the-mud like him.

Sheetal, on the other hand, was *charmed*.

"He's such a gentleman," she gushed. "Have you noticed how his eyes are always respectfully lowered when he talks to girls?" To which Zara countered that Sunny was neither timorous nor modest – he was just staring at her boobs.

As she shrugged into her white coat, Zara had a fleeting vision of her mother collapsing from shock if she ever mentioned Vaibhav. He with his droopy eyes, that could switch from playful to wounded in a blink, his permanently creased shirt, and that stupidly disarming grin. There *was* something in all that. Or maybe not. He hadn't exactly made a declaration. No poetry, no proposal, not even an awkward 'I like you' in the canteen. Just flirtatious banter and... vibes.

Typical.

But for the time being, she laid aside all such thoughts. This was the first day of clinics!

The first year of MBBS had been no different from the pre-degree years, with just lecture classes and practicals. But the second year of MBBS was significantly different as they would start interacting with real patients. They had become *real* medical students!

With a spring in their step, Zara and Sheetal crossed the skywalk that linked the college building to the hospital wing. On the other side, the main corridor stretched out before them, branching into wards at regular intervals. Stepping into it felt like entering a parallel universe – one that was charged with chaos and noise.

The corridor buzzed with energy. People chattered, wheelchairs and trolleys rattled past, hospital staff shouted instructions, senior students weaved through the crowd, and doctors marched along, lost in thought.

Absentmindedly, Zara touched the stethoscope tucked into her coat pocket – a brand-new grey Littmann Classic, gifted by her parents. It had cost them a small fortune. She longed to wear it around her neck like the house-surgeons and staff doctors, but there was an unspoken rule: medical students were not to wear their stethoscopes like badges of honour. Not yet.

They checked the schedule pinned onto the hospital office notice board and groaned. Two weeks in Orthopaedics. Great. Bones and bandages. So, the two girls made their way to the Ortho OP, where they found Tarachand waiting nervously outside the Head of Department's room. A few patients sat nearby, observing him with mild curiosity.

The HOD, Professor KO Vijayan, arrived around 10:30 a.m. – a large, bear-like man with an imposing presence and a bushy, greying moustache sprouting under a fleshy nose.

"Where's are your posting orders?" he growled.

The three students exchanged panicked glances. Sheetal stepped forward and explained that most of their batchmates hadn't turned up because of the bandh, and so they hadn't received the posting orders either.

Dr Vijayan grunted and waved them into his office. The room was dim and sparsely furnished: a worn wooden desk, a creaky chair, and a stool for the patients. Along one wall stood an examination table, partially hidden behind a metal screen which was draped with a faded green curtain. A small sink clung to the adjacent wall. The window panes looked as if they hadn't seen any water since the hospital was built, and the mosaic floor screamed to be polished.

"You're lucky," Dr Vijayan declared as he took his seat. "Orthopaedics as your first posting – and me as your teacher."

He launched into a monologue, detailing the daredevil surgeries he had performed, his uncanny ability to crack complex referral cases that had stumped every other orthopaedician and how the rest of Kerala's orthopaedic community should just retire out of sheer respect. Zara was astonished that anyone could be this pompous. She kept her lips tightly pressed to prevent any giggles from escaping.

A few patients peeked in timidly, only to be told to wait. But as the murmurs outside grew louder, Dr Vijayan finally relented and called the first patient, an elderly woman with a painful knee. He asked her to lie down on the examination table and began an elaborate demonstration of the four golden tenets of clinical examination: Inspection, Palpation, Percussion, and Auscultation.

"During palpation or hands-on examination, the physician uses his hands to examine the patient," he explained. He beckoned them over. "Come, come. Amma, these young doctors want to have a look, okay?"

The woman nodded nervously. Tarachand stepped up and gently rotated the woman's patella with his fingers. "Grmpf! Not like that!" Dr Vijayan placed his big, meaty paw over Tarachand's hand to help him palpate the knee joint. Then he beckoned to Zara.

She came forward and placed her hand on the knee. Dr Vijayan clamped his hand down over hers, but instead of guiding her, he massaged her hand sensuously with his fingers.

Zara's ears grew hot with confused embarrassment while the bear continued talking about knee joint examination as if nothing untoward was happening. Wondering if it was only her imagination, she glanced at her unit mates – they looked equally embarrassed.

"You will appreciate the technique better if I stand behind you," Dr Vijayan said, moving around without taking his hand off hers. Zara nimbly sprang away, saying, "I have understood the technique, sir."

"Eh? Oh okay." He sat down, scribbled a prescription, growled some advice to the patient and told her to leave.

The next patient was a young man with a visible deformity at the elbow. Once he'd left, Dr Vijayan turned to the group.

"Do you know what the carrying angle of the elbow is?" he asked, then gestured toward Sheetal. "Help me demonstrate."

Sheetal stepped forward hesitantly.

"Stand straight. Arms by your sides. Palms facing forward." He circled her slowly as he spoke. "Normally, the forearms should angle about 5 to 15 degrees away from the body. This is the carrying angle – it lets your arms swing freely past your hips when you walk."

As he explained, he rested one hand on her shoulder, and with the other, began tracing slow, deliberate lines along the inside of her elbow – up and down, again and again.

Zara watched as tiny goosebumps rose on Sheetal's pale skin.

"Certain elbow fractures can alter the carrying angle," he explained, his fingers gently tracing her arm as though demonstrating on a mannequin. "If the angle increases, the arm sticks out from the body – what we call an excessive carrying angle. But if it decreases, making the arm point inward, it's known as gunstock deformity."

Sheetal's face turned beetroot red, her eyes brimming with tears.

Just then, there was a knock, and a group of postgraduate students entered.

"Hrmpf, what is this? I told you all to come at noon, no?" the bear growled. Sheetal escaped from his grip.

"Sir, it is already 12 o'clock."

"Hrmpf, Grmpf?"

Seizing the opportunity, Zara said, "Sir, we have to go now. We have theory classes at one." The three of them rushed out of his room without waiting for a reply.

Afternoon classes were cut short owing to the bandh, and at 3.30 p.m., the girls gathered in the mess hall to discuss their first day of clinics over tea.

"Hey, did any of you get 'Kozhi Vijayan'?" asked Sreedevi of the '94 batch from the adjacent table.

"Er… do you mean KO Vijayan Sir in Ortho, *Chechi*?" asked Zara.

"The same. Did he give any of you a massage?"

"How do you know that?"

Sreedevi laughed. "He's a notorious *njarambu rogi*. Just tell your batch representative to adjust postings so that only boys are in his unit. That's what we all do."

Sheetal spoke up. "Chechi, if everyone knows about him, why doesn't anyone complain?"

"Students have complained in the past, some bystanders and patients as well," Sreedevi said, "but nobody does anything about it. Kozhi Vijayan has political clout. He's been suspended once or twice when the allegations were extreme, but he always returns unfazed."

The first years stared at her in shock, and Sreedevi laughed again. "I'll give you all some advice. There are many 'Kozhis' in this world. Fighting them is a waste of time. Worse, the girls who complain are ignored, ridiculed, isolated and failed. Your best option is to avoid Kozhi Vijayan."

***

At 6 p.m., the *bandh* was declared a 'success' and called off. Almost all the girls had arrived at the hostel by then, and the rooms were alive with chatter, sounds of unpacking and the smell of homemade goodies. Everyone had stories to tell. The biggest sensation was Waheeda, who was the first bride in their batch. "My *nikah* is over, so I'm officially married to Ahmed *ikka*," she said, her cheeks colouring, "but I will be staying at my house till the *kootti kondu pokal* ceremony is over. That's when his family members escort me to their house. They have postponed that to next year when *ikka* completes his course." She took out a photo of Ahmed from her bag, and the girls crowded round.

"You're now this guy's wife, eh?" Daisy said thoughtfully. "Did you both go anywhere together?"

"Not a chance! Our parents won't allow it before the ceremony. But we did go to a flower show near home. It turned out to be a total fiasco, though."

"What happened?"

"Well, ikka is a gardening enthusiast. He selected some earthen pots, and I thought I would impress him with my bargaining skills to make up for my total ignorance about gardening. I told the shopkeeper to reduce the price as all his pots were damaged; they had holes at the bottom!"

The girls screamed with laughter. "You're too much, Waheeda!" Daisy said, holding a stitch in her side. "Where's Zara, by the way?"

***

On the sole bed unoccupied by bags and clothes, Nayana spilled out her woes to Zara as the two of them worked on the puzzle. Nayana got home for the vacation to find her younger sister Meghana occupying her room.

"My parents explained I shouldn't be upset because I stay at the hostel, and since Meghana is in high school, she needs a bigger room. But my room is my personal space! They *always* favour her over me!"

Zara cocked an eyebrow. "Oh, come on, you don't really believe that, do you?"

"I'm not sure I don't," Nayana said, fidgeting with the puzzle pieces. She unburdened herself some more. Meghana was the prettier sister and resembled their parents. She was fair and dimpled with thick, curly tresses, and all their relatives mooned over her. By comparison, Nayana was lanky and brown-skinned with straight hair. "You don't even look like sisters," was the oft-heard comment in family circles. Speculation was rife about the cause of Nayana's dark complexion:

1. Her mother had not ingested enough saffron milk while pregnant.
2. Nayana had been conceived during the scorching summer heat.
3. Mustard oil had been used to massage baby Nayana instead of coconut oil.

Speculation was usually followed by suggestions for skin lightening, which included weekly milk baths, ayurvedic face packs and the infallible *Fair and Lovely*. Nayana's sole consolation was her intellect. When she came second in the SSLC exam, her proud family was interviewed by every major Malayalam newspaper. Her parents encouraged her to try for medicine as they hoped at least one child would become a doctor, but Nayana had no such aspirations.

Nayana's pre-degree years had been rocky, with frequent nervous breakdowns. Yet she managed to clear the entrance exam and qualify for admission to the Calicut Institute of Medicine. Nayana's recollection of her unhappy June vacation was interrupted by Daisy, who came in waving Ahmed's photo.

"Let me see!" Zara grabbed it eagerly and sat down, looking dejected. "I guess he's, well… okay."

Nayana peeped over Zara's shoulder. "Hmm, a typical Malayali guy. I always imagined Waheeda would marry someone like Aamir Khan, considering how pretty she is."

Mala entered the room. "Hi, everyone. My exams are only a few weeks away. I took a few minutes off to see you all."

The girls flocked around, hugging her tight.

"Hey, relax! I'm not terminally ill or anything," Mala said with a giggle. "By the way, I have some *other* news for you." They waited expectantly, wondering if Mala was finally going to tell them the truth about her family.

"I have a 'line'! It's Madhu Mohan."

There was heavy silence followed by weak noises of surprise. Mala didn't seem to notice, though; she was too caught up in her own 'hot' news. "I guess it's not much of a surprise to you all since we were bodymates, right?"

"Umm, have you both told your parents?" asked Daisy.

Mala shook her head. "My parents are very likely to object, considering he's not from an NRI background. His whole family is in government service. But Madhu said not to worry, we'll figure it out."

Zara, Nayana and Daisy exchanged glances; she had lied to Madhu Mohan, too! Minutes after Mala left, Sheetal came in, toweling her hair. "Anything going on?" she asked, seeing their expressions.

"Mala has a line with Madhu Mohan, and she has fed him the NRI story," summarized Daisy.

Sheetal hung her towel on the clothesline strung between two windows. "Great! The girl is not only a liar but also a thief! The less we see of her, the less the chance of theft."

"That's not fair," Zara said, wagging a finger, "you can't just pin the thefts on her..."

"All I know is that every time a watch, a book or a bangle went missing, Mala was in the vicinity. It's been like that since last year – she's always around when anything vanishes. A lot of girls have noticed it."

"Okay, that's enough of that," declared Nayana, looking uncomfortable. "I'm going to Waheeda's room to hear about her romance."

"Hey Zara, want to read notes with me?" asked Sheetal.

"What! Read notes when there's hot gossip? No way!"

"Aren't you coming, Sheetal?" Daisy asked on her way out.

"No, I have to read Ortho."

"Ortho? Zara told us that all you learned today was to stay away from that *njarambu rogi* HOD. It's a good thing that our batch representative announced he would only put boys in his unit."

"Yeah, but Vijayan Sir did mention a few things, like the carrying angle of the elbow. I thought I would read that up."

"Okay then." Daisy left.

Sheetal sat down at the table and opened Maheshwari's Textbook of Orthopaedics. Involuntarily, her eyes fell on Nayana's college satchel, which lay open on the bed. She got up, popped her head into the corridor to make sure no one was around and bolted the door shut. Then she opened the satchel and leafed through Nayana's books, hoping to find what made her roommate so smart.

Whatever the secret, Sheetal was determined to find it.

***

Clinics was a whole new world to the second years. They grappled with foreign concepts like case-taking and physical examination, and piecing together their findings to arrive at a diagnosis.

"Just like Sherlock Holmes, except there's no crime scene, only a body." Vaibhav had received an earful from the Assistant Professor for that remark.

The students quickly realized that case-taking was an art which depended as much on the finer conversation skills as on asking the right questions. Many patients were aware that students had no role in their actual treatment. Hence, the approach was crucial in winning their cooperation. In his welcome address, the HOD of General Medicine had told them, "The three professionals who rely on public support for success are actors, politicians and doctors." Over the years, the students would come to wonder if one also had to be a bit of the first two in order to succeed as the third. Elderly patients who longed for a sympathetic ear were overtly willing to cooperate, but the vast majority were reluctantly cooperative, and a smaller number were outright hostile.

Then there were the tricksters, those who liked to take the naive students for a ride. "What made you come to the hospital?" Kenza asked Khaderkutty in bed seven, whose case sheet said he had rheumatoid arthritis.

"Nothing, really." Khaderkutty waved his hand as if he didn't take his situation seriously.

"But there must have been something," insisted Luqman, who

was on the case along with Kenza. "Let's see." He looked at the date of admission on the cover of his case sheet, "You were admitted on the 17th at 10.45 a.m. What happened that morning?"

Looking thoughtful, Khaderkutty said, "I got up at seven. I usually get up at five for the morning prayer, but I had attended a marriage function the night before, and I was late getting back. It was raining heavily at the venue…"

"That's all okay," interrupted Kenza, "Just tell us what happened on the morning you came for admission."

"Oh yes. After I got up, I went to brush my teeth and found the toothpaste was over. I told my son to go to the shop down the road and buy one. But he came back saying the shop was closed…"

"Yes, yes, *then* what happened? After all your morning bathroom activities?"

"Then I had breakfast, *puttu* and *kadala,* I think. Or was it *vellappam* and stew?" He turned to his wife. "*Edi*, what did you make that day?" And for the next few minutes, the couple was engaged in a guessing game about that day's breakfast menu. Kenza and Luqman looked helplessly at each other.

Just then, a voice behind them said, "Khaderkutty, what have I told you about talking to the students?" They turned around, and Kenza gave a start. It was the same postgrad she had accompanied to the veterinary centre last year.

"This is a teaching hospital," he continued. "Those who don't cooperate do not get beds. You will have to lie on the floor."

"No, no, doctor, I'll tell them anything they want!"

After that, they had no problem with Khaderkutty. An hour later, the postgrad was writing out case sheets at the nurses' station. The stethoscope around his neck bore a name tag: KT Jayachandran.

"*Chetta*, is it true that patients who don't cooperate lose their right to a bed?" asked Luqman.

Jayachandran gave them a smile and winked.

***

College elections rolled around soon after the new batch of MBBS students arrived. Festoons of banners crisscrossed the campus, colourful billboards brightened the corridors, and candidates darted around frantically, canvassing for votes. Classes were relaxed to accommodate the campaigning, and the '96 batch students roamed among the freshers with a swagger born of newfound seniority.

As in previous years, the main contenders were ASU and Integrity. ASU, the student wing of a prominent leftist political party, had once considered the Calicut Institute of Medicine its stronghold. Back then, it wasn't unusual for ASU members to consult directly with party leaders on campus matters – a practice that didn't sit well with everyone. Tensions often erupted into clashes with students who resented political interference.

Over time, discontent with ASU's aggressive tactics grew louder, eventually leading to the formation of a new group – Integrity. With its popular slogan, "No politics on campus," Integrity quickly gained traction. At present, it was riding a wave of popularity, thanks to its fiery speakers and magnetic leaders who had a way of electrifying their audience.

Then there was the KKPP – short for *Kittiya Kitti, Poya Poyi* – a spoof party floated by King-Kong and his two sidekicks. No one took them seriously.

All eyes were on whether Integrity would finally dethrone ASU. The atmosphere on campus was electric, and the excitement was infectious.

The only one in a foul mood was Sheetal. Her favourite charm bracelet, the one her didi had brought for her from Dubai, was missing. She was always extra careful with it, but the previous evening she'd forgotten to stow it away before going for her bath. Much later, when she remembered, she combed through the room, but the bracelet had vanished. As usual, Sheetal had only one suspect – Mala. Lately, she had been hanging around the hostel quite often.

Wondering if there was any way to secretly check Mala's bags, Sheetal climbed the steps of the nearly empty lecture hall behind Sunny, who made his way to one of the back rows. They sat down, and he opened his textbook – Tripathi's *Essentials of Pharmacology*.

The last lecture of the day had been unexpectedly cancelled. While most students either headed back to their hostels or joined in the election campaigning, Sheetal and Sunny had opted for group study.

The first internal assessment of the second year was scheduled right after the elections, and Sheetal was struggling with Pharmacology. In the first year, it had been Biochemistry that tripped her. One day, during dissection class, Sunny had overheard her telling Waheeda that she planned to memorize the entire textbook cover to cover. "Do you honestly think you can memorize the whole *Lippincott* – or any other reference book?" he asked her later. "Those things are big enough to kill you if they fall on your head."

"It worked for me in school. Just memorize and regurgitate."

"Well, even if you could, it wouldn't make you a better doctor. You're supposed to arrive at a diagnosis, not recite a textbook to your patient."

He pulled his copy of *Lippincott* from his bag and flipped it open. "Start with the diagrams and graphs; they explain entire concepts beautifully. In exams, draw them, and write just enough to make your point. That's what I do."

As Sunny shared his study tips, Sheetal felt like her entire school education had been a waste. Her teachers rewarded those who reproduced their notes word for word. Any deviation was struck down with the dreaded red pen.

But Sunny's approach made sense. She took his advice to heart, and her marks improved dramatically. After that, group study sessions with Sunny became a regular part of her routine.

Forty-five minutes later, Sunny left for cricket practice, and Sheetal decided to head back to the hostel. Campaigning activities had died down, but some ASU candidates—like Mubashira Gafoor, who was running for vice chairman—were still around, engaged in discussions. King-Kong was prancing around, dressed as an Arab with flowing white robes and matching headgear, elaborating on their party name KKPP (*Kittiya Kitti Poya Poyi*) to a group of fourth-year girls.

Mala and two senior girls from the '95 batch were in the portico, chatting with a few first-year MBBS boys. Mala had a 'Vote for ASU badge' while the seniors wore 'Vote for Integrity' badges. As Sheetal walked past, she heard one of the girls tease, "We won't let you go until you sing the alphabet in reverse."

The boys chuckled nervously. Mala and the seniors giggled. Sheetal rolled her eyes and kept walking. Ever since ragging had been made a punishable offence, harmless flirting disguised as 'getting to know your juniors' had become the new norm.

Still, there were stray incidents of actual ragging, especially in the hostels. Sheetal, Zara, and Tarachand had once been caught on their way to RamCo and forced by some seniors to participate in an imaginary three-legged horse race down the road. Tarachand came in last – not surprising, since physical exertion wasn't his thing – but the seniors decided he was being chivalrous by letting the girls win and threatened to 'catch him later' at the hostel.

Vaibhav, on the other hand, *lived* to recount his ragging tales. He was particularly fond of retelling one story during dissection class – how he had once been forced to perform the 'medical salute' at the main road traffic junction. His crime? Being too engrossed in a chicken drumstick to stand and salute King-Kong when the senior entered the mess hall.

"The medical salute," Vaibhav explained with relish, "is the traditional way juniors greet seniors in the hostel. You raise one hand in a salute, grab your crotch with the other, and jump."

"Why hold your crotch?" The question slipped out of Waheeda's mouth before anyone could stop her.

"To protect the seniors' ears from the sound of our balls clanging together," came the prompt reply.

Sheetal still remembered the exquisite shade of red that spread across Waheeda's face and the unmistakable pride in Vaibhav's tone as he claimed this *achievement* had earned him a spot in the Djangoes club.

Sheetal could never quite understand why so many boys seemed to consider public humiliation a rite of passage. To her relief, Sunny didn't share that sentiment. He hadn't been ragged at all; maybe because the seniors simply hadn't found him interesting enough to bother.

When Sheetal entered the room, Zara, Nayana and Daisy were gathered noisily around a red-faced Waheeda. She saw a notebook with some crudely drawn but sexually explicit sketches. Her eyes widened. "What's going on here?"

"We are educating Waheeda," said Daisy. "You won't believe what she said to me today when I told her to sit next to a boy during common class." Sheetal looked expectantly at Waheeda, who said in a small voice, "I said I couldn't sit next to him because I might get pregnant from the sperms running up and down his pants."

The girls screamed with laughter, and Sheetal's mouth fell open. "But… but… Waheeda, you're a second-year MBBS student! And you're married! What did you think? How do you…"

"Never mind," cut in Zara, waving the notebook with diagrams explaining different positions. "We have taught her all that she needs to know about what happens after *kootti kondu pokal.*"

Waheeda hid her face in her hands. "*Ya Allah*, how can I look at Ahmed *ikka*'s face now?"

This sent the girls into more peals of laughter.

Sheetal couldn't believe a girl could be this naive! Her own mother had explained everything when she was in high school. But being a gynaecologist, talking about body parts and their functions came easily to her. It was only when the others started discussing how they had figured out about the birds and the bees that Sheetal realized that having a parent willing to give you 'the talk' wasn't a privilege every child had.

"I already had some vague notions from the hurriedly fast-forwarded scenes in movies," Zara said, "We didn't own a VCR (video cassette recorder), so Daddy rented one occasionally, and we'd see movies at a stretch. Once, when we were watching 'The Day of the Jackal,' he was called urgently to his office. Mama was busy in the kitchen, so he left me in charge of the remote after a hurried explanation of how to use the crucial fast-forward button. I stayed alert, and suddenly there was this nude woman in bed with a man. Panicking, I pressed the button. But I didn't realize I had actually pressed the slow-motion button. We, kids, watched the nude scene saucer-eyed and open-mouthed!"

"I found out by accident when I was around eight," said Nayana. "We were staying at our cousin's home during one vacation, and I found an unopened condom under the bed while playing hide and seek. I looked up the word in a dictionary, one word led to another, and then I knew." She grimaced. "It was quite a shocking discovery at that age, and I felt really nauseated for a long time afterwards."

"Same pinch! Same pinch!" Daisy said excitedly, "I, too, found out in an under-the-bed hide-and-seek situation, but much worse!"

Waheeda covered her ears.

"Oh, don't be such a prude!" Daisy swatted Waheeda's hands off her ears. "It's an interesting story. I was around 10 at the time. There was a wedding in my ancestral home, and the entire extended family was there. We, kids, were playing hide and seek, and I hid under a huge four-poster bed in one of the farthest rooms.

Suddenly, Litty Aunty and Ouseph Uncle entered in a tearing hurry, locked the door and started flinging their clothes off. I felt like an intruder, so I kept quiet. A few minutes later, the bed started creaking ominously, and both of them were making a lot of grunting noises. I thought they were trying to kill each other; I started bawling. They discovered me, and a really awkward situation followed."

"Poor Daisy and the loss of her childhood innocence!" Zara laughed so hard that tears ran down her face.

"Well, it wasn't a total loss. They stuffed me with chocolates so I wouldn't go around the house with a megaphone. And they still send me treats; that huge tin of roasted cashews I brought last month was from Litty Aunty."

"They are still bribing you after so many years?" Sheetal asked in surprise.

Daisy gave several winks. "Because they're not married to each other."

"Ooooh!" Zara said,

"Phone call for Waheeda, second year!" came a shout from the corridor.

"That must be Ahmed ikka!" Springing off the bed, Waheeda bounded out of the room.

Sheetal giggled. "She's going to have some trouble talking to him now, thanks to your lessons."

"The lesson just happened by chance," Daisy said. "She actually came to ask if anyone had seen the Sheaffer pen Ahmed gifted her. It's missing."

***

A week prior to voting day, the hostellers woke up to scandalous news on their notice boards: an official complaint had been made to the college Principal against two girls from the '95 batch, both Integrity supporters, on the grounds of ragging first-year students. The witnesses were Mubashira Gafoor and – much to the shock of the '96 batch – Mala Diwakaran.

At the first stroke of eight, the HOD of General Medicine, Dr Gayathri Vasudevan, marched into the ward trailed by an Assistant Professor and three postgraduate students. The students posted in the unit quickly assembled in front of her.

"Is everyone present today?"

"Yes, ma'am," they chorused.

Dr Gayathri was a stickler for punctuality, so even incorrigible latecomers arrived five minutes early. The students flipped through their notes for details of the patient they had examined the previous day – symptoms, clinical history, past history, family history, treatment history, physical examination findings and finally provisional diagnosis. They also had to list the investigations that helped them arrive at a final diagnosis.

But that day, the students weren't as prepared as they normally would be, owing to the Pharmacology spotting exam in the afternoon.

As Dr Gayathri led the group through the ward from patient to patient, Kenza trailed behind, wondering how on earth Mala had become mixed up in this. As Mala was now in the additional batch, they hardly saw each other. She glanced sideways at Madhu Mohan; he seemed preoccupied, worried even.

"Who took this patient's case?" Dr Gayathri asked, stopping at a bed.

Latheef raised his hand nervously.

"Okay, present."

He cleared his throat. "Sixty-two-year-old male, chronic alcoholic, chronic smoker ..."

Dr Gayathri stopped him with a wave of her hand. "What's your name?" She searched his coat lapel for a name tag and, not seeing one, looked at him in quiet fury.

"Sorry, ma'am, I accidentally ironed over it this morning."

Dr Gayathri was not amused. "Well, at least tell us your name!"

"Latheef KP."

"Tell me, Latheef KP, is that how you start your clinical history?"

He blinked in confusion, and Dr Gayathri clucked pityingly. "This patient has a personality, a profession. But you chose to sum him up in two unkind terms – chronic alcoholic, chronic smoker. Can't you show the courtesy of saying his name or what he does for a living before revealing his vices?"

Looking contrite, Latheef started again. "Swaminathan, sixty-two-year-old male, chronic, err," he paused to avoid the same mistake and quickly switched words, "*sanyasi*." Everyone burst into laughter.

"*Chronic sanyasi, eh? Then what is an acute sanyasi*?" Dr Gayathri asked, smirking. "This is *exactly* what I mean when I warn you people about mindless case-taking."

The next case was a cardiac patient whom Luqman had seen. "What is balanced vasodilation?" she asked, sending shock waves through the group. Luqman rattled off the answer, and the other students exhaled in relief. Only Luqman or Kenza could handle fireballs like that. Gayathri madam was impressed. Her next fireball fell on Latheef. "You, Acute *Sanyasi* – give me another example of balanced vasodilation."

Latheef looked clueless. Then he blurted out, "Smoking and drinking. Smoking causes vasoconstriction, and drinking causes vasodilation. So, it's balanced."

Everyone burst out laughing again while Dr Gayathri looked as if she were debating whether to laugh or cry. Then she seemed to decide that exam stress was the reason behind these horrific blunders and excused them so they could revise for the spotting exam.

That afternoon, the Pharmacology spotting exam was interrupted by a noisy procession of Integrity supporters on the main road shouting slogans against ASU. As soon as the exam was over, they raced outside to hear the news.

Scuffles had broken out earlier in the day when Integrity accused ASU of trying to tilt the election in their favour with a fraudulent ragging complaint against two of their key supporters. ASU had refused to back down, projecting Mubashira and Mala as witnesses to the incident. Finally, the Principal called both groups for a meeting. ASU agreed to drop their complaint if Integrity agreed to withdraw the complaint of vandalism they had made a week earlier against some of the candidates in the ASU panel. After the complaints were dropped from both sides, Integrity organized a procession to vent their ire.

At the Ladies' Hostel, every room was buzzing. "Those senior girls and Mala were just talking to the boys. I saw and heard them. How can Mala be a witness to a ragging that never happened?" Sheetal looked perplexed.

"What I heard is Madhu Mohan compelled Mala to stand as witness at Mubashira *Chechi*'s insistence," said Daisy. "Those senior girls are the 'lines' of two Integrity candidates. The purpose of this whole drama was to get the complaints against the ASU candidates dropped. They *made* Mala lie."

"Once a liar, always a liar," Sheetal said disdainfully.

"Even worse, now that Mala is in the spotlight, many of the boys have come to know that she lied about her NRI background."

"Does Madhu Mohan know?" asked Waheeda.

Daisy shrugged. "Either way, Madhu took advantage of their relationship to use Mala as a dispensable tool for ASU."

The girls fell silent. Finally, Nayana sighed and changed the topic. "How was the exam?"

"I guess it was okay, but the fifth spotter was ridiculous," Waheeda said.

"How so?"

"Don't you remember? It was a ruler placed on a piece of paper with the question – Write two uses of this instrument. I wrote – To measure. What else do you use a ruler for? My school teacher used to hit us with one, but I can't write that!"

The girls burst out laughing.

"You fool, that spotter was Dale's water bath!" shrieked Nayana. "It was placed at the back next to the wall, and that ruler was placed on the question paper to prevent it from flying off!"

Waheeda looked mortified. She had missed seeing an instrument as gigantic as Dale's water bath!

"What do I do now? Shall I go and tell the HOD tomorrow?"

"Leave it," Zara said. "She'll pack you off to Ophthalmology if you say you didn't see that dinosaur-sized thing!"

***

As expected, Integrity won the election and the union. But the ragging issue had created a dent in their image which was big enough to lose them two key posts and three minor posts. It was the biggest gain for ASU in recent years. Mubashira Gafoor, the newly elected vice-chairman, proclaimed to one and all her continued efforts against ragging. In every speech, she mentioned Mala's 'bravery' and encouraged others to be like her. But her praise did little for Mala's tarnished image. Especially when the whole campus came to know she had been lying about her family background.

The results of the Second MBBS first average exams were out. The students rushed to the department notice boards to check their marks. They ran their fingers over the microscopic lettering and jabbed at their names, some victoriously, some dejectedly. Several students had performed abysmally in the Pathology practicals, because the faculty had wisened up to the tricks they used to identify tissue sections and placed a fresh set of slides for the exams.

"But the slide with a scratch in the left corner *was* Hepatocellular carcinoma, and the slide with the half-torn sticker *was* Amoebiasis, and the slide broken in the centre *was* Granulomatous lymphadenitis," insisted Vaibhav. He couldn't believe he had failed.

"I told you guys not to depend on such stupid shortcuts," said Zara. "Hey Tarachand, what's up with you?"

Tarachand was flipping through his answer sheets, his face reddening. Sunny wrestled them out of his clutches, found the source of his embarrassment and read it out, much to everyone's merriment. Tarachand had identified four out of 10 histopathology slides as lesions of the cervix in the hope that at least one would be correct. The faculty who evaluated his paper had written a little comment, 'I understand you may have a fascination for certain things, but don't make it so evident on paper!'

Sheetal took one look at her marks in Pathology and ran back to the hostel before she bumped into anyone. Bolting the door shut, she fell on her bed, tears dampening her pillow. She had scraped through in Microbiology, Pharmacology and Forensic Medicine, but had fallen flat on her face in Pathology. Sunny had cautioned her endlessly against using Vaibhav's technique of identifying slides. But the shortcut had seemed like the perfect solution to gain more study time for Pharmacology and Microbiology, subjects she found extremely difficult. How could she face Sunny now? Disheartened, she dozed off until a knock on the door awoke her a little later. It was Daisy.

"Hey Sheetal, Mubashira *Chechi* has asked you to meet her at the blood bank for a donation."

The surprise on Sheetal's face must have been evident because Daisy asked curiously, "What blood group are you anyway?"

"B-Negative. But how does Mubashira *Chechi* know that? I never registered myself with the Blood Donor's Forum (BDF)."

Daisy shrugged. "No clue. I guess these BDF members can just sniff out rare blood types. You'd better get going. You wouldn't want to refuse a request from our new vice chairman."

When she reached the blood bank, it became clear at once how the BDF knew of Sheetal's blood group. Nayana was there talking to a few of the members. Sheetal saw red. She knew Nayana was obsessed with blood. She was always the first to volunteer in Clinical Pathology to make peripheral smears; she was possibly the only one in their batch who already knew how to draw blood with a needle and syringe; and she knew the blood groups of all her roommates!

"Hi Sheetal," said Nayana. "I'm sorry I told Mubashira Chechi that you are B-Negative, but there was no time; it's a small kid with leukaemia, and he's critical."

"Shut up, you bitch!"

Mubashira walked in just then. "Ah, glad you volunteered, Sheetal. Come this way."

Sheetal lay on the couch and watched blood flow from her arm through a plastic tube into the collection bag rocking in a motorized tray. The rocking motion made sure that the blood was mixed thoroughly with the anticoagulant in the bag.

A few minutes later, a small beep emanated from the machine signifying the blood bag was full. The nurse disconnected the bag, removed the needle from Sheetal's arm, stuck a plaster and led her to a small recovery room near the exit, where she helped herself to the biscuits and Frooti packs on the teapoy.

A few seconds later, Nayana entered and sat in the adjacent chair. Sheetal concentrated on her drink so that her rage wouldn't show.

"Hey, I'm really, really sorry that I told…" began Nayana, but stopped seeing Mubashira come in.

"Blood donation is our duty to our fellow human beings," she lectured. "That little boy's parents were at their wits' end trying to arrange blood for him. You are his hero, Sheetal."

Sheetal continued slurping her juice with downcast eyes. Mubashira sighed. "I'll put it this way, Sheetal – you should not B-Negative about blood donation, you should B-Positive!" She chuckled at her own joke, and Nayana forced a weak laugh.

Sheetal stopped slurping and looked up. "*Chechi*, I have a doubt. Can parents with A-Positive and O-Positive blood groups have a B-Positive child?"

Mubashira frowned. "That's impossible. They would have either A-Positive or O-Positive children, but never B-Positive, unless it's the extremely rare Bombay blood group. You need the B antigen in at least one parent. It's Mendelian genetics. We've been studying this right from our pre-degree years, haven't we?"

Sheetal nodded. "Yes, Chechi, you're correct. It's impossible."

***

Zara pressed the phone receiver to her ear and bit her lip to stop her giggles.

"Don't play games with me, Zara," came her mother's terse voice over the phone. "Just last week, you told me you had broken up with that boy, Arthur Guy-something. And you've found a new Orthodox Syrian Christian boy this fast? People will say you have loose morals if you run after boys like this."

"Chill, Mama. They're all running after me!"

"Not funny! And what kind of a family name is Papan... Papini... oh what was it?"

"Papanicolaou. It's derived from the colloquial name of George's hometown, Papani Kollam. So will you talk to Daddy about him?"

"*Eshoye!* Wait till your father hears this news," her mother groaned before the phone went dead.

Zara chuckled merrily at the thought of her agitated mother pestering her father with the news that their daughter had a new 'line' with a certain George Papanicolaou. It seemed only appropriate to use the name of the founder of the Pap smear, as she was currently posted in Gynaecology. Her eyes drifted to the window of the visitors' room, through which she could see Nayana at the far end of the garden, sitting on the rim of the broken fountain.

Zara usually left Nayana alone during her crying spells. She would spend a few nights weepy and sleepwalking around their room, then slowly return to her usual self. In their first year, this had been a weekly routine, but by the second year, the spells came less frequently, sometimes with gaps as long as two months. Daisy, whose antennae missed nothing, had once told her that Nayana was on medication for depression. Not knowing how to comfort her, Zara had chosen instead to respect her space.

But today, Nayana seemed worse than usual. Zara was debating whether to go into the garden when Kenza appeared. She closed the textbook she was carrying, sat down beside Nayana, and gently wrapped an arm around her shoulders. Kenza often stayed at the hostel for group study; one of those overly studious types, Zara thought. Nayana seemed to respond to her words, and Zara exhaled in quiet relief. For all her extroverted charm, Zara had never known how to console someone.

Zara was the Medical Officer in charge of Casualty, and in the dead of night, she was called to see a patient who was brought in with multiple rib fractures. He said he'd fallen from a wall. The man looked vaguely familiar.

"Why were you clambering up a wall in the middle of the night?" she asked, proceeding to examine him. The man remained silent. Just then, something fell out of the folds of his lungi onto the floor. Zara saw it was a slender stainless-steel torch.

That's when it clicked – this was no ordinary man, this was the showman! The guy who waited behind bushes to flash unsuspecting girls and scaled the wall of the Ladies Hostel at night to shine the torch on his private parts.

"Ha! You are done for now, you njaranmbu rogi!"

Suddenly, his chest collapsed inwards, and from the great gaping hole, a river of blood poured out and pooled all around the Casualty floor. The man turned his head and gave her an evil grin. Horrified, Zara backed away. The blood level kept rising inside the room; it was up to her chest, then her neck, then her forehead; she took a deep breath, and the blood flowed into her lungs, drowning her.

Zara shot up in bed, gasping for air. Wiping her sweaty forehead with a shaking hand, she waited for her erratic breathing to slow down.

God, what a nightmare! The clock on the wall showed 2.50 a.m. She got up for a glass of water and moved past the other girls fast asleep in their beds… and stopped. Nayana was not in her bed. She reflexively looked at the door – it was ajar.

She hastily stepped out of the room and made a quick search of the verandah. Nayana was nowhere to be seen. Zara's sleep-fuddled brain couldn't make head or tail of the situation. They always padlocked their door at night, so who had opened it?

But where on earth could Nayana be? *Maybe she's in the toilet!* Zara made her way to the toilet stalls, but all were empty. *Could she have gone outside the hostel?* Unlikely. Both the front and back entrances were padlocked.

A bat flew close overhead, startling Zara, and she looked up at it.

That's when she saw her.

Nayana was on the terrace, her head bent, blue nightgown flapping in the breeze, and she was slowly but surely walking towards the edge of the terrace… one slow step after another, towards thin air. Then she fell.

Time slowed to a crawl.

Like a movie in slow motion.

The girl in the blue nightgown drifted down slowly, landed on a clump of shrubs, breaking branches, and floated to the ground, where she bounced twice before coming to rest. Clouds of dust flew everywhere, twinkling in the moonlight, and settled around the girl who lay like a broken doll.

All of a sudden, time caught up to speed.

Zara screamed.

The whole hostel was wide awake. The watchman called an ambulance while the hostel secretary summoned the Warden. Nayana, unconscious and bleeding, was bundled into the ambulance and taken to Casualty. Zara had to be restrained from going along and was weeping inconsolably, her head in Daisy's lap. A little later, the Warden called from Casualty to say Nayana had regained consciousness but was immediately sedated. She had fractured her pelvis, both arms and a leg, and was being prepared for surgery. Her parents had been informed, and they were on their way.

"Thank God those branches broke her fall," remarked Waheeda, shaking her head. "Did anyone see her sleepwalk?"

Daisy glanced at Sheetal. "Sheetal was the last, as usual. She slept at 2 a.m. She forgot to padlock the door. Nayana was in her bed at that time."

"But how did she open the door to the terrace? And after she entered the terrace, how did it get bolted from inside?"

"We asked the watchman about that," said Mohini. "He said workers were cementing a leak in the roof, and though they returned the key to him as usual, the lock on the door is ancient and rusty and perhaps hadn't been properly locked. After she entered the terrace, it must have slammed shut, and the rusty bolt must have fallen back on itself and jammed."

Everyone fell silent. Outside, those who hadn't heard the news were being updated by their friends, and some were inspecting the area where the accident occurred.

One of the senior girls appeared in the doorway. "Come on, everyone, the mess hall has been opened. There's coffee and biscuits. The Warden called to say the police will be here soon."

Mohini pulled Zara up from Daisy's lap. "What's happened has happened. There's nothing we can do for Nayana except pray she makes a full recovery. Come, freshen up."

Daisy turned to Sheetal, who sat hunched up in bed, staring at the wall. "Aren't you coming?" Sheetal didn't reply.

"Look, I know you didn't get along with her, but we all knew Nayana sleepwalked and…" Daisy hesitated, "she had depression."

Sheetal looked up sharply, her eyes widening. "How do you know that?"

"Her prescription from the Psychiatry OP fell out of her bag one day, and I picked it up for her."

Sheetal went back to staring at the wall. "Do you know if there was a cause? For her depression, I mean."

Daisy shook her head. "No idea. All I know is that in her first year, she was either getting constant phone calls or crying in the garden. She seemed better when the second year started. But over the past few days, she turned gloomy again and started sleepwalking."

Wrapping herself in a shawl, Daisy left the room.

Sheetal sat staring at the wall, her chin on her knees, unsure of how she ought to feel.

6. Daisy, 2016

17th March, 2016
Calicut

The boys were off to their grandparents', and Zara and I had just polished off an excellent dinner of appam and mutton stew that had turned out even better than I'd hoped. By 10 p.m., we were sprawled on the lounge chairs beside the pool, cradling our vodkas. The breeze was cool, and the water rippled in gentle waves.

Zara was scrolling through her phone; her eyes narrowed with that familiar mix of curiosity and judgement.

"You're checking the comments on Vaibhav's apology post, aren't you?"

She gave a noncommittal "Mm," still staring at her screen.

I turned toward her, grinning. "Want to know a secret? I called him."

Her eyes flew wide open. "No way! You're bluffing."

"I'm not!" I said, laughing. "I actually picked up the phone and asked him straight up what made him post that public apology."

"And?"

"He didn't say much. Played it safe. Said it felt like the right thing, even if it was too late."

Zara snorted. "Typical."

"But I *know* there's a story there. A juicy one. And not knowing is killing me. You know how I get – if there's gossip I'm not privy to, I get the worst belly aches," I said, holding my stomach.

Zara laughed. "Your stomach is protesting the way you devoured all that mutton stew."

"Hey!" I said, pretending to be offended, then brightened when she added, "But it was delicious."

"True," I said smugly. "Now, maybe I'll just make up a reason for Vaibhav's apology, as I did for Tarachand's divorce. For *mann ki shanti*, you know?"

She giggled. "Taru's first wife left because she couldn't take living with a makku. Maybe Vaibhav's wife caught him flirting with his neighbour."

"See?" I said, delighted. "I'm already feeling better."

Zara smiled. "It's been so good. I wish I didn't have to leave tomorrow."

"Then don't! We could go to Thusharagiri or even drive to Muzhappilangad beach. Come on."

"I'd love to, but I've got a string of people to visit. Mama's asking when I'll be in Kottayam. Vivian's invited me to his son's baptism. Mala's been sending these guilt-trip messages about her housewarming, and Waheeda… well, she'll kill me if I don't meet her."

"You see?" I said, trying to pout but failing. "This is what happens when you're so loved."

She leaned back, then I asked the question that had been burning in my head.

"So, who's 'The Prince'?"

Zara choked on her drink. "God damn you, Daisy! Were you spying on me?"

"Excuse me! *Your* phone was lying on the kitchen table. Some guy called, the call got cut, and I saw 12 missed calls from him. So, tell me – is he one of those clingy admirers who can't take a hint?"

Zara shrugged, trying to play it cool. "You could say that."

Just then, my phone rang. I answered with an exaggerated, "Hi Achachan! Enjoying New York?" Zara smirked as I slipped into my high-pitched wifey voice.

Ten minutes later, I hung up. "He says he misses my cooking. See? A little distance, and he realizes my worth."

Zara looked straight at me. "Can I ask something? Doesn't it bother you, being stuck at home while he flies off to conferences all over the world?"

"Not really. I enjoy myself here – shopping, movies, eating out."

"But always in Calicut. Don't you want to travel alone sometimes? Why not visit me in the UK during the kids' summer vacation?"

I laughed but quickly added, "I'll have to ask Achachan, and also check with my in-laws."

Zara's smile vanished. "Did *he* ask anyone's permission before flying to New York?"

I didn't have a reply to that.

"Look," I said finally, gesturing at the house, the garden, the pool. "I focus on what I *do* have. How many women live like this? I just ask, and he hands me his credit card, no questions asked. Sure, our relationship has rough edges, but *adjusting* is the key to happiness."

"Are you happy?" Zara asked softly.

I hesitated. She raised her hands, backing off. "Never mind. It's your bubble. I'm not here to pop it."

"You'll understand when you get married," I said, trying to lighten the mood.

"God, you sound like my mother," she groaned. "Maybe I'll marry if I find Mr Right."

"So, I take it 'The Prince' is Mr Wrong?"

She grinned. "Ex-boyfriend. Brit. Hence the nickname. He wants to get back together, but…"

"But?"

"Never mind. Just be glad I have the freedom to land up on your doorstep at 2 a.m. if I want to."

Later that night, I locked the patio doors and started washing our highball glasses. Upstairs, I heard Zara packing.

The ache crept in.

By morning, she'd be gone. And I'd go back to the routine – school runs, groceries, meal plans, managing two boys who bicker like politicians on TV.

My phone buzzed. A message from Achachan. *'Mutton biryani in New York! No match to what you make at home. Can't wait to be back.'*

The photo below showed him and his colleagues grinning with plates piled high.

I sent a heart emoji. Reflex.

And then just stared into the darkness outside the kitchen window.

Fourteen years of marriage. Two demanding boys. A house that ran like clockwork. Somewhere along the way, I'd lost track of who I was supposed to be.

Before the wedding, I was obsessed with learning to cook and draping a sari – so much so, I'd bungled my first attempt at the postgraduate entrance. When I suggested using contraception, till I cleared the exam, his horrified "No!" had been the end of that.

I got pregnant within a month.

By the time my son was two, I began to despair about ever clearing the exam. To add salt to my wounds, he often downplayed my efforts to study.

"Don't expect to pass the exam if studying is only an afterthought," he'd say when he walked into the kitchen, seeing me balancing an MCQ book next to the stove while flipping dosas.

"When I was studying," he launched in, pacing like a man about to quote his own success story, "I didn't move from my desk. Day and night. Books open. Nose in them. Not even bathroom breaks unless strictly—wait a minute—"

He stopped mid-heroic monologue to peer into the curry bowl. His face twisted in shock.

"Is that… *chammanthi podi*?"

A beat.

"I hate it. Why isn't there any coconut chutney? Is that so hard?"

And just like that, my crime wasn't poor time management or subpar prep – the real betrayal was the missing coconut chutney on his crisp dosa.

The following year, I became a mother again, while he got selected for a two-year fellowship course in Germany. I was left alone with two small children, a home to run, unreliable maids and parents on both sides with health too fragile for babysitting. And I failed. Again. I gave up completely.

Eventually, I became the wife he expected – home manager, school admin, plumber wrangler, queen of chutneys, disaster fixer. Everything and everyone came before me. I cheerfully managed everything that threatened to interfere with the career graph of a fledgling neurosurgeon.

In his eyes, I was perfect. "My wife, my life," he'd boast to his friends. And I'd smile, pretending it didn't sting.

A few years ago, I joined the government health service as an Assistant Surgeon in the district hospital. It was my colleagues who encouraged me to start the YouTube channel – initially just a lark.

But it took off. The subscribers poured in. Then came the book deal. And suddenly, I wasn't invisible anymore.

He hated it.

"YouTube is juvenile."

"You'll attract creeps."

"A cookbook? You're a *doctor*!"

"Shouldn't you be preparing for the entrance exam?"

Now, as I brushed my teeth, his voice echoed in my head. *"Mutton biryani… coconut chutney… Shouldn't you be studying…"*

I spat hard into the basin and washed my face. In the mirror, I saw a jaw set in steel and eyes that had stopped flinching.

After Zara left, I would start work on that book.

And I'd see it through. Come hell or high water.

I pulled the bedroom door shut and heard Zara's voice floating down from upstairs. She was pacing the hall, talking on the phone. She sounded irritated.

British ex-boyfriend, my foot.

I'd seen the number. It was an Indian one.

Why had she lied?

What could be so secret?

Knowing Zara, it could be *anything*. A cult. The Illuminati. A politician's son.

Maybe someone *we both* knew?

I made a mental note to pester her about it later.

Whatever it was, I'd find out. I always do.

7. Third year, 1998-1999

'Yes, you CAN but you MAY not!'

10th March, 1998
Calicut

Dear Pappachen,

We've all caught a bad case of Third Year Syndrome. It's not an official diagnosis, but it might as well be. Basically, you spend enough time reading about diseases and start believing that you or someone you sit next to – has them.

Tarachand was convinced he had cerebellar ataxia because he kept bumping into door frames. Turned out he just needed glasses. One visit to Ophthalmology and the drama evaporated. He still walks like a duck, but now it's with clarity.

Arundhati self-diagnosed herself with fibromyalgia and uses it as a reason to make Anand, her long-suffering boyfriend, carry every single one of her bottles and bags. (He's started limping slightly, though no one's sure if it's real or symbolic). Anand now functions exclusively as a human pack mule. If she ever breaks up with him, he might need physiotherapy.

And Latheef has dragged his parents to the hospital so many times that they've started threatening to legally disown him. We're all waiting to see if they'll follow through.

But the gold medal, without question, goes to Waheeda.

During our General Medicine posting, she offered to be the test subject while we practised clinical examination. Sheetal listened to her heart for all of 20 seconds and casually mentioned, "Hmm... could be mitral stenosis." Waheeda immediately dove headfirst into Cardiology textbooks, became her own private patient, and emerged with a self-diagnosis of Ortner syndrome. She spent a week checking her own pulse like it was a religious ritual. She even mustered the courage to consult the Head of Cardiology himself. A man who looks like he hasn't smiled since the 1980s – who threw her out and

threatened 'dire consequences' if she ever darkened his door again with 'this nonsense'. (His words. Or close enough).
She hasn't mentioned Ortner syndrome since, so I suppose she's been 'cured'. But give it a week. A new malady will arrive, and Waheeda will welcome it like an old friend.
As for me, I seem to have escaped the Third Year Syndrome. But not the nightmares. I still get them sometimes. Nayana falling. From rooftops. Trees. Ledges. Always high places. Always falling. I think it's because I keep thinking about her. After the accident, I used to call her home now and then, just to check in. No one ever seemed to mind. But then, one fine day, no one took the calls. When a few of our batchmates went to visit during the holidays, they found the house locked. Neighbours said the family moved away, that too, suddenly. No forwarding address. No explanations. Nothing.
I keep telling myself there's probably a simple explanation. But that's the thing about silence – it never actually sounds simple.
Will write again soon.
Your loving granddaughter,
Zara

A nervous Kenza sat outside the examination hall, flipping through the Dhingra ENT textbook, her eyes taking in nothing. It wasn't the exam that rattled her – it was the question waiting for her after it. Jayachandran wanted an answer.

She wasn't sure when exactly their separate paths had begun to blur. Maybe it was during her second year when she was posted in his unit. He taught their classes with an air of stiff competence, answered their endless questions with saint-like patience, and peppered lessons with dry medical anecdotes. Or maybe it was that day when she'd finally mustered the nerve to ask him about the dog they'd saved together in the first year.

"Tripod's at my house now," he'd said matter-of-factly. "His leg couldn't be saved, so we amputated."

"You named him Tripod?" she asked, raising an eyebrow.

"Yeah. Three legs. Felt accurate."

He then launched into a detailed account of Tripod's quirks;

his love for anything yellow – mangoes, jackfruit, butter cakes. His tendency to bark at kittens. As if Kenza were the only person in the world who needed to know. She was struck by this oddly warm version of Jayachandran. In class, he was all protocol and punctuality.

Then, just like that, he said, "Want to grab a coffee?"

Startled, intrigued, and mildly hungry, Kenza followed him to the Coffee House. They ended up talking for over an hour – college, medicine, and the various ways house-surgency could derail one's soul.

"If you're aiming for a civil surgeon post in the government sector," he advised, "you'd better take your house-surgency seriously. Learn the Casualty work, medicolegal stuff, sutures, common antibiotics – all of it. But if you're planning to specialize, do the bare minimum and pour your soul into PG prep."

Kenza listened quietly. The truth was, the odds of her academic story extending beyond MBBS were laughably slim. In her family, daughters were groomed for marriage, not medicine. Her parents weren't opposed to her studies, as long as it didn't interfere with the sacred duty of getting married on time. Continuing studies after marriage depended on her husband's goodwill and his family's tolerance.

Her own marriage had ended before it had really begun. Her father had scraped together every spare rupee to arrange it. The groom had been older – 28 years. He ran a small *palacharakku kada* and lived with a bedridden mother. Kenza entered that household at 18, with psoriasis hidden under her long sleeves and a headscarf.

One day, over lunch, Jayachandran asked the inevitable: "Why did your marriage end?"

She stirred her coffee. Then, with a quiet defiance, she let her headscarf slip back, revealing the angry red patches along her hairline and ears.

"Psoriasis," she said. "It's worse on my body. My parents knew no one would marry me unless they did it quickly. My husband… he wasn't cruel. Just very methodical and rigid. When I got selected for BSc Nursing, he said no. Called it immoral, because I'd have to care for men."

Jayachandran blinked. "What about his family?"

"His mother had Multiple Sclerosis. I was her primary caregiver. His sisters dropped by once a week, at the maximum. If I left, the care would fall on them. I cried and begged him for days. He finally slapped me. So, I walked out."

Her voice trembled. "Then I had an abortion. I didn't even know I was pregnant. My husband was furious. My parents begged me to go back. I threatened to kill myself if they didn't let me study."

"Did they believe you?"

"Enough to panic. They asked my husband to wait. But once I joined college, I never went back. He divorced me. I took the entrance again the next year and got an MBBS. Now my parents are desperate to remarry me before my younger sister turns 18."

Jayachandran didn't say anything. His face was unreadable.

That weekend, Kenza spiralled. Why had she told him everything? He would disappear like Mala and Nayana. After the college election drama, Mala had turned invisible, refusing to acknowledge even simple gestures like a wave from across the road. Nayana had been kinder, often leaning on Kenza (literally and emotionally), and had once even asked her to move into the hostel. But then she'd left too.

Now Jayachandran would vanish.

But the next week, Kenza began her ENT posting, got consumed by the upcoming average exam and to her surprise, he reappeared. Showed up one afternoon outside the ENT OPD just as she was signing out."I'm going for lunch," he said. "Coming?"

From then on, they often lunched together. And with each meal, Kenza grew more aware that what they had wasn't just coffee and casual conversation. Other people noticed too. When a classmate made a suggestive comment, Kenza panicked. She stopped meeting him.

One afternoon, a junior approached her in the mess hall. "Chechi, someone's here to see you."

Jayachandran was waiting in the visitors' room, arms folded, face set.

"Why are you avoiding me?" he asked. "I'm not leaving without an answer."

She looked away. "People are talking."

He rolled his eyes. "I'm juggling a hundred things – finals, shifts, sleep deprivation – and I still make time to see you. And now you're dodging me. Why? Don't you like me?"

Kenza blinked. Did he just say that?

"Do you like me or not?" he asked again, this time softly.

She didn't reply.

Jayachandran picked up his helmet. "I'm doing a double shift starting tomorrow. After that, we'll meet – maybe for the last time. It's your call."

Now, that moment had arrived.

"Kenza Abubacker!" called the Tutor from the doorway.

She snapped out of her thoughts and walked into the hall. The exam was easier than expected. But more importantly, she had made up her mind.

Jayachandran was waiting in the portico, sitting astride his bike. He didn't dismount. Kenza stood there, heart thumping. Then, slowly, she walked over and climbed on behind him. He started the engine, and they rode off, with the eyes of the entire portico watching them.

***

"Letter for you, Zara," Daisy said, entering the room with a brown envelope. Zara took it, surprised that Pappachen had replied so quickly.

"Oh!" It wasn't from Pappachen; it was from Rishab Manchandani, her colourful school friend. Letters from him were rare, but they always carried explosive news. She tore open the envelope, stepped out of the room and sat on the steps leading to the garden.

25th April, '98

My Z-weetheart,

What's up, ya? You won't believe the kind of Ladakh trip you missed last year. No tents collapsing this time, no getting locked out of hotel rooms, and we even had proper food.
But chhod all that. I've got BIG news. Ready?
Your boy has officially finished his Hotel Management course! Campus placements were wild – lots of fancy options – but I went with the one that felt right in my gut: The Taj. Kovalam. Yes, madam. Kerala. Beachside. Five star. Me in uniform. Try not to faint.
And I already know what you're thinking:
"Why Kovalam, yaar? Why not Mumbai or Delhi?"
Okay, so… I did a small detour to your house before finalizing things. Just thought I'd give your folks the good news. You know – polite beta things. Aunty looked sweet as always, but the moment I mentioned Kerala, she got that oh-no-he's-coming look in her eyes. Started mumbling about 'good grooms from respectable families' and 'distractions' and I was like, "Arre Aunty, relax. I'm just talking about a job, not a honeymoon."
But THEN she casually drops that line of 'khandaani' rishtas are waiting to meet you. I laughed. Until I realized she wasn't joking.
So yeah. Decision made.
Kovalam it is.
I mean, if your family is so scared that I'm gonna show up and sweep you off your feet… maybe I should just go ahead and do it, na?
Also, Trivandrum's kind of vibey, ya. Caught a quick stopover at Kochi too – sending you pics! Wait till you see me in a mundu.
Next stop: Calicut. You, me, beach.
Call me when you stop laughing.
Yours in full glam and slight delusion,
RM

Zara snorted. Knowing Rishab, the most likely reason was that he had found a new girlfriend with a connection to Kovalam, and once he broke up with her (which was the routine), he would pack up and leave. She went through the photos – vivid colourful snaps of his stay at Bolgatty Palace and his visits to Fort Kochi, Sree Padmanabhaswamy kshethram, Shanmugham beach and Vizhinjam port. He was an excellent photographer with an eye for the unusual.

Behind a photo of the famous *Jalakanya* sculpture on Shanmugam Beach, he had scrawled – *You always keep telling me South Indians are so conservative, so orthodox. I totally agree!* Zara laughed. Truth be told, she admired the rebellious air of that nude mermaid sculpture – a spirit free of the shackles of morality. In one of the photos from Bolgatty Palace, a svelte girl in a strappy top and shorts posed beside a snooker table. Her laughing face and body language clearly told Zara she was the reason for Rishab's interest in Kovalam. The photo had a professional quality to it, owing to the dim overhead lighting and the large framed picture on the wall behind her. She went through all the photos, around 10, but her eyes kept going back to the one with the girl at the snooker table. There was something odd about the photo, but she couldn't put a finger on it.

A few days later, Zara spotted Kenza at the hostel, carrying a heavy duffel bag out of Waheeda's room. She lent her a hand in dragging it to the entrance.

"Thanks," said Kenza, "It's some of the books I brought to the hostel last year. I'd forgotten all about them once exams were over."

"How are you taking them home – on the bus?"

Kenza blushed. "My, er, friend will help."

"Okay," Zara said, keeping a straight face. The Kenza-Jayachandran 'line' was hot news all over campus, but Kenza still tried to play innocent.

Sure enough, Zara spotted Jayachandran come by on his motorbike a little later, and Kenza climbed on behind him with the bag balanced between them. Earlier, Kenza's reason for occasionally staying at the hostel had been group studies, nowadays it was her evening rendezvous with Jayachandran. Zara didn't know Kenza too well, but she was nice and got along with everyone. She had been especially close to Nayana, being body and unit mates.

Zara suddenly realized that more than a year had passed since Nayana's accident. There was still no news of Nayana's whereabouts, but she no longer thought about her as often as she used to, and her nightmares had stopped entirely. The demands of college life had taken precedence, gradually pushing Nayana out of her mind except when someone made a comment or shared a memory. Like Daisy recalling how she had toppled face forward over Nayana's puzzle box and landed on the floor with puzzle pieces stuck all over her face.

Zara giggled, then stopped abruptly, eyes widening. She tore down the corridor and into her room. "What's up with you?" Sheetal asked in amazement as Zara searched frantically in her duffel bag. She found the envelope from Rishab and rushed outside with it. Heart hammering, she took out the photo of the girl near the snooker table and peered at the framed picture on the back wall. Except it wasn't a picture – it was a large framed puzzle! More specifically, *The Allegory of Sight and Smell* by Jan Brueghel.

"How can you be sure it's Nayana's puzzle? A lot of people could have the same," said Sunny. The thought had crossed Zara's mind. But Bolgatty Palace was known for its frequent Kathakali performances, Nayana's father was a professional Kathakali artist, and the very same puzzle was at Bolgatty Palace. It was too much of a coincidence.

"Why not just ask Rishab for the contact address? He stayed there, didn't he?" pressed Sunny. This too had occurred to Zara, but even if she did contact Rishab, he was the laid-back type who wouldn't understand the urgency. Her only option was to get someone in Kochi to look up the number for Bolgatty Palace. Her two close friends from Kochi were Daisy and Sunny. Since she didn't want Nayana's secrets to meet the same fate as Mala's, Sunny was her only choice.

Sunny relented. "Okay, I'll tell my brother to look it up. But you'll have to wait; he comes home from his college hostel only on some weekends."

Zara's patience wore thin as the days dragged by. Sunny's impassive demeanour during clinics and classes made it worse.

After what seemed like eons, Sunny finally suggested they meet at the Milma booth during morning break.

"I've told you several times not to make Kathakali eyes at me during clinics! If I had any info, I'd have told you," he said, frowning.

"Sorry, I couldn't help myself. Did your brother get the number?"

Sunny smiled. "He did better. He asked the manager to enquire about the puzzle, and when he called again, guess what – you were right! The manager said it had been donated by one of their Kathakali artists, Vadakedath Krishnakumar. That's Nayana's father, isn't it?"

Zara was astonished; she couldn't believe her hunch had proved right. "Can your brother get his number?" He took a piece of paper from his coat pocket and handed it to her. "Already got it! He pretended he was interested in booking Mr Krishnakumar's troupe for a performance."

She looked at the number. The area code was not for Kochi.

"It's Thodupuzha," Sunny explained, "Just one thing though…"

Zara looked up at him.

"In all this time, Nayana hasn't tried to get in touch with you. Have you considered that maybe it's intentional?"

That evening, after class, Zara hurried to the college junction looking for a phone booth. The hostel pay phone was in too public a space. She found a vacant booth, stepped inside and dialled the number. As she heard the phone ring at the other end, her heart began to race.

Sunny's comment about Nayana's possible lack of interest came to mind, but she didn't want to believe it. When the ringing stopped, Zara put the receiver back in the cradle. Maybe no one was at home. She picked up the receiver and dialled the number one last time.

On the seventh ring, the call was answered. "Hello?"

Zara stiffened. It was a girl's voice. *Nayana's voice!*

"Is this Nayana Krishnakumar?"

"Is this from the hospital?"

"What? No, No. It's me, Zara!"

Silence.

"Hello? Nayana, it's Zara Ann Mathew, your batchmate at Calicut. Remember?"

"Of course I remember. How could I forget?" Her voice sounded soft and sad.

Zara wiped the tears from her eyes. "How are you, Nayana?" she asked, her voice thick with emotion.

"I'm good. I'm much better. How did you get this number?"

"From the manager at Bolgatty Palace. I saw your framed puzzle in one of the photos a friend took while he stayed there."

"Oh! You went to so much trouble."

"You disappeared, Nayana. What happened? Aren't you coming back? Can I come visit you? "

There was a pause. "Umm, listen." Another pause. "I need more time, Zara. And distance."

"Nayana, I didn't mean to…."

"It's okay. I'm really touched that you all still think about me. But I'm trying to forget a lot of things, so I'm avoiding everything and everyone that is related to my past. You understand, don't you?"

"I… well, okay."

"So please don't call me again. Okay?"

Zara felt a thunderbolt strike her. "Okay, I won't." Her voice was close to inaudible.

"And don't tell anyone you found me or talked to me."

"Of course not."

Nayana sighed at the other end. "Thanks for understanding, Zara. Bye then."

The line went dead. Zara crumpled in a heap on the floor of the phone booth and sobbed her heart out.

***

It was post-admission day in Surgery Unit 6, and the wards and corridors were overflowing with patients. The postgraduates were responsible for filling up the case sheets, but when the number of patients got too high to handle, they enlisted the help of students. It was a demanding task, talking to the patients and their bystanders, sifting through their complaints to identify the real problems and doing examination for appropriate signs.

"Sisterrrr …"

Zara gritted her teeth and swung around, stethoscope dangling from her neck, and glared at the bystander who had just addressed her. "If you are looking for the nurse, she is in that room," she said, pointing in the direction of the nurses' station.

The man scratched his head. "I thought you were the sister."

"And why is that – because I'm a female?" She pointed to Vaibhav at the adjacent bed. "Does he look like a nurse to you?"

Looking contrite, the bystander beat a hasty retreat.

"Chill Zara, it was just a silly mistake," said Vaibhav.

"That's one too many to ignore! Any male in a lab coat is addressed as 'doctor', and any female in a lab coat is addressed as 'sister'. Because a doctor *has* to be a male and a nurse *has* to be a female – that's the public's attitude."

Vaibhav started to reply, then, deciding against it, he went back to taking the case history of his patient.

From across the ward, Sheetal looked curiously at Zara; such outbursts were so uncharacteristic of her. But for a few days now she had been sullen and moody.

And she was hanging out with Sunny quite a bit. Over the past few weeks, the two of them had often been seen whispering in corners and occasionally slinking off during breaks.

Were they a 'line' now? Had Zara ditched Vaibhav for Sunny?

Sheetal wondered if Zara ever penned down her feelings in the letters she constantly wrote to her grandfather and God-knows-who-else. Maybe she could have a look through them when Zara was not around.

Sheetal felt miserable. Although Sunny still met her for group studies, he had neither explained his recent interest in Zara nor 'proposed' to Sheetal in all this time.

With a deep sigh, Sheetal went back to her case-taking.

***

The following day was Minor OT (operation theatre) where cases like lymph node biopsies, skin grafting, hernia repairs and haemorrhoidectomies were posted for surgery. Towards the end of a hernioplasty, they were observing, Vaibhav turned to Zara and whispered, "Shall we take a break?"

They walked down the long corridor past the other OT rooms, past the pre-op room where several patients clad in white *mundu* and *thorthu* or blouse sat on wooden benches awaiting their turn, past the changing rooms and the reception and reached the entrance of the OT complex where the canteen staff sat with a large, stainless-steel tea container and a box full of fried snacks.

Sipping their tea, they walked to the males' changing room, which was empty. It was a makeshift cubicle with plywood walls, and the clothes weighing down the lines gave off a smell of starch and washing soap mixed with body odour.

Vaibhav sat down on the metal cot. "Have you heard? Sheetal coined a new Malayalam word this morning. *Garbha-bandham*! She couldn't remember the Malayalam word for contraception, so she improvised. Since the Malayalam word for constipation is *mala-bandham,* literally 'shit-stop', she asked the patient if she had *garbha-bandham* or birth-stop!"

Zara laughed despite herself. Putting her tea down on the cot, she pulled her mask off and tried to undo her OT cap, but the knot had become entangled in her thick hair. Vaibhav got up to lend her a hand, and they laughed and made silly comments, enjoying the feel of their fingers brushing together.

Finally, Vaibhav declared, "Only a wide local excision can sort this mess." He went outside, returned with a pair of surgical scissors and cut the knot along with the hair it was entangled in.

Zara giggled, brushing aside strands of hair loosened out of her plait and adjusting her large maroon *bindi*. She noticed that Vaibhav's face wore an undecipherable expression. "Hey, latch the door, will you?" he said.

"Why?"

He just motioned with his head towards the door, and she did as asked. When she turned around, Vaibhav was standing right next to her. She shivered. He leaned forward, his face close to hers, and whispered, "Can I kiss you?"

Zara's breath caught in her throat; she was hypnotized by Vaibhav's smile and his deep brown droopy eyes. He leaned in closer, his eyes on her lips. But just then, Zara's mother popped into her head and said in her English teacher's voice, "You CAN, but you MAY not!"

"No," Zara said mechanically.

Vaibhav backed away, looking embarrassed. "I'm sorry, but back in the OT during the hernioplasty I, er, felt you pressing against me, so I thought...."

Zara was horrified. "I was just leaning over your shoulder to get a better view!"

"Oh shit. Shit!" Vaibhav murmured, staring at the veins on the back of his hands. "I think I'd better get back." Opening the door, he left.

Tears stung Zara's eyes, but she took a few deep breaths and went back to the OT. When they broke for lunch, Vaibhav was waiting for her. They walked silently until they reached the road to the Ladies Hostel, when Vaibhav said, "Just forget what happened, okay? Are we cool?"

She nodded. "It's just that I never expected it from you. I was a bit shocked that you could even think that way about me... that I was deliberately pressing against you"

Vaibhav suddenly looked irate. "Oh, you're taking the moral high ground now, after your secret romance with Sunny over the past few weeks."

"It's nothing of the sort!" Zara said, flabbergasted. "But why should you care anyway? It's not like I'm your girlfriend."

Vaibhav's face flushed deeply. "Not everyone is good at spelling things out, Zara." She stared at him. Had he just indirectly admitted his interest in her?

"If it really is nothing of the sort," continued Vaibhav, "then tell me what you and Sunny are up to."

"I can't."

"Why not?"

"Because," Zara groped for words, "because I don't want to betray a trust."

Vaibhav's eyes bored holes through her. "So you trust Sunny to keep a secret but not me."

Zara's face threatened to crumble. "I'm sorry I can't say anything, Vaibhav. It's complicated."

"It's always complicated with you, Zara. You keep giving me mixed signals, just like you did in the OT."

He walked off with Zara staring after him, mind numb and eyes blurred with tears.

***

Kenza rushed along with her unit mates to the common lecture hall to grab seats in the front row. They were crushed to see that students from another Surgery Unit had beaten them to it, and they settled for the second row. At exactly 11 a.m., Dr Gopan Sreekumar, Professor and HOD of the Department of Surgery, entered the room. He was a demigod – worshipped by students, adored by patients and envied by peers of lesser calibre. Every Thursday, he held a class for all the students posted in the Department of Surgery. More often than not, the hall overflowed as even house-surgeons and postgraduates came to attend his lectures.

Dr Gopan was followed by a middle-aged, sickly-looking lady. She was ushered to an examination table at the front of the hall by a final year student, who then thumbed through his notes and commenced his case presentation on carcinoma of the breast.

When he reached the physical examination part, Dr Gopan stopped him. "Demonstrate the physical findings." The student faced the woman and gesticulated in front of her chest, while discoursing on the irregularity in shape and size of both breasts. Dr Gopan sprang up from his seat.

"When you present a case, you should do it in the proper way!" He turned to the woman. "*Amma*, please remove your top."

Low-key murmurs erupted throughout the hall. Kenza felt Mohini nudge her. "Is Sir really going to make her bare her chest in front of this crowd?"

"*Amma*, please remove your top," he repeated. The woman looked from Dr Gopan to the sea of students, then back at him. She slowly dropped her *sari pallu*, unbuttoned her blouse and brassiere, and peeled them off. The murmurs were louder this time, punctuated by anguished exclamations of 'Ssho! Ssho!'

"Silence!" The students fell quiet, and Dr Gopan proceeded to explain the physical findings. "Look at the size and shape of both breasts. Look at the position of the nipple." The woman's right breast was of an irregular shape, and the nipple had disappeared within a thick, angry-looking, reddish-purple patch of skin.

But Kenza's eyes kept returning to the woman's face – there was no embarrassment or anger. Just resignation.

"How could Sir be so unethical?" Kenza complained to Jayachandran that afternoon as they sat sipping coffee at the Milma booth.

Jayachandran shrugged. "Sir's theatrics at a patient's expense are common knowledge. He's an egotistical ass. Thinks he's God and expects everyone to fall at his feet. Like you and several others do."

"I guess I fell for his surgical expertise."

"Expertise does not equate with compassion."

Kenza sighed. "I don't think I will ever be able to see Sir in the same light again."

Jayachandran laughed. "That's because you think of people in black-and-white terms, with no shades of grey. Acceptance or rejection of a person actually depends on how much grey you can tolerate. Every human being has shades of grey, and doctors are humans. I don't agree with what Dr Gopan did today. At the same time, he doesn't charge much for private consultation at home, he never consorts with private laboratories for commissions, and most importantly, he never pulls patients off the elective surgery list just because they didn't bribe him. That's why patients flock to him despite the theatrics." Jayachandran threw away his empty paper cup. "Now, there's something important *we* need to discuss."

Half an hour later, Kenza made her way back through the crowded hospital corridors, mulling over Jayachandran's plans for their future. He had passed his finals and had a month before his course was over. He planned to find a job in Calicut, and then perhaps they could get married using the Special Marriage Act because that was the only way possible for them.

Kenza knew Jayachandran's parents weren't too enthusiastic about her, but they did not object to their son's decision. If her parents came to know, she was sure to be imprisoned at home. Secrecy was her only option. Lost in thought, she almost collided with Mala, who was headed towards the Department of Pathology.

"Hey Mala! It's been so long. How are you?"

"Hi. Yeah, I'm good. You?"

"Great!"

At a loss for something to say, they smiled at each other. Time, distance and misadventures had strained their once close friendship.

"What are you doing here this late?" asked Kenza.

"I came to collect my mother's lymph node biopsy report. She hasn't been feeling well for some time now, always tired, and losing weight." Mala wrung her hands.

Sensing she was distraught, Kenza offered to accompany her.

"Oh! You don't have to, it's probably nothing…"

"No, I insist."

They stepped through the swing doors above which a sign read Reporting Room. The pathologists had left for the day, and the large central table was occupied by postgraduates huddled over their microscopes, their eyes fixed on the monocular eyepieces, their fingers adjusting the stage controls and fine-tuning knobs. The silence was occasionally broken with short conversations on Greek and Latin terms. To Kenza, it felt like a secret convention of sorts.

A diminutive, bespectacled girl rushed past them carrying several tomes heavy enough to qualify her for a weightlifting championship. "Yes, what do you want?" she asked, depositing the books on the large central table.

"My mother's biopsy report." Mala showed her the discharge card.

The girl took it and beckoned them to follow her. They left

the Reporting Room and went further down the hall to the much larger and airier Grossing Room. While the girl searched through the several registers piled high on a table, Kenza looked around.

In one corner was a huge marble slab stacked with numerous bottles and buckets, containing organs removed in the operation theatres. A postgrad was inspecting the containers. He opened one, pulled a gastrectomy specimen onto a wax-coated wooden block and inspected it closely. Then, with a heavy cleaver, he chopped away enthusiastically. Kenza's stomach did a somersault, and she quickly turned away.

The bespectacled girl found the biopsy report and copied it out on a blue report form that she handed to Mala. "Who did you say this patient was?"

"My mother."

"Oh, I'm sorry. It's not good news."

Seeing Mala tremble, Kenza looked at the report. It read *Metastatic adenocarcinoma, supraclavicular lymph node biopsy.* Kenza gasped and laid a hand on Mala's shoulder, but she brushed it off and walked away, wiping her eyes.

The following evening, Mohini called all the girls for a meeting in the common room.

"As many of you must have heard from Kenza, Mala's mother has been diagnosed with an advanced malignancy, and we need to help them financially. The boys have been informed as well, and our Warden has agreed to let her stay indefinitely in the hostel if the need arises. I have asked Mubashira *Chechi* to sound out the union for possible donations from other batches and the faculty."

There was a low rumble of dissent at the mention of Mubashira (who now held the post of University union Councillor), but Mohini countered that Mubashira's clout would work in Mala's favour. The girls dispersed, carrying the discussion back to their rooms.

"Mala could stay with us," suggested Daisy. "Nayana's bed is still free."

Sheetal smirked. "Then get ready for the next round of thefts."

The other three gave her shocked looks. "How can you be so

insensitive at a time like this?" Daisy asked angrily. "Don't you have any empathy?"

"Look, I really am sorry about Mala's mother, and I'm willing to help her," said Sheetal, "but no one can deny that when she stopped coming to the hostel, the thefts stopped too."

"But Sheetal, there is no solid evidence to show she was responsible," countered Kenza.

"Whatever!" Sheetal said huffily. "But if she is moving into this room, I'm moving out. I don't want to walk in on her rifling through my bags."

Daisy's face was paper-white, and her mouth trembled. "But it's perfectly fine for *you* to rifle through everyone's bags, right?"

Sheetal looked as though she'd been slapped. "Wha… what did you…?"

"Did you think no one knew?" Daisy said her voice tight with anger. "I've seen you going through Zara's bags. If I were to suspect anyone of being a thief, it would be you, Sheetal."

Zara and Kenza looked thunderstruck.

"I stayed quiet to give you the benefit of the doubt," continued Daisy, "but now that you're hell-bent on framing Mala, I may as well speak out."

"I'm no thief," blubbered Sheetal. Tears flowed down her cheeks.

"Then why were you rummaging through Zara's belongings?"

Sheetal didn't reply; she hid her face in her hands, and her body shook with sobs. Kenza couldn't tolerate it any longer. Putting an arm around Sheetal, she led her outside with soothing words.

Zara stood rooted to the spot in shock.

Daisy gave her a disgusted look. "For God's sake, get off your fence for once and take a stand!" she hissed as she left the room.

***

Morning rounds in Surgery Unit One were underway, and the HOD, Dr Gopan Sreekumar, was tossing out questions to the postgrads, shaking them up.

"Come on, come on, we don't have all day. How are you going

to manage this patient with cholecystitis?" he asked the trembling first-year postgrad.

"Sir, we can start the patient on antibiotics and adopt a wait-and-watch policy, or we could operate before his gall bladder is perforated."

"But what will you do in *this* case? Treat conservatively or open him up?"

The postgrad beat around the bush again, and Dr Gopan lost his patience. "Sir, I want just *one* answer." It was never a good sign when the HOD addressed students as 'Sir' or 'Madam'.

Dr Gopan gave him a piteous look and smirked. "My dear sir, you would do well to remember that if you always sit on the fence, you will end up with a perineal tear!" Stifled giggles arose from the faculty and students alike.

Zara felt a slight jolt at the word 'fence', and was reminded of Daisy's rebuke many months ago. Several events had occurred since then. Their batch hired two minibuses for a trip to Thalassery to celebrate Waheeda's *kootti kondu pokal* ceremony. Since her husband's home was only half an hour from college, Waheeda vacated her hostel room. Sheetal seized this opportunity to shift rooms as she could no longer bear the tension in theirs. Daisy hardly spoke to Sheetal, and Zara had tried a few weak attempts at reconciliation that seemed to irk Daisy even more.

Shortly afterwards, Mala's mother succumbed to a severe lung infection following two cycles of chemotherapy, and their batch hired the same minibuses to attend her funeral at Mala's home in Nilambur. Zara was stunned to see the remote village and the primitive brick structure that Mala called home.

Sheetal, of course, hadn't joined in either trip. She had become something of an outcast, more so after Mala's mother's demise, as Daisy just couldn't help dropping hints about Sheetal *not being who you think she is, but don't tell anyone this, okay*. Sheetal spent most of her time in Sunny's company or at the library.

Occasionally, Zara would pause to look at the Scopegoats poster on their door. In the first year, she and Daisy had almost written 'Except Sheetal' on it, but backtracked as the words might imply a lack of unity among them. Now that memory brought a wry smile.

The only silver lining in these tumultuous times was Kenza, who now stayed in their room whenever she spent the night at the hostel. She was warm and forthcoming, yet sagacious enough to deflect Daisy's intrusive questions about her romance with Jayachandran. On one such night, while Daisy was in the TV room watching a rerun of *Dilwale Dulhaniya Le Jayenge*, the topic shifted to Nayana. Zara disclosed how she had painstakingly deciphered her whereabouts only to be rebuffed over the phone.

"You never told your roommates any of this?" Kenza asked, surprised.

Zara shook her head. "I don't think Nayana would have wanted me to. Only Sunny and I know. And now you."

Kenza bit her lip hesitantly. Then she asked, "Can you keep a secret?"

Sleep evaded Zara that night. She stared at the ceiling, listening to Daisy's light snore as she rewound the story Kenza had divulged. She turned her head to look at Kenza, curled up on Sheetal's cot. It transpired that all those nights she spent at the hostel the previous year had been more about Nayana than about group study or Jayachandran.

Zara felt a weight in her chest. Despite being her roommate and close friend, Nayana had chosen to reveal her innermost turmoil to a unit mate whom she met for just a few hours every day. She had opted not to tell Vaibhav about her efforts to trace Nayana because she didn't expect him to show much interest or support her efforts.

Had Nayana felt the same about her?

8. 2016, Mala

18th March, 2016
Nilambur

There are some mornings when the hills feel like they're listening.

This was one of them. The light was soft, the air already thick with the smell of overripe jackfruit, and Rafeekka stood before me with his latest offering.

"Rafeekka, how many jackfruits do you think one doctor can eat?"

He didn't answer, just smiled his gummy smile and held it out like a sacred gift. The nurses stood around us, trying not to giggle. I took it with both hands, even though my arms ached from the weight of too many small kindnesses like this one.

I didn't see her approach. I just heard the voice.

"Playing passing the parcel?"

I turned, startled. "Zara!" I shrieked. The jackfruit slipped from my hands, landed with a dull *thump*, and split clean into two. "Ayyo!" I muttered, seeing the disappointment on Rafeekka's face. "It's okay, we'll all share it." His face broke into that gummy, endearing smile, and he hobbled away, victorious.

"He's my oldest patient," I told Zara, brushing my palms on my sari. "He has asthma, so shows up religiously for the cough syrup. I think he's more addicted to my attention than to the medicine."

One of the attenders piped up, "He's always bringing her gifts, too. We call him Dr Mala's boyfriend."

I rolled my eyes.

"I'm so glad you called before coming," I said, slipping my arm through Zara's. "Mornings are mad here. Come, let me show you around our humble little PHC."

She looked around, shielding her eyes against the sun. "Looks more like an old house."

"That's because it was. After a terrible dengue outbreak some years ago, when too many people died and the panchayat kept ignoring us, the locals staged a huge protest. There was no access to healthcare here; the nearest hospital is still miles away. So, the authorities hurriedly converted this abandoned house into a PHC to pacify the people. But they didn't care about maintenance. Everyone who came here got transferred – on request. Nobody wanted to stay in a place like this. When I joined as Assistant Surgeon, the place was falling apart."

"You didn't want a transfer?" she asked, looking around at the faded walls and chipped floors of the OP room.

"I did," I said honestly. "At first. But then… the land held me. The people taught me how to stay."

"How long have you been here?"

I smiled. "Ten years and counting."

I told her how the locals rallied around me once they realized I wasn't going to leave. How they helped fix doors and windows, clean the premises, and dig a compost pit. How an NGO stepped in with supplies once they saw our progress.

"All it takes is one person willing to stay," I said. "One stubborn person."

Zara looked at me with something close to awe. For a moment, I caught a glimpse of the old college days in her eyes – confusion, admiration, guilt.

We drove to my favourite spot afterwards, the one place I go to collect my thoughts. I led her down a dirt trail, up a steep hill, until we reached the banks of a large, gleaming pool with a waterfall at one end.

"Oh wow!" she gasped, wading into the water like a child.

We sat in the shade with our feet in the water, admiring the emerald moss-covered stones. For a while, the silence was easy until she spoke.

"Mala, I need to tell you something."

She stumbled through an apology, trying to find the right words. I stayed quiet.

"That was such a long time ago," I finally said. "I've made peace with it. And honestly, I gave you reason to doubt me."

"I never understood why you lied to us."

I sighed. "Because I always felt like an *outsider.* All of you were from upper-middle-class families, parents employed in white-collar jobs, good homes, cars.... What was I by comparison? So, I lied to fit in."

Zara said softly, "Oh Mala, we would never have judged you—"

"Wouldn't you?" I interrupted, more sharply than I intended. "Do you really think everyone would've embraced me had I said on day one that I was a Scheduled Tribe quota candidate?"

She tried to protest, but I held up a hand.

"I lived in that hostel for just two months. In that time, I was privy to occasional conversations about the reservation, and I could invariably sense the simmering resentment. In college, the boys were more vocal than the girls on the topic. There were a handful of staunch supporters on either side of the debate, but the vast majority just sat on the fence. Contempt can be an unobtrusive thing, Zara. It's like that sneaky neighbour quietly burning plastic in his backyard. You may not see or hear it, but you sense it because of the toxic sting that lingers in the air."

She fidgeted, visibly uncomfortable. "I'm sure no one meant any offence. It's just that... many feel reservations eat into their opportunities."

I turned to her. "Can I ask you something? Did you ever live in a home with no electricity or running water? How many of your clothes were handouts from total strangers? How many kilometres did your parents walk carrying a convulsing child, only to be told there was no doctor available at the PHC? My sister died on the way to the next hospital."

My throat closed, but I forced myself to go on. "And how many thousands did your parents shell out for your medical entrance exam coaching? Did you ever have to work part-time to support your MBBS course? After two months in the hostel, my parents could no longer afford to keep me in college. If it weren't for our ward councillor, who got the Koya family in Kuttichira to lend us financial support in exchange for household help, I would have had to discontinue the course. Yet people like me are seen as the reason the rest of you have to toil so hard for the MBBS entrance exam. I was the one who would eventually steal your postgraduate seat, the one who would snatch away your government job."

"No, Mala!" interjected Zara. "Nobody would discredit an honest candidate like you; it's the undeserving ones that everyone talks about, the ones from wealthy homes who claim reservation."

"I agree that for every handful of candidates who genuinely require upliftment, there are one or two who misuse the system. But to catch a few rats, do you really need to burn the whole house down?"

Zara flushed but didn't respond.

"And is wealth enough when there is no social equality? Do you remember Waheeda being called a *mandoos* Mapilla by one of the seniors? Although it was in jest, the implication was crystal clear."

"Yeah, I was there with her then," Zara said. "She got upset and shouted back that her medical entrance exam rank was two hundred and six."

"Exactly! Even if you secured a seat through merit, the assumption was *always* biased against a quota seat based on caste and religion."

Zara looked crushed. "We were wrong. We judged you so harshly."

"Yes," I said, softer now. "But I forgive you. Because I've forgiven myself, too. I shouldn't have lied. It wasn't just you. *I* dishonoured my parents' sacrifices. And Madhu… after that election mess, when he learned the truth, it gave him an excuse to walk away instead of standing up for me."

I didn't say it, but the betrayal still stung.

"You know what hurt most?" I continued. "I was accused of the hostel thefts – just because I'd lied. But when the real thief was caught, you gave her a mental health pass. Why? Because she was one of you. She was an *insider*."

Zara's silence said everything.

"But I rose from that," I said, brushing a hand across my knee. "My village gave me a hero's welcome when I returned after MBBS. I'm the first doctor in my tribe. The first to study beyond school. Today, I'm a symbol of what's possible."

I told her about my outreach work – health camps, hygiene

awareness, mobile clinics, and immunization drives. About visiting schools to speak to children, to let them know that they, too, can dream big.

"And all this was made possible by the 'unfair' policy you all hated. Reservation didn't give me an unfair advantage; it gave me a fighting chance."

Zara looked uncomfortable, "If only I could go back and make it right."

"You can," I said. "Not with apologies. But with action. With empathy. With listening. You have a voice. Use it."

She nodded, eyes wet.

My phone buzzed, snapping us back. I smiled. "That was Rakesh. Wondering where we've disappeared. Shall we?"

In the car, Zara asked, "So how did you and Rakesh get together?"

I laughed. "He came to my OP twice. On the third visit, he proposed! His family runs a furniture business in Nilambur town, and they are well off. He's from a backward caste too, and guess what? My father opposed the marriage because he thought Rakesh's caste was beneath ours!"

Zara burst out laughing. "The irony!"

"Exactly. My brothers managed to knock some sense into him."

As the trees zipped past outside, Zara murmured, "Do you think anything will *ever* change?"

I turned to her, smiling. "Change starts like this. Two people talking by a waterfall with understanding and empathy. Small steps, Zara."

I told her about the tribal kids who now know how to spell their names and read a thermometer. I told her about the girls who used to be married off at 15 but now come to my centre with questions – bold, unafraid.

"This work," I said, gesturing to the hills, the PHC, the waterfall. "It isn't redemption. It's reclamation. Of my pride. Of my story."

We sat in silence again. But this time, it felt like healing.

9. Fourth year, 1999 – 2000

'So that's the bottom line – No one will help us.'

14th February, 1999
Calicut

Happy Valentine's Day, Pappachen.
I know, I know – you think it's a ridiculous Western import designed to sell chocolates and sin. But I'm still wishing you. Because, despite your disdain, I think even you, beneath the layers of gruffness –might secretly enjoy a good love story.
We've had our own, after all. Heer-Ranjha. Shahjahan and Mumtaz. Bajirao and Mastani. All doomed, all passionate, and all definitely not exchanging Hallmark cards, which makes them more respectable, apparently.
Anyway, Valentine's Day on campus is a full-blown spectacle. The college union has institutionalized it with something they call The Rose and Chilli Exchange. It's as elegant as it sounds. Red roses for love, yellow for friendship, and green chillies for people you'd happily trip in a corridor.
I received enough green chillies to season a family-size fish curry. But also, some yellow roses. Which I'm choosing to interpret as proof that I am, in fact, not universally despised.

Zara stopped short of writing about the red rose from Tarachand. Between afternoon lectures, he had bounced over to her row, reciting *shayari* and presented the rose with a flourish, much to her absolute embarrassment and everyone's merriment. Zara had glanced surreptitiously at Vaibhav, who seemed uncharacteristically absorbed in his textbook. Although they had patched up, they still walked on eggshells around each other. And Tarachand sensed a window of opportunity with Zara. She resumed writing.

In other news, my Paediatrics posting is finally over, and am I relieved!
It was... horrifying.
Screaming kids, cooing parents, musical toys of all sorts going

off together endlessly – I invariably ended up with a headache by noon. Examining children needs triple the effort required with adult patients because kids don't understand that we are trying to help them. Gaining their cooperation requires a strategy, and the strategy needs to keep changing. And all the while, we are worried about not having a case to present by 11 a.m.

The kids who are grievously ill break my heart. I wonder what kind of God wants kids to suffer like this. This morning, a boy in the leukaemia ward developed shortness of breath. I thought he was gasping, but the Assistant Professor on rounds rushed to hold a plastic bag around his face. Later, the Assistant Professor told us that the child had been hyperventilating from a panic attack. He had witnessed the death of another leukemic child just that morning, and that triggered his panic attack.

The other day, I saw a postgraduate doing a bone marrow procedure on an infant in the side-room. The baby's screams of pain and the sight were so ghastly that I vomited in the sink in the nurses' room. I don't think I will ever, ever, ever take up Paediatrics. It's too depressing.

But there are those who are absolutely fascinated with it. One example is Charles Varghese Palakkunnu, a senior who was posted along with us. You were right, Pappachen – he is distantly related to our family, although neither of us can figure out the exact relationship. He and his friends ragged me when I was in my first year, but during this posting, I realized he's an okay guy. Except for his maddening tendency to quote from the Bible at every opportune moment – like you do, and like Ammachy and also Mama – Oh wait, now I see the family connection, Ha ha ha!

Waiting eagerly for your reply.

Hugs and kisses, Zara.

Daisy sulked in a corner of the common room. The movie *Hey Ram* starring Kamal Haasan was running in town, and being a huge fan, she was determined not to miss it. But none of the other girls were interested, as it was rumoured there were steamy scenes in it, which meant the crowd would undoubtedly be all male and mostly the lecherous kind.

"It's not just *any* movie; it's a magnum opus!" Daisy pleaded again with Zara.

Zara buried her nose in the Sunday newspaper and remained silent. Arundhati, who sat on the window ledge painting her toenails, looked up. "I'll come with you if Anand can also come along."

Daisy hesitated; taking a boy along to watch a movie which might have adult scenes did not sound proper. But left with no choice, she agreed. Arundhati pranced away to phone her boyfriend.

Done with the newspaper, Zara headed off to their room, pretending not to hear Daisy, who tagged behind her imploringly. The last time she had fallen for Daisy's persuasion, they had ended up watching *Fire* by Mira Nair. As Daisy had predicted, there were no familiar faces at the 11 a.m. show. But when they exited the theatre, there was a long queue of boys from their senior batch waiting for the matinee show. For many months after that, the two of them had been subjected to chants of 'Lesbo, lesbo' any time they passed the senior boys.

Zara was determined not to take that type of risk again. She reached for her Neelibhringadi oil from the shelf and pulled the hair claw out of her bun, letting her thick locks tumble free. Daisy panicked – once Zara commenced her Sunday *champi*, there would be no way of getting her out of the hostel.

It was time to play her trump card.

An hour before the matinee started, Zara and Daisy got down at Hotel Paradigm, famous in Calicut for its biryani and seafood cuisine. Hotel Paradigm was Zara's weakness, and as Daisy watched her devour crab *malabari* and *vellappam* with gusto, she sincerely hoped the movie would be worth this bribe.

When they reached the theatre, Arundhati and Anand were waiting outside. The place was thronged with men, and the queue at the gents' ticket counter snaked all the way out of the theatre compound. The girls were the only ones at the ladies' ticket counter. Some of the men gave them once-overs while others jeered lewdly.

"I don't think this is safe. We should go back," whispered Zara.

Daisy held her ground. "Let's wait for the ticket counter to open. If at least one other woman turns up to see the movie, we'll stay. If not, we'll leave." She didn't want to have paid for a fancy lunch for nothing.

As if in answer to Daisy's prayers, an elderly woman turned up just as the ticket counters opened. She was around 60, dressed in a plain orange cotton sari and her forehead was smeared with ash. She looked like the last person to be a Kamal Haasan fan. But one can't be too sure about Tamilians, thought Daisy; they treated their movie stars like gods. Daisy helped her get a ticket while Arundhati got a ticket for Anand, and they all took seats together in the last row of the gallery.

Half an hour into the movie, Daisy started feeling uncomfortable. The bedroom scenes more than justified the hearsay, and the crowd was going berserk, wolf-whistling and shouting expletives. Equally discomfiting was the hanky-panky in the corner between Arundhati and Anand whenever they thought Daisy's attention was riveted on the screen.

Zara nudged her from the other side. "I don't think our elderly friend is handling the movie too well." Indeed, the woman was trembling in her seat.

"*Amma*, are you ok? Don't you like Kamal Haasan?" Daisy asked, leaning across Zara.

"Who's Kamal Haasan?" the woman asked miserably. "I came thinking this was a movie about Bhagwan Sri Ram. And what am I seeing! *Ayyo*, *Ayyo*, Ram, Ram!" She started weeping quietly.

Zara gave Daisy a distraught look, and Daisy sighed resignedly. "Fine, let's leave." The two girls escorted the woman out of the theatre, with a reluctant Arundhati and Anand following them.

There seemed to be no point in returning to campus just yet, so the four of them caught a bus to Manachira Park and loitered around munching peanuts and drinking falooda. On their way back, they spotted Madhu Mohan, Tarachand and Luqman sitting at the back of the bus with several lumpy gunny sacks between them.

"Where are you guys coming from?" asked Madhu Mohan

when they got down at the college junction.

"Manachira Park," blurted out Daisy before anyone offered the real answer. Seeing Tarachand's woebegone expression at the missed opportunity, Zara quickly changed the subject before he made any embarrassing comments. "What's in the gunny sacks?"

"Make a guess," Tarachand said playfully.

"Pirated CDs?"

"Cannabis seedlings?"

"Kidneys for the black market?"

Luqman and Madhu Mohan laughed. "The girls have such a great image of you, Tarachand," said Luqman. He opened one sack for them to see. "These are all sample medicines given to doctors by representatives of medical companies. Every Sunday, we collect the unused medicines from the homes of doctors and take them to the Drug Bank – it's that small room under the staircase near ward seven. The medicines are distributed to patients who can't afford to buy any. Antibiotics are the hardest to source, but we try."

"Wow, that's a great initiative!"

"It was actually the brainchild of Charles *ettan*," said Madhu Mohan, "The charge of the Drug Bank is handed down to each successive batch, and this year it's our turn. Why don't a few of the girls also volunteer?"

"Sure, we'd love to," said Zara, "I just can't believe there's a side like this to a rascal like Charles Varghese Palakunnu."

Just then, Arundhati clutched her stomach and doubled up. "Arghh, cramps. Must be the falooda, I have milk allergies." She groaned in pain and swayed, alarming everyone.

"Come on, let's get you to Casualty," said Daisy.

They trooped there, and the duty Medical Officer (MO), after examining Arundhati, gave her a shot of Cyclopam to settle the cramps. He also insisted on twenty-four-hour observation just to be on the safe side.

"I'll be her bystander," Zara whispered in Daisy's ear, "or else on the way back Tarachand will stick to me like a fly on jackfruit."

A little after dusk, Daisy arrived at the Casualty side-room with a bag of essentials. Anand also arrived to check on his girlfriend, and the four of them talked for a while. Daisy left shortly, but Anand stuck around with Arundhati. Zara settled into the other bed in the room with her novel. The excitement of the day soon got to her, and she fell asleep with the book over her face.

Some time later, she awoke with a start. It was pitch dark in the room except for a bright bluish glint in the pale light streaming through a crack in the solitary window. There were muffled noises and movements coming from Arundhati's bed.

She must be in pain, thought Zara, propping herself up on one arm. Then her eyes got accustomed to the dark, and she froze, watching wide-eyed. A few seconds later, she quietly turned on the other side and went back to sleep.

Around six in the morning, Zara left without bothering to inform Arundhati, who was sleeping peacefully.

"Is Arundhati back? Is she feeling better?" asked Daisy when she opened the door for Zara. She told her about the night's events, and Daisy's eyes popped. "You weren't dreaming, were you? Anand was sitting in bed with a topless Arundhati…"

"… and playing a very hungry infant," added Zara, "I didn't bother to watch after that."

"Hmm. The cramps proved convenient, didn't they?" said Daisy. She told Zara of the petting she'd witnessed in the theatre and then threw her hands in the air dramatically. "To each her own. Just don't tell this to anyone, okay?"

Zara nodded, quite aware that before long Daisy would spread the news to the entire hostel. She was glad she hadn't mentioned the blue crystal pendant around Arundhati's neck; the glint from it was what had caught her eye. Last month, one of the junior girls had gone around the hostel asking if anyone had seen her blue crystal pendant. Could this be the same?

***

The sports ground at the far end of the campus was buzzing with practice sessions for the inter-collegiate sports meet. This year, in addition to the regular events, there was a cricket match for girls, and the Calicut Institute of Medicine, whose boys' cricket team regularly lifted the champions' cup, was determined to put up a competitive girls' team.

When the girls showed up for the try-outs, Zara surprised everyone with her bowling and batting skills.

"You play quite well for a girl," commented Tarachand, who'd been hanging around her ever since she arrived at the pitch.

Zara gritted her teeth. "Has cricket been a boys-only game? Girls can play cricket just as well as any boy."

"Of course, of course," he agreed hastily.

She made for the steps surrounding the ground and purposefully sat down between Sunny and Vaibhav. Looking dejected, Tarachand sat down next to Sunny.

"You hit some great shots, Zara," Sunny said. "Did you ever go for cricket coaching?"

"Actually, Waseer Akmal taught me those moves personally."

The boys stared at her like she was mad. "The Pakistani fast bowler Waseer Akmal?" Sunny asked, "*Chumma*! *Gundu*! No way!"

Zara laughed. "I'm not fibbing. Waseer Akmal came to my house in Bombay. For as long as I can remember, I used to play gully cricket with my brother and his friends. In those days, I had a huge crush on Waseer Akmal and every time he played, I would pray for the Pakistani team to win (unpatriotic, I know). I started sending him fan mail, well, more like love letters really, in glittering ink with hearts and stars and flowers, and doused with my mother's perfume."

Vaibhav gave a snort. "Celebs never read such letters."

"True. But I told him I was terminally ill, slowly dying from a hole in my heart, and it was my last wish to meet him. Anyway, sometime in late 1992 (that was the year Pakistan lifted the World Cup after defeating England, if you remember), my neighbour Rishabh came looking for my brother in the midst of our match with an urgent request to rush back home.

"There was a huge crowd outside our apartment complex and several policemen, and I bounded up the stairs, fearing the worst. Instead, I got the shock of my life – Waseer Akmal was sitting next to my father on the living room couch! Amidst the tea cups on the teapoy sat the small stack of love letters I had written to him. I was so embarrassed that I prayed for an instant earthquake to flatten our apartment."

The boys fell over laughing. "What happened after that?"

"Well, my father made me apologize to Akmal first. Then we took some photos, he signed a few autographs and asked to see our pitch. There, he showed us kids some slick moves, including his famous reverse swing. After he left, my father took me to task." Zara winced at the memory.

Just then, the sports captain whistled to signal that girls' practice had ended for the day. With a hasty goodbye to the boys, Zara darted off before Tarachand could follow her.

Vaibhav caught up with Zara just as she exited the gates. "That was a pretty tall tale."

"Well, next time I return from Bombay, I'll bring the photo we took with Akmal."

"Okay, never mind. I believe you. By the way, er, my *Chechi* wants to meet you."

Zara stopped walking and turned to look at Vaibhav. "Why?"

"I have told her about you, several times actually, so now she's curious about the girl with the eyes of a cow." He gave a silly grin.

"Cow?"

"Yeah, haven't you observed their eyes? Large, innocent and beautiful."

"Oh, thanks." She had read of doe-shaped eyes in novels, but eyes like a cow? A riddle that Tarachand had asked long ago suddenly popped into her head – How do you spell COW using 13 letters? See-o-double-you.

Zara told her brain to shut up.

"You see," continued Vaibhav, "I also told *Chechi* that we are, er, more than just friends." His face flushed.

Zara's heartbeat sped, but she kept her head clear. "What's the point, Vaibhav? Our families will never agree, they are poles apart."

"But *we* aren't poles apart, Zara. There *is* something between us, isn't there? You can't deny it. We could have a little world of our own." He spoke rapidly as if afraid his nerve would fail him if he slowed down.

"Vaibhav, I... I don't know what to say."

"It's okay, just think it over. Shall we discuss this tomorrow?"

"Okay." Then she slapped her forehead. "Tomorrow is Friday; I've been asked to compere for a conference at the Taj. It will be over only by 7 p.m."

Vaibhav's eyes lit up. "Can I pick you up on my bike?"

Her mother's pet quote boomed in Zara's ears yet again – *You CAN, but you MAY not.*

Zara suppressed a chuckle; if she ever hooked up with Vaibhav, her mother would be correcting him till kingdom come.

"The organizers are providing transportation, Vaibhav."

"Doesn't mean you *must* return with them, does it? I'll pick you up. We can go to the beach, watch the waves and talk in peace."

Zara shuffled her feet. The thought of riding pillion with Vaibhav on his gleaming black, beautiful bike was a big temptation. But she composed herself. "Sorry, no."

"No?" Vaibhav tilted his head playfully, and his eyes crinkled.

"No," she replied with as much firmness as she could muster.

***

Friday turned out to be an extremely unconventional day. Early in the morning, before they left for clinics, Daisy received a call from home. Her mother did not bother with her usual niceties. "Daisy*mol*, that proposal for your *Chechi*, the software engineer in America whose parents own acres of rubber," (Daisy rolled her eyes; her parents were obsessed with rubber and coconut estates), "they are asking for too much dowry."

"Oh, how much?"

"In addition to 50 lakh in cash and a car, they want our house in Rose*mol*'s name," wailed her mother.

Daisy felt like she had walked into a brick wall. "What! Hand over our house to them?"

"Your *Appa*'s blood pressure has skyrocketed thinking about it," her mother wailed again, "but it's such a good proposal for Rosemol, and if we don't agree, they will back out of the proposal."

At that moment, Daisy understood exactly why her mother had called her so urgently. As per tradition, their house was for the younger child, meaning Daisy. If they buckled under pressure now, Rose would have a smooth marriage, but Daisy would be left high and dry.

Then again, breaking off the marriage at this late stage would not bode well for either Rose or Daisy. Theirs was a small rural community, and the immediate reaction to such news would be to cast aspersions on Rose's morals, which in turn, would have a domino effect on Daisy's marriage prospects.

What made the situation worse was that Rose had only half-heartedly agreed to the proposal. After the *pennu kaanal* function, she had confided to Daisy that the guy was a bit of a *makku*. His remarks had conveyed a narrow outlook on life; he had spoken mostly about the dollars he earned, and when Rose told him her favourite author was Gabriel Garcia Marquez, he had commented, "Gabriel *Maakri?* Never heard of him."

But as their families seemed to have taken to each other, Rose had not objected to the alliance. A week later, elders from both families met again for the *vaaku parayal* function to finalize various important matters – the marriage date, availability of the church, number of expected guests, hotel details and, of course, the dowry. That was when the demand for the house came up.

"So, what are you going to do?" Daisy asked her mother.

"God only knows! Your Appa has asked for time to think it over, but we have to let them know our decision by the end of the week. The boy has already seen two other girls, and his parents are determined to finalize his marriage before he returns to America."

They talked for another 10 minutes before Daisy hung up. She sat on the armrest of the sofa, lost in thought, trying to imagine going back to a house that was no longer theirs.

The other girls had started to leave for clinics by then, so she rushed to grab her coat and bag from her room. Hurrying along the sidewalk, Daisy spotted Sunny and Sheetal walking together much ahead of her. After Sheetal changed rooms, their conversations had dwindled to exchanging pleasantries in the mess hall. She was also rarely seen at the hostel, spending almost all her time with Sunny and hurrying back just before the hostel gates were locked at night.

Despair washed over Daisy – it was such a shame that a perfectly eligible Christian boy like Sunny was besotted with a North Indian Hindu girl. It was rumoured that he had 'proposed' to Sheetal by gifting her a pocketbook on General Medicine.

Daisy was aware of where she had erred. She had put too much faith in Linda Goodman and star signs when they were clearly not working in her favour. But that was about to change. She had recently discovered a medium more powerful at predicting futures, and tonight she was going to test it.

***

That evening, Waheeda helped Zara get dressed for her stint at the Taj. While Zara balanced on high heels and arranged the *pallu* of her pink silk sari, Waheeda teased out the pleats, all the while declaring how jealous she was. "Do you know how much a cup of tea costs at the Taj?"

"Er, no."

"Forty rupees!"

"Wow! Then I'll make sure I savour every drop of it."

Waheeda sighed. "You're so lucky. How did you get this opportunity anyway?"

"It's all thanks to Sreedevi *Chechi* of the '94 batch. She suggested my name because I'm one of the few Malayalis who can pronounce the word 'memento' properly. Most people pronounce it as 'mo-mento', and since there will be a lot of mementos to give away at the conference, they're really particular about the pronunciation."

Waheeda giggled. "Sreedevi *Chechi* is such a joker."

"You think she was joking?"

"Well, didn't she once tie your dupatta to the backrest of a chair in the mess hall, toppling you over when you got up?"

"Oh yeah." Feeling foolish to have fallen for the 'mo-mento' explanation, she quickly changed the subject. "How long will you be staying in the hostel?"

"A week," said Waheeda. "Until Ahmed *ikka* gets back from the workshop at Jaipur. His mother is a real taskmaster; *ikka*'s absence is a valid excuse to escape from her clutches for a few days."

Zara stuck pearl hairpins in her long braid. "Where's Daisy, by the way? She agreed to help with my makeup."

"I saw her entering Mohini's room earlier. Shall I call her?"

"Never mind, my pickup will be here soon." With one last dab of lipstick and a final look in the mirror, Zara grabbed her sequined clutch and left.

***

Darkness had fallen when Daisy returned to Mohini's room as planned. Waheeda tagged along after promising to remain a mute spectator. Daisy placed the crude homemade cardboard Ouija board on the floor while Mohini and Arundhati lit candles and incense sticks. They shut the door but left the windows open as the room was stiflingly hot. Waheeda joined a few other spectators on the closest bed.

Daisy, Mohini and Arundhati sat cross-legged on the floor around the Ouija board and using a coin for a planchette, they started the séance. The smell of incense filled the room, and the flickering candles threw leaping shadows on the walls, creating a sinister ambience. A few minutes into the séance, the coin started moving of its own free will among the alphabets, numbers and words. The excited spectators jotted everything down on paper and tried to string the alphabet together to form meaningful words.

"O, friendly Spirit, what is my future husband's name? Where is he at this point in time?" asked Daisy in a high tinkling voice. The coin slowly zigzagged back and forth across the floor.

B – E – N –

"*Daivame*! It's your unit mate, Benny!" whispered Arundhati.

Daisy winced. Benny Thomachan was as appealing as unsalted rice water. To her relief, the next alphabet was not another 'N'.

'B – E – N – E – D – I – C – T'

Daisy looked confused. The only Benedict she knew was Benedict's reagent, a chemical used to test the presence of sugar in urine samples.

"Look, Daisy!" Waheeda whispered, "The second part of your question is being answered." The coin moved slowly to 'E', and Daisy held her breath. Was he in Europe? Would her dream of a home in England come true? Of afternoon tea with hot, buttered scones? Of girls in white dresses with blue satin sashes?

Slowly but surely, the coin spelled out the place in full: E – R – N – A – K – U – L – A – M. A town smack in the heart of Kerala.

Daisy's English cottage crumbled before her eyes. "So my fate is to marry some Benedict from Ernakulam." She sagged like a deflated balloon.

"You know, Benedict sounds like the name of a bishop!" teased Waheeda.

Amidst giggles, a gravelly voice boomed in the darkness: "Don't worry *chakkare*, if no one will marry you, I will!"

All heads turned simultaneously to the window – there in the pale moonlight was a silhouette hanging from the window bars. Screams shattered the air. Mohini quickly flicked on the lights, but the showman had vanished.

"Must… complain… to… Warden," panted Daisy, as she and Waheeda tumbled into their room and fell flat on her bed. A minute later, the clickety-clack of heels sounded in the corridor, and Zara entered. She stared at the two girls. "Did you two run a marathon?"

"Sort of," Waheeda said, sitting up. "Why are you so late? The conference got over at seven, right?"

"Umm, it got delayed a bit." Zara undid her sari, removing the multitude of safety pins holding it in place.

Daisy got up, put on her slippers and then looked at the floor. "Hey, where did all this sand come from?"

She peeped outside the door. Zara's high-heeled sandals were full of sand.

***

The labour room at the Calicut Institute of Medicine occupied the entire third floor of the hospital. It was a world of its own where almost a hundred deliveries took place every day. The students of the '96 batch who arrived for their month-long posting were greeted by a cacophony of wails, screams, clanging and banging. Seeing their stunned faces, the house-surgeon at the reception rushed to instruct them. "Go along the corridor marked Third Stage and find the nurse in the Register room."

"New students, eh?" asked the nurse as she showed them the shelves on which the OT shirts and pants were stored. "All are free size," she added, pointing to the changing rooms. Waheeda inspected the rents and holes in her heavily starched green OT shirt.

"I wouldn't be surprised if these have been here from when the hospital was built," said Sheetal. She closed the smaller holes with safety pins and taped the larger ones with Micropore. "Hey Zara, fixed your dress yet?" Zara chuckled. After four years in Calicut, Sheetal had started pronouncing 'fixed' as *fix-ed* and 'mixed' as *mix-ed*. "Yes, I have fix-ed mine. Let's go."

The duty MO was waiting for them in the First Stage Hall. She gave them a short lecture on the do's and don'ts of the labour room and what they were expected to learn during the posting. "The patient's history is taken at the reception, followed by a cursory examination. In the First Stage, we monitor the contractions and measure the cervix till full dilatation. The Second Stage is where we deliver the baby. The Third Stage is post-delivery care for the mother and baby. Since there are 11 of you, two can sit at the reception, and the rest can divide themselves among the three Stages. You can rotate between stations each day. Got it?"

Zara felt Vaibhav tug at her sleeve. "You and me, let's take the reception." The house-surgeon at the reception was amiable but too busy to socialize beyond cursory introductions. They watched him talk to the patients and examine their bellies. In between, he had the unenviable task of shooing away bystanders who kept poking their heads inside the front door.

"How I wish we had a security guard here," he fumed.

Zara saw an old lady poke her head in nervously. "What is it, Amma?" she asked, going over.

"Please, it's my daughter's first delivery, and she's been inside for five hours now. Is she okay?"

"What's her name and age?"

"Sumitha Prakash, 20 years."

"I'll find out. Stay here, Amma." She returned after five minutes. "Sumitha has been given medicine to help her deliver more quickly. She is doing all right and asked you not to worry." The woman thanked her profusely and retreated. That's when Zara noticed the horde of bystanders jostling behind the old woman. "Laila Ashraf, 20 years; Sreeja Madhavan, 23 years; Suhaila Mohammed, 18 years; Khadeeja Beevi, 17 years; Siji Johny, 28 years," they called out.

Zara sighed. She got paper and a pen from the reception table and went back to note down the names.

Vaibhav sneered at her. "Sweetie, why bother? Their daughters will deliver one way or another. Tell them all to shove off."

Zara hesitated for a moment, but then went off to the First Stage, paper in hand.

This month is not going to be easy, thought Sheetal as she looked through the case files in the First Stage, trying to ignore the assault on her senses by the pervasive pungent smell of blood and antiseptic. She empathized with the pregnant women lying on bare metal cots with IV tubes stuck in their arms, moaning softly and looking frightened. She too would have been just as frightened by the huge, cold hall, the constant wails and screams from the adjacent Second Stage, and the mechanical behaviour of the labour room staff.

"I need to go to the toilet," said one woman, rolling over on her side and standing up. Sheetal disconnected her IV tube and accompanied her, but just as they reached the toilet door, a gynaec postgraduate yelled, "*Stop!* What are you doing?"

She made the woman lie down on the nearest cot, parted her legs and motioned to Sheetal to have a look. "See? She's crowning," said the postgrad, "The baby's head is putting pressure on her bowels. Good that I caught you both, or else she would have delivered in the toilet. She needs to go to the Second Stage right now. *Trolley!*"

"The day shift is bad enough; I don't know how I'm going to survive the night shift," whispered Zara to Vaibhav. "I can hear you!" warned the house-surgeon taking the delivery in the Second Stage. "I allow only attentive students to assist me. Not those who waste time chatting."

Zara pulled a face behind the house-surgeon's back.

"As soon as the head is visible, you insert two fingers, stretch the perineum and put in the episiotomy incision," said the house-surgeon, demonstrating the procedure. She coaxed the patient – "*Mukku! Mukku!*" – and all of a sudden, there was a gush of fluid and the baby popped out with a cry, followed by a deafening thud.

Everyone turned around – Tarachand had fainted. The house-surgeon cut the umbilical cord and carried the baby away, while the boys carried Tarachand away.

All the staff and students were gathered in the duty MO's room for a treat by a house-surgeon who was to get married shortly.

"Quiz time – who knows why the position of childbirth is called the Lithotomy position?" asked Sreedevi of the '94 batch, one of the house-surgeons on duty.

"Lithos means stone," said Tarachand, "So unloading a baby is like popping out a huge stone from the belly?" Sreedevi laughed. "I love your imagination, but no. Lithotomy refers to the prehistoric technique where patients for bladder stone removal were made to lie in this position for...." She stopped short as Vaibhav entered the room, sporting a big maroon *bindi* on his cheek. Everyone burst into laughter.

"Vaibhav, who were you with, eh?"

"Tell us your secret girlfriend's name, *yaar*!"

"We all know who wears a maroon *bindi* around here, don't we?"

Waheeda slipped out and hurried to the ladies' changing room, where she dug in Zara's bag for her *bindi* packet. She found Zara in the Second Stage, pulled her aside and stuck a *bindi* on her bare forehead.

"How did you know my *bindi* had fallen off?" Zara asked, surprised.

"Because it walked into the duty room on your hero's cheek! Now go show your face there before people start connecting the dots!"

Zara entered the duty room looking as innocent as possible. "Any snacks left?" Seeing the intact *bindi* on her forehead, everyone resumed teasing Vaibhav, speculating about who else in the labour room wore a maroon *bindi*.

"I swear it must have stuck to me accidentally," Vaibhav said in a pleading voice. "You know how girls are always sticking their *bindis* on walls and mirrors."

Zara noticed Tarachand sitting quietly in a corner. He averted his eyes, but not before she saw the heartbroken expression in them.

When the night shift started, the students realized sleep was a luxury in the labour room. Sheetal had fallen into an uneasy slumber when a shriek from the Second Stage woke her up. Then came the shouts of '*trolley, trolley*' followed by the sound of rattling metal and running feet. Conceding defeat, she sat up and looked at her watch – 1.50 a.m. She squeezed past the other beds and realized Zara was missing. Stepping outside and not seeing Vaibhav either, she made an educated guess.

Just then, Sreedevi called to her from the Third Stage. "Hey, I need some help here. You record the pulse and temperature while I take the blood pressure." Sheetal took the case files and went about the task. The third stage was the post-delivery area – the happy mothers cradled their cooing babies while the bystanders fussed around them. Sheetal was jotting down the details of the second patient when Zara materialized at her side. "Hi, up already?"

"Don't think you're fooling anyone, okay?" hissed Sheetal.

Zara blushed. It was exhilarating and unnerving, this cat-and-mouse game with Vaibhav. Furtive kisses, hurried embraces – she was slowly but surely losing her mind.

"Are you two mad to carry on like this inside the labour room?"

"Don't be so matronly," Zara shot back. "It's only because Sunny is in the other shift and not with us that you are being so prim and proper."

"We would NEVER!" Sheetal slammed the case files down on an empty cot and walked away.

Zara picked up the files and went over to Sreedevi, who was examining the abdomen of a patient. "I'm checking for uterine retraction. A retracted uterus will feel like a cricket ball. If it's not retracted, the patient's bleeding will persist."

The patient's mother came up to them with a paper box. "We got this for the doctors here as a token of our gratitude. Please accept it." The box contained a sizeable number of *laddoos* and Zara wondered how much they had cost. Neither the patient nor her mother looked well off; they were using scrap cloth for the newborn's nappies.

Sreedevi was absolutely delighted. "Wow, thank you!" Holding the box up with one hand, the *laddoo* in the other and in a voice loud enough for everyone in the corridor to hear, she said, "See this? This is how you all should be thanking your doctors."

Zara flushed deeply at Sreedevi's callousness. She excused herself. Waheeda was the only one in the changing room when Zara entered. "I've been meaning to ask you something," said Waheeda, "Why are you carrying on with Vaibhav when you know your families will object? You're just going to end up in tears."

Zara fiddled with her fingers. "I'm quite sure of us. I love him, and he loves me, and that's all there is to it."

"Be practical, girl!"

"Love *is* impractical, isn't it?"

"Then why not come clean with your parents? Give them time to get over their objections and accept your decision."

"As a matter of fact, I already talked to Vaibhav's sister. She is nice, seems okay; said she would support Vaibhav when he talked to their parents about me."

"And what about your parents?"

"I'll tell them after the labour room posting is over. I mean, they have to accept that this is *my* life, don't they?" But Zara was aware of the lack of conviction in her tone.

***

The following Sunday, Zara paced nervously inside the hostel, trying to imagine the unrest in Vaibhav's home. No matter how gently he broke the news, and despite his sister's support, his parents were bound to be upset about welcoming a Christian daughter-in-law into a Hindu household. Her conversation with Mama in the morning had not been too encouraging either. At first, her mother thought she was being pranked as usual, but then realized her daughter was serious.

"So, he isn't a Christian. Is he a Brahmin or a Namboodiri or a Nair?"

"Why should that matter, Mama?"

"What caste is he, Zara? Tell me."

"I don't know. I've never asked him. He isn't an Orthodox Syrian Christian. Isn't that the only issue?"

Her mother gave a deep sigh. "*Mol*, you won't understand things like social status because you didn't grow up in Kerala. Do you know which family you come from?"

"I know, I know," Zara said bitterly, "My great-grandfather drove around Kottayam town in a horse-drawn chariot. Big deal!"

"It *is* a big deal," her mother replied tartly, "Things like ancestry, background, education, and wealth *do* matter."

"In that case, our families aren't that different, Mama. His parents are government employees; they, too, have ancestral property, his grandfather was a well-known Malayalam poet, and we are very much on par as far as finances are concerned. I'm extremely lucky to have met a guy like him."

"No, Zara, *he* is extremely lucky to have met a girl like you, and I'm sure he knows that. One's birth status makes a *huge* difference."

"You mean if he is a Namboodiri or Brahmin or Nair, you will feel better about our relationship? Is that what you're saying?"

"I never said that!"

"But you did *imply* it. So no matter how nice he is or how great his achievements are, you won't accept him if he isn't noble-born or upper caste, right?" There was a long pause. Finally, her mother said in a reluctant tone, "*Mol*, for your sake, we can try."

Zara spent the entire morning deciphering the nuances of the conversation and concluded that her Mama had taken the middle ground only because she feared a point-blank objection might push her daughter into a rash decision. But she was sure that once her father and Pappachen got involved, Mama's tune would change. Her hopes were now pinned on Vaibhav convincing his parents. If one set of parents agreed, there was a chance things could work out.

The day passed in a daze, and at 6 p.m., she rushed to meet Vaibhav in the portico as planned. He was already there, leaning against his bike. The grim expression on his face did little to loosen the knot in Zara's stomach.

"It was total bedlam," he stated without any preamble. "Amma became hysterical and wouldn't even hear of it. You know she's a cardiac patient, so I couldn't pressure her beyond a point. The bottom line is that if we marry, I will be your only ally in my home."

"I don't need anyone else, Vaibhav," she said as she tried to read his eyes, but he refused to look at her.

"It's not that simple, Zara. Marriage is a union of two families, and ours are poles apart. Truth is, we need our families. We both have to do our postgraduation, right? If we elope, how will we support ourselves?"

Zara felt tears sting her eyes. "We discussed this, didn't we? We agreed that one of us would work while the other studied for the entrance exam. Once we pass, we can manage on our stipends."

Vaibhav shook his head. "It's easier said than done."

"Or, we could wait until both of us got into postgraduation courses," Zara suggested.

"Do you think your parents would let you stay unmarried that long?"

"Or, we could both write the PLAB and leave for the UK."

"I will never leave my country. Let's be practical – we always knew this wouldn't work out."

Zara's heart pounded from the anger that was welling up inside. "Then maybe it's best to call the whole thing off, right?" she suggested in a tight voice.

"Yes, yes, I agree."

Zara couldn't believe his nerve! Vaibhav had dragged her out of her initial scepticism with promises of walking through fire for their relationship; he'd had her talk to his sister; he'd sworn to convince his parents at any cost. And now *he* was trying to convince her that their relationship wouldn't work.

"We can just go back to being good friends," Vaibhav said in a tone tinged with relief.

Zara's eyes flashed angrily. "No, Vaibhav, don't *ever* expect, even in your wildest dreams, that we can go back to being good friends." She turned on her heel and walked off without waiting for a reply.

***

Kenza was having a bad day. In the morning, she arrived in the ward to find that the Surgery Unit chief had been nabbed by the vigilance department for bribe-taking. While the students were debating this spectacular news, one of the postgrads poked his head into the side-room to say they were wanted by the HOD.

Dr Gopan Sreekumar was on the phone, fuming at the ears when they entered. He slammed the receiver down and gave them an irate look. "Your Unit Chief has created a mess, and now I have to pick up the pieces. Until he returns, you lot will present cases along with the students posted in my unit, understood? Now go."

On his best days, Dr Gopan was a perfectionist who chewed out even those who presented their cases quite well. Today, his wrath would be of volcanic proportions. Understandably, no one wanted to volunteer to present their case. They decided to draw names to see who the sacrificial lamb would be. It was Kenza.

As soon as class was over, Kenza ran to the staff toilet, where she closed the door and let her tears flow. When she returned to the side-room, puffy-eyed and exhausted, Luqman was waiting for her. "Don't take it personally," he said. "A lot of these old goats get their kicks out of terrorizing their students."

Kenza sniffed. "I used to be in such awe of him."

"Yeah, me too. But I've come to learn that we needn't respect *all* our teachers as we were once taught in school, only the ones who deserve the respect. Take our Unit Chief, for instance."

"Did he really take a bribe?" asked Kenza.

"Of course! And from what the postgrads say, it's not his first time getting caught either. But he doesn't mind because the newspapers print his name and address, which gives him free publicity for his private practice!"

"Won't patients hesitate to consult a doctor who takes bribes?"

"Why do you think patients bribe him in the first place?"

Luqman asked, shrugging. "So that they can cut the queue and get their surgeries done ahead of others. The heavier the bribe, the earlier your surgery."

"What a messed up system!" Shaking her head, Kenza made to leave, but Luqman lingered.

"I've been meaning to ask you something," he said, cheeks colouring. "I, er, I really like you. Do you think we can be a couple?"

The world crashed around Kenza. She remembered fantasizing about Luqman in their first year, watching him from behind her Cunningham's during Anatomy dissection.

Luqman kept talking, groping for words, his fair face intensely flushed. "I know you were close to that medicine postgrad. I used to hear the gossip, but now he's gone, so I thought..."

Kenza found her tongue. "We're not a good match, Luqman. My family isn't as well off as yours; I'm two years older than you, and I have a medical condition." Seeing his alarmed expression, Kenza added, "Nothing fatal. It's psoriasis."

Luqman considered this for a moment and then smiled. "My feelings remain unchanged. Think it over and let me know, okay? I'll be waiting."

I'll be waiting. The exact words Jayachandran had used over the phone two days ago.

I'll be waiting near the bus stop in front of the Registrar's Office with the witnesses. It was unimaginable that they were going to be married one month from now! Her stomach did somersaults every time she thought about facing her parents afterwards. Although Luqman was a more acceptable match, she doubted his infatuation would withstand the knowledge of her previous marriage and its aftermath. Jayachandran was the only person to whom she had disclosed her miserable past, and he had accepted her unconditionally. Would Luqman be as magnanimous?

After classes that evening, Kenza decided to stay overnight at the hostel. She couldn't go home. She needed solitude to sort out her thoughts. She had a spare toothbrush in the hostel and could always borrow a nightie from someone. Weighed down by her worries, Kenza didn't quite register the smell when she opened the number lock to Zara's and Daisy's room. Then it hit her – the stench of urine.

"This is just too much, too, too much," Daisy said, angry tears welling up. Several girls stared in shock at the smashed window and the urine which had trickled down the wall and pooled on the floor.

"I think this is the showman's revenge for the hot water bath we gave him last time," said Zara. Following the interruption of the Ouija board séance the girls had complained to the Warden, who said there was little she could do. It wasn't as if she hadn't tried – street lamps had been placed several times, but these were invariably found broken a few days later. Twice, security guards had been appointed, but neither ever saw anything untoward, even though the nuisance persisted. The main reason was the ease of escape for the voyeurs – large tree branches hanging low between the hostel and the adjacent buildings, whose terraces and parapets were almost at the same height.

The Warden advised the girls to keep all their windows shut after dark, and this infuriated them further. It was bad enough that they had to face showmen in broad daylight on the roads. Didn't they have a right to feel safe, at least inside their rooms?

In their outrage, the girls decided to set a trap for the intruder. Each day at dusk, they faked a séance in a random room and waited for the showman to show up. On the fourth day of this routine in the glow of candlelight, Daisy and Zara spotted something falling from the compound wall. As planned, they flattened themselves on either side of the window, saucepans in hand.

A few seconds later, a gravelly voice called out: "*Aarumille*?"

"Now!" Both girls flung the boiling water in the saucepans through the window to surprised howls followed by the sound of running feet. They had obviously been too optimistic in thinking that no voyeur would ever dare to set foot inside the hostel compound again.

Daisy's lips trembled with rage. "I'd much rather clean cat poop from my bed every day than mop up this *thendi*'s pee." Mubashira Gafoor, who was now the hostel secretary, materialized from the group gathered around the room. She took Daisy and Zara to task for their idiotic plan. “Since there’s been an intrusion, it’s better we phone the police,” Mubashira said. “I’ll inform the Warden.”

An hour later, a burly man in a kakhi uniform arrived on a motorbike, and the watchman hurried to unlock the hostel gate.

“Who called the station?” asked the policeman, stepping into the lobby.

“I did, I’m the hostel secretary.” Mubashira went on to explain the recent incidents and the broken window. The policeman listened with a blank expression, nodding ever so slightly at times, but he seemed more preoccupied with making a surreptitious inspection of the girls. “Is he sizing us up?” whispered Mohini to Sheetal.

“I think he’s a little drunk too,” whispered Zara, “His eyes are congested, and he’s slurring slightly.”

Finally, the policeman said, “It seems only you girls have this problem. We have never received such complaints from the general public. See how many ladies are here in the hospital area – patients, bystanders, shopkeepers, staff – and not one similar complaint so far.”

The girls wondered where this was going.

“When you cannot even describe the appearance of the perpetrator, how can the police help you?” he continued. “The only thing I can advise is that you all behave more decently. You’re always walking around with boys and riding on their bikes, morning and night. Is it any wonder then that these fellows are targeting you?”

Everyone was so stunned that they remained silent. Even the fiery Mubashira lost her voice. The watchman spoke up. “Sir, they are good kids. It’s not their fault…”

“Who asked your opinion?” the policeman barked. “I have a good mind to take you down to the station for questioning. You are the sole male at night in this women’s hostel – I strongly suspect your handiwork behind these incidents.”

The policeman turned to the girls. “Unless you have a description of the miscreant, don’t call the station again to make baseless complaints. Understand?” He swung on his heel and marched out of the hostel.

One by one, the girls dispersed, silent and subdued.

Daisy stopped in the doorway to her room. Zara and Kenza

brushed past her, carrying dustpans, mops and a bucket. Seeing them clean up the mess, tears started down Daisy's cheeks again. "So that's the bottom line – no one will help us. The college authorities have no permanent solution; the police turn out to be the moral police, and we have to suffer these perverts in silence."

A hand patted her shoulder, and she turned around to see Mohini. "Buck up, dear, no battle was won in a day. Mubashira *Chechi* says she's going to get the college union involved and force the college authorities to take notice." She took Daisy's arm. "Come on, you all need some cheering up. Maggi noodles, my room!"

10. Kenza, 2016

20th March 2016
Chittur

I was sprawled on Waheeda's sofa, trying to stay cool under the full blast of the ceiling fan, when I heard the gate creak. The sound of footsteps followed, and I jumped up with a grin as the door opened.

"Surprise!" I yelled, throwing my arms open.

Zara's face lit up as she hugged me tight. "Congratulations Kenz! I'm so proud of you!"

Waheeda ushered her in and led us on a quick tour of her beautiful two-storey house. We ended up in the upstairs bedroom, where she left us to get lunch ready. Zara and I sank into the little alcove, catching up like we were still in college.

We were so deep in conversation that we both jumped when a yellow helmet popped up outside the window.

"God!" I gasped, clutching my chest.

Then we realized it was a KSEB worker fixing the wires on the electric pole, and we burst into laughter.

"For a second, I was back in our hostel," I said, shaking my head. "I never really got over the shock of seeing that showman peeping through the ventilator."

"Oh, I'll never forget that incident!" Zara said. "I wonder if they still creep around the campus."

"I'm not risking it," I replied firmly. "That's why I'm looking for a flat. Besides, Jayachandran and the kids will visit. I'll need the space."

I noticed Zara's slight pause – she wanted to ask something. I could sense it. Probably something Waheeda had told her. I'd heard them whispering earlier, and I had a fair idea.

"I think it's amazing that you have the drive to do postgraduation after all these years," she said instead.

"I hope I survive it!" I laughed, though the truth was I was terrified.

"You will," Zara said. "You'd be mad to give up an MS Gynae

& Obs seat at Calicut."

"Yes, especially when Jayachandran is so supportive."

That was a lie. A neat, convenient lie. One that stopped Zara from probing further.

Just then, Waheeda poked her head in. "Bad news – KSEB's cutting power for a few hours. And we don't have an inverter yet. Might get a bit hot, especially for you, Miss Zara from the UK."

"That's alright," Zara said. "I'll just change into my bikini if Ahmed won't mind."

Waheeda looked briefly horrified. "Very funny. Come on, lunch is ready."

That evening, after lunch and long conversations about batchmates and gossip – particularly about Vaibhav's cryptic Facebook apology – I excused myself and went upstairs for the evening prayer. I lingered on my prayer mat afterwards, scrolling through my phone.

Jayachandran's WhatsApp display was a photo of him with our children. My heart twisted. Our eldest son video-called me every other day, sweetly assuring me that he wasn't mad at me like his father. The twins, still eight, just said they missed Amma. Jayachandran hadn't called me once since our fight.

I had bent myself backwards for him. For years. After house-surgency, I followed him to Abu Dhabi. We had our first child, and I barely had time to breathe between diapers and bottles. When I tried to apply for jobs, I found I lacked the experience required. Every hospital wanted a year post-house-surgency. When I told Jayachandran I wanted to return to Kerala to get that experience, he dismissed it.

"What about our son? Where will you stay? Who'll look after him?" he asked.

So, I made do. Observerships, short contracts – nothing permanent. When our son turned five, the twins were born. Again, I gave up everything. But I didn't stop dreaming. Quietly, I studied, waiting for the moment I could try again.

Then came Uppa's stroke last December. My sister's message was brief but urgent. I flew down immediately.

The man lying on the cot in our parents' house didn't resemble the one I remembered. He didn't even recognize me.

"Does Uppa recognize anyone?" I asked my mother.

"I can't say. Sometimes I think he does," she said softly. "But he hardly speaks."

I stayed on to help my mother, and maybe – to my surprise – start healing what was left of our relationship. The postgrad entrance exam happened around then, and on a whim, I wrote it.

Two months later, I checked my results. 241. I nearly dropped my phone. Good enough for a seat. A real one.

But Jayachandran had other plans. A fellowship in Canada. The paperwork was already underway.

"Believe me, I know what's best for us, Kenza."

"Just do as I say."

"No arguments."

"You trusted me to bear my children, didn't you?"

"I've made up my mind."

That night, I packed a suitcase and booked a one-way ticket. I couldn't stay with my parents. I couldn't go back to our house in Abu Dhabi. So, I came here. To Waheeda's. To safety.

Sitting on the prayer mat, I stared at the ceiling. I'd mistaken control for care, obedience for love. Jayachandran, in the end, wasn't all that different from Uppa. But this time, I wouldn't be the trailing spouse.

The call for the last prayer of the day sounded. I stood up to pray.

Then my phone rang. Jayachandran.

I stared at the screen for a few seconds before picking up.

"Were you sleeping?" he asked.

"No," I replied, trying to keep my voice even. "Is everything okay there?"

"Yeah. All good."

"How are the twins?"

"Fine."

The silence stretched.

"When does your course start?"

"May first week."

"Hmm."

Another pause. Another silence. I didn't fill it.

"Do you have any money? Shall I send you some?"

I closed my eyes for a second. "I'm doing night shifts at a hospital nearby. So… I have some."

He didn't respond immediately. I could hear the faint sound of the fan in his room, the hush of someone pacing, maybe.

"I've been thinking," he said finally. "And you're right. It's not fair to hold you back now. Canada can be put on the back burner."

My breath caught. "Are you serious?"

"I just said so, didn't I?" he answered. "You've sacrificed your academics and career long enough. It wouldn't be right to make you give this up now."

A lump formed in my throat. I didn't trust myself to speak. The years I'd waited, the compromises, the quiet ache of ambition – suddenly they had a place again.

"I'll send you a flight ticket," he said. "Once you're back, we'll talk. Plan your future together."

Plan your future. Not *my future.*

I whispered a quiet *Insha'Allah* under my breath. For the first time in years, it felt like maybe, just maybe… something was turning.

11. Fifth year, 2000–2001

'Because she was asking for it, that's why.'

3rd January, 2000
Calicut

The internet arrived in Calicut in 1999, and its popularity surged as the new millennium rolled in. Small internet cafés mushroomed in every nook and cranny. Most students had personal email IDs – even if they didn't have anyone to write to. Some, like Vaibhav, chose colourful addresses: *hotmale@hotmail.com.*

"So do girls sign up at *hotfemale.com*?" Waheeda had asked once, leaving Vaibhav uncertain whether she was being sarcastic or just clueless.

For most, the internet was just another frivolous pastime – perfect for sending pointless e-greetings and chain-mail jokes. Zara was an exception. She actually received regular emails from Pappachen. Thrilled to be alive at the dawn of a new millennium, he had taken a solemn oath to become 'modern' and bought himself a desktop computer. Now, he used it to send Zara long emails – mostly filled with proposals from eligible bachelors – and demanded explanations when she turned them down.

That afternoon, Zara strolled past RamCo to a newly opened internet café, rumoured to be faster than the one near Milma booth. It was a ramshackle little place, with cramped, half-partitioned cubicles painted in garish, headache-inducing colours.

"Twenty rupees for half an hour," announced the receptionist.

As she squeezed into a cubicle, she noticed Charles in the one next to hers, hurriedly minimizing his screen. Zara grinned.

"I didn't know you were such a fan of women's beach volleyball."

"What? No, no – that's just the screen saver here," he said, giving her a wink.

Zara typed out her Rediffmail address in the URL and waited for the bar at the bottom of the screen to turn blue. Her inbox popped open, displaying a variety of e-greeting cards, all from

Vaibhav. Cards declaring *I miss you, Friends forever* and *Let's make up* with dancing hearts, flowers and teddy bears. She remembered him whispering in her ear during clinics, "No matter how much you overreact, I still care about you."

She selected his messages, 32 in all, and clicked Delete. There was an email from Rishab Manchandani, her friend in Mumbai, with the subject line 'I conducted a cycle tour'. She clicked it open and saw a dozen photos of Rishab leading a group of cyclists along the lanes of Mumbai.

Zara felt a stab of jealousy. Although she loved hearing about Rishab's adventures, his photos underlined her scopegoat status. The last photo showed him beaming, surrounded by a bunch of young women. She stuck her tongue out at him and closed the email. Then she clicked on the Compose button.

From: zaraZAM96@rediffmail.com
To: eipeootty2000@rediffmail.com
Subject: No more boy photos, please!
Dear Pappachen,
My dream of becoming a star cricketer has come to an end. Our cricket team failed miserably in the semifinals, and we're out of the competition. I'm not too upset, though, as we never had high hopes to begin with. There were just three of us – me and two junior girls – who actually knew how to play. The rest of our team didn't even know how to hold a bat, so it was a surprise that we even made it to the semifinals!

Zara stopped typing and considered how to word her frustration with her grandfather's unsolicited efforts to get her a husband. While she'd fooled her mother several times with Arthur Guyton, George Papanicolaou and others, she didn't have the heart to trick Pappachen. She thought for a moment and decided it was better to be direct.

Speaking of romance, please don't send any more pictures of prospective husbands. My focus is on getting over the last hurdle in MBBS – the dreaded finals. It's a tough exam, and the failure rate is quite high. I'm also thinking of writing the PLAB exam for speciality training in the UK. So, I really don't want any distractions, Pappachen.

Not even the kind with good genes and land in Kottayam. I hope you understand.

When she exited the internet café later, Charles called out, "Hey Scopegoat, wait for me!" Zara rolled her eyes. "I've told you several times not to call me that. And where are your buddies?"

"James is in Paediatrics, and Kamaraj is suspended."

"What! Why?"

"You didn't hear? He slapped that loafer clerk in the B2 section."

Zara stared. "Oh! So that was the reason for the sloganeering outside the Principal's office."

"Correct," Charles said with a nod. "The staff demanded his suspension. In my opinion, that clerk had it coming – never around when you want to pay fees, shirking work and chatting in the Coffee House."

"Hmm. Can't say what King-Kong, er, Kamaraj did was right. What's going to happen now?"

Charles shrugged. "Such skirmishes are nothing new in this institute. Kamaraj will be back after a few weeks. By the way, I'm posted with you in Medicine next month. Want me to take care of your boyfriend problems?" He made a fist and hit the palm of the other hand.

Zara frowned at him. "I don't have any boyfriends or problems."

"That's not what Taru told me," Charles said with a chuckle as he strolled off towards the Men's Hostel.

Zara decided she had to corner Tarachand at the earliest. She didn't have to wait long. A few days into their Medicine posting, as Zara headed to the side-room to fetch a pen from her bag, she overheard Tarachand and Charles talking in hushed tones within. She flattened herself against the wall and listened.

"...my only consolation is they're still not talking to each other."

Oh! Tarachand means me and Vaibhav, thought Zara.

"Romans 8:25 – But if we hope for what we do not see, then do we with patience wait for it," recited Charles. "See Taru, you and Zara are like parallel lines. "You share the same thoughts and walk the same path, and therefore hope to meet at some point in time in infinity. But infinity, being something abstract and intangible, you never meet."

"That's a real shame." Tarachand sighed. "But frankly, I don't even feel like a line. I feel invisible, like an insignificant dot. Can a dot dream of becoming a line?"

"Hmm, let me put it in a different way," said Charles. "A person's life is like a circle. Each tangent that hits it and continues on its way is an affair or an acquaintance. True love is that line that continues with the circle, spiralling inwards, closer and closer, until they collapse into each other and form – guess what – a DOT! So Taru, what you should do is focus on becoming the dot in the centre of Zara's circle of life."

Charles is good at mixing philosophy with geometry, Zara thought, suppressing a giggle.

"Then there are the intersecting lines," he continued. "They meet at one point in time, there is a brief spark, and then they separate, never to meet again. Mark my words, Taru – if I know Zara's grandfather, she and Vaibhav are doomed to be an intersecting line no matter how entwined they are now."

Zara stopped smiling. It had been amusing when Charles was doing a Sigmund Freud on Tarachand, but it didn't seem as funny when the analysis involved her.

As soon as class was over, Zara cornered Tarachand. His eager smile disappeared when she gave him an earful. "Who I choose to walk around with is none of anyone's business!" she concluded, breathing fire.

"Okay, fine, I'm sorry, I won't talk to Charles *ettan* about you," he said, "But there's something about Vaibhav you need to know. Something I should have revealed a long time ago."

Zara rolled her eyes. "Please, Taru, not again."

He was forever leaking silly hostel secrets about Vaibhav in the hope that she would ditch him. But details like Vaibhav sleeping in his sweaty tracksuit in other people's beds or pinching someone else's toothpaste had not dampened Zara's interest.

"No, this is different, not about toothpaste or soap."

Zara sighed. "Okay, what then?"

"Remember that *Sheher ki ladki* dance during our first Batch Day and the *Nayana-Vagina* song at the end? Vaibhav was behind that. He was the one who started singing *Nayana-Vagina,* and the rest of the boys joined him."

"What bullshit!" Zara snapped, "You're jealous as hell! Vaibhav would *never* do such a thing."

Tarachand looked horribly embarrassed. "If you don't want to believe me, don't. I just felt that as your friend, I should warn you about the person you are getting so intimately involved with."

Zara's face flushed, and she resisted the urge to land a tight slap on Tarachand's chubby cheek.

"I know you always thought it was King-Kong or his friends," he continued, "but I can assure you one hundred per cent that it was Vaibhav." He strode off quickly towards the hostel.

From somewhere inside Zara's head, a doubtful voice asked – *What if it's the truth?* Tarachand's demeanour had been serious this time, not his usual buffoonish style. She fished out a coin and dialled the Men's Hostel from the pay phone in the college portico. The boy who answered the call could be heard hollering "Vaibhav, phone!" down the hostel corridor. When Vaibhav picked up the receiver, she said, "Hi, Zara here. Come to the portico, it's urgent."

Ever since she'd broken up with him, Zara avoided Vaibhav as steadfastly as he tried to make up with her. But the sight of his warm smile and droopy eyes was so familiar and reassuring that Tarachand's story suddenly seemed far-fetched. She felt silly.

"Hey sweetie, you sounded serious on the phone. What's up?"

"Don't call me sweetie."

"Okay, salty then." He grinned.

Zara remembered the last time they kissed – he said her lips tasted salty. She steeled herself. "I know this is going to sound ridiculous, but I really need to ask you this question."

"Why so much drama, *ishta*?" he drawled, "Ask away."

"During our first Batch Day, during the *Sheher ki ladki* dance, was it you who started the *Nayana-Vagina* song?"

He blinked in surprise. "That was such a long time ago!"

"Was it you?" Zara repeated.

"Why are you bringing this up now? That girl is not even here anymore."

"Just tell me – Yes or No."

Vaibhav sighed, folded his arms across his chest and gave her a defiant look. "What if it was?"

Zara felt the breath leave her. "What! Why did you do that to Nayana?"

"Because she was asking for it, that's why. Don't you remember the way she was pouting and pirouetting on stage?"

Zara couldn't believe her ears. "Only because that's what you boys told her to do!"

"Oh. Come on, Zara. There's a *big* difference between a simple catwalk and the kind of slutty strut she was doing. Nayana knew *exactly* what she was doing. How can any girl behave like that and expect guys not to react?"

"Not *guys*, Vaibhav, *you*! You sang that dirty song! And you made everyone sing it with you."

"And they did. Look, we guys just had a bit of stupid fun that day. It was no big deal, really." He shrugged.

Zara was too shocked to speak. Finally, she found her voice. "All this time, when I was blaming King-Kong and his buddies, I would never ever have guessed that *you* could sink that low."

Vaibhav laughed. "You girls are *always* like this. Digging up something insignificant from the past and turning it into a fight. I'd totally forgotten that silly episode until you brought it up now."

"*Shut up!*" Shivering with anger, Zara marched off.

Mind numb and eyes blurring with tears, her legs carried her to the Coffee House. She couldn't go to the hostel mess, not when she was too distraught to fake cheerfulness. Zara sat in a corner facing the wall, and all through her meal, Vaibhav's words kept echoing in her head: 'a bit of stupid fun… no big deal really…'

She remembered how miserable Nayana had been after that public humiliation. She clenched her fist so tight that her sharp nails nearly drew blood. When Zara left the Coffee House, her thoughts were interrupted by a shout, "Hey Scopegoat, over here! Give me a hand?"

Charles waved from the post office next door; an envelope stuck to his hand. The post office made its own glue (speculated to be made of *maida*), which was placed in a large bottle with a stick for an applicator. It was a strong, gooey concoction that looked like phlegm and gave off shimmering strands on coming in contact with air.

Charles was in a sticky mess – his hands, the envelope, the stamps and the stick were all stuck together in a cobweb of glue strands. "Tried to scratch my nose and this happened. *Post-Mortem*, that's what I call this mess; death by post office glue; POST-mortem, get it?" Charles chuckled.

Zara remained silent. She held down the glue bottle while he tried to paste the stamps that were adamant on sticking everywhere except on the envelope. "It's a challenge getting the right things to stick together, isn't it?" he said softly.

Zara gave him a sharp look.

"What happened, Scopegoat?" He winked. "Fought with your 'line'? I saw you both in the portico."

"Will you just leave me alone?" she hissed.

With another wink, Charles posted his letter and went his way.

Zara was about to leave when her eyes fell on a square plastic container near the exit filled to the brim with post office glue.

An image flashed before Zara's eyes and possessed her – Vaibhav, overcome with rage at an unknown someone who had doused his precious bike with sticky, post office glue. It wasn't impossible to execute. She knew where Vaibhav kept his bike during clinics – in a remote corner of the OP building that was hardly ever patrolled by the security staff. All she had to do was carry the container in an oversized bag and sneak off in between on the pretext of visiting the toilet. In a sudden rush of adrenaline, Zara bent down near the exit as if picking up something she had dropped, snatched the container and made off hurriedly.

"Why are you sprawled out on your bed so early?" asked Daisy. She folded the kurta she was ironing and spread out another one.

"No reason," replied Zara.

"You're not fooling me. You may look like a wilted flower, but

I can see the fire burning in your eyes."

"Uff! When did you become so poetic?" Zara got up and put on her slippers to go to the bathroom. Her mind was still revolving around the container of glue locked inside an oversized duffel bag under her bed as she entered one of the toilet stalls. A scream from the shower cubicle froze her in her tracks. Kenza ran out, wrapped in a towel, face paper-white, and pointing with a shaking finger at the ventilator. Zara felt an icy chill course down her spine – there was a forearm dangling through the ventilator slat, and there was grunting and cursing as the owner tried to free it.

She raced outside, shouting down the corridor: "Girls! Girls! Come quickly! The showman is stuck in the bathroom ventilator!"

Several doors opened all at once, and everyone came running, including the watchman. By now, the showman was struggling violently to free himself, and blood was oozing from his gashes.

Murmurs arose within the crowd.

"What do we do now?"

"Should we call the police?"

"What for? To hear another moral science lecture?"

"There's a ledge above this bathroom," said the watchman, "I'll see if I can tackle him from there." He ran off.

Zara suddenly remembered the glue. She ran to her room, retrieved the container and ran in the direction of the door that led to the ledge. Just then, a guttural scream followed by a dull thud was heard. The showman had fallen! Changing direction, Zara raced outside the front doors and towards the side of the building where the bathroom was located, with several girls following her. The showman was holding his injured arm and struggling to get to his feet.

"Don't let him escape!" bellowed Zara, triggering a chain reaction among the girls who ran shouting and yelling and grabbing whatever they saw along the way – brooms, sticks and rakes. Hearing the ruckus, a few of the hostel staff joined them.

Zara slammed into the man, toppling him over into a pile of leaves, and dumped the whole container of glue over his head. He rolled around, screaming in confusion, and the brown leaves stuck to his body, making him look like a grotesque bird.

The watchman reappeared carrying a large rug, which he threw around the man. Then he slammed the man against a nearby tree and bound him with a length of rope. Exhausted, the showman stopped struggling and hung his head in defeat.

The watchman sat down on the ground to catch his breath while the girls and the staff gathered around their prisoner. He was small and wiry.

"Is it the same *thendi* who pissed all over Daisy's room?" asked one of the girls. Daisy shrugged. "It was dark. All these *thendikal* look the same in the dark."

"Stand back!" ordered the watchman. He approached their prisoner with a bucket of water. The showman howled in shock when the cold water hit his face.

"Who are you? How did you get your hand stuck there?" asked the watchman. The man screamed a string of expletives at him.

"Okay, I'm calling the police."

"No! Please don't!"

"Then tell us how you got onto that ledge!"

The man deliberated for a moment. "There's a large tree in the compound of the bank adjacent to this hostel," he said, "and a big branch overhangs your terrace. It's easy to scale the wall of the bank. From the hostel terrace, I slid down the main water pipe. The girl who was bathing had hung her gold chain on a knob near the shower head. I was trying to grab that when my arm got stuck."

Zara heard a junior girl whisper: "Two birds with one stone – a *kuli* scene and a gold chain."

"So, you're a thief too," growled the watchman, "All the more reason to hand you over to the police."

"No, please!" begged the man, "Forgive me! I made a mistake. It's my first time here. I'm not a regular customer like the others."

Shock reverberated through the group.

"Who are all these others?"

"The customers are brought here by the agent," the man said. "I ran into this agent by chance near the OP entrance. He charges a fee to show customers the route to the ledges above the bathrooms."

"*Hey bhagwan*, so the rumours *are* true!" said Mohini, horrified.

"Please forgive me," beseeched the man.

The watchman shook his head. "Handing you over to the police is the only way to prove these girls were not hallucinating about showmen."

The man began to weep. "My wife is pregnant. I have a small daughter and an ailing mother. What will they do without me?"

Zara felt disgusted by his miserable drama. His wife, daughter and mother were precious to him, but every other female was nothing more than an opportunity.

However, there were sympathetic voices among the crowd.

"He *does* look genuinely repentant, doesn't he?"

"It's the agent and regular customers who should be caught. Not people like him."

"The college authorities are as much to blame. They never trim the trees, no matter how many times we ask them to."

"I think we should let him go. *Paavam*."

"Yes, if the police beat him up, his family will really suffer."

Zara's self-control snapped. "Are you all mad? This guy is peeping at us in the shower, he tried to steal Kenza's gold chain, and you want to let him go?"

"What if he becomes a better person after this incident?" asked a senior girl.

"Yes, Chechi, we should give everyone a second chance," said a junior. Zara shot her a scathing look, and she lowered her eyes.

"You all do as you please!" Zara declared, trembling with rage.

She stormed off to the hostel. An hour later, she awoke hearing chatter outside. The clock said 8.40 p.m. She got up hurriedly and rushed to get dinner before the mess hall closed at nine. Kenza was the only other person there. She looked up as Zara entered and gave a weak smile.

"I've lost my appetite, forcing myself to have a few bites. You know, Zara, it's the biggest shock I've ever had in my life. I didn't see him at first, I just *sensed* him, you know, like an ESP (extra sensory perception) that I was being watched."

Zara nodded. "What happened after I left?"

"They let him go."

"Yeah, I thought as much." She tore up her *chappathi* viciously.

"The majority voted to release him, and they made him swear that he would take psychiatric treatment."

Zara laughed so hard she choked on her food and went into a coughing fit. "Too much!"

On their way back, they passed the watchman who was going to check the hostel gates. "Chetta," called out Zara, "thanks for all your help. Too bad he was let off."

The watchman gave her a worldly look. "The police would have beaten him to a pulp, and his family would have suffered. Let's hope he mends his ways. But the agent and the other customers are still out there. Warden madam has been informed. She said she would take up the matter on a war footing."

By the following evening, the entire campus was buzzing with the news. A journalist came to the hostel enquiring if anyone was interested in an interview. A few days after the incident, a column in the local evening newspaper reported that a group of workmen descended on the hostel. They cut off the limbs of all the overhanging trees, increased the height of the hostel compound wall, placed a barbed wire fence on top of the wall, repaired the broken streetlights and boarded up the bathroom ventilators.

"Perhaps the embarrassment created by that paper column prodded the college authorities into action. Better late than never, I guess," Waheeda said as they sipped coffee at the Milma booth.

Zara nodded.

Kenza's home was a mere 50 metres from the bus stop, and as she got down from the bus, she saw an unfamiliar car parked outside the gate. She quickly loosened her headscarf, unfastened the gold chain around her neck and put it in her shoulder bag.

There was quite a din emanating through the open front door, and Kenza walked smack into a *pennu kaanal* session.

"Mol, we were waiting for you," said her father. He beamed from ear to ear as he introduced her to the prospective groom, his parents and his paternal uncles. Kenza was told to serve tea and snacks to the guests; then the prospective groom requested to speak with her privately (during which she learned he was a businessman and a widower with three small children); there was more banter and merriment (which abated slightly when the marriage broker suggested a generous amount as his commission); and an hour later the guests left in a flurry of handshakes and promises to fix a date for the *vaaku parayal.*

While her excited parents discussed marriage plans and her siblings finished the leftover snacks, Kenza slid upstairs to her bedroom and locked the door. From her shoulder bag, she took out the thin gold *thaalimaala* that Jayachandran had tied around her neck roughly two months earlier at the Registrar's Office.

The time had come for her to make yet another decision. Jayachandran stayed in the quarters of the hospital he worked in, roughly 25 kilometres from her house, and she'd been over there a few times. What stopped her from moving in was his idealistic, but totally impossible, demand that she come clean to her parents before walking out the door.

She knew why Jayachandran was being adamant – his own parents had blown a fuse when he'd told them of their registered marriage. But ultimately, he'd managed to placate them enough to ensure they wouldn't be unwelcome visitors in his parents' home. He expected Kenza to have the same conversation with her parents, and this was a point of argument every time they met.

Kenza got up, pulled a duffel bag from under the bed and started packing clothes while giving thought to her plan. She had to leave, and the sooner the better. If she waited until after the *vaaku parayal*, her parents' humiliation would be absolute.

She would shift her belongings to the hostel a little at a time. Their average exams were nearing, and it was usual for her to stay in the hostel on and off during exams

She zipped the bulging bag shut with an air of finality. If Jayachandran wouldn't make the decision, she would.

Waheeda was back in the hostel for group studies, but she spent more time gossiping about her in-laws to the eager listener, Daisy. They were seated near the common room windows.

"Ahmed ikka's second sister is the meanest of the lot. Once she came into the kitchen when I was making tea and offered me a *peda* from a box. After I ate it, she asked if it tasted good. When I said yes, she told me there was fungus in the box and she gave me one to find out if they were still edible."

"*Shho*!" Daisy made sympathetic clucking noises.

Sheetal looked up from her notebook. "Aren't you both in the least bit worried about the surgery exam tomorrow, especially since Gopan Sir is on the warpath?"

Waheeda shrugged. "If he has already decided to screw us all, why bother to study so hard?"

A month earlier, Dr Gopan Sreekumar had walked into the lecture hall one Friday afternoon to discover half the batch missing. There had been multiple factors for the bad attendance that Friday – the release of Salman Khan's latest movie *Chal Mere Bhai*, a crucial ODI cricket match and the wedding of a batchmate's brother. But what made Dr Gopan see red was that when he took the roll call at the end of class, nearly all students were present! Infuriated, he demanded that the proxy-callers reveal themselves. When no one stood up, he stormed off ominously.

"How tough a question paper can he set anyway?" asked Daisy, "Besides, there will always be some kind postgrad invigilator willing to give us hints."

The following morning, the tension in the exam hall was thick enough to cut with a knife. Everyone had the same thought – how bad would Dr Gopan's payback be?

At 9 a.m., the question papers were distributed and shocked gasps sounded throughout the hall. The essay question for 10 marks was: Significance of S.T.A.R.T in routine hospital practice.

Sheetal blinked. What on earth was S.T.A.R.T.? How could you write an essay on something you had no clue about?

The short notes were equally cryptic:

1. F.A.S.T.
2. S.I.R.S.
3. M.O.D.S.
4. L.A.H.S.H.A.L.

5. Persistent Priapism.

Sheetal knew the meaning of the last one – it was a persistent, prolonged, painful erection.

But what caused it? Drugs? Infection? Trauma? She checked on the others. Everyone looked like they had been clubbed over the head. Someone sobbed quietly behind her, in the adjacent row, Madhu Mohan was pleading with a postgrad for clues. The postgrad shook his head, saying Dr Gopan would know if they helped, because he was confident not a single student knew what the abbreviations meant.

Sheetal sighed in defeat. Waheeda and Daisy's decision to put in minimal effort had been the right one. There was no point wasting time here when she could be studying for the next exam. She wrote out a few sentences for the fifth short note, handed her paper in and joined the students leaving the hall.

Sunny was waiting outside and asked if she wanted to catch the latest Aishwarya Rai movie *Kandukondein, Kandukondein*. Vaibhav had bought a few 'first day-first show' tickets from some seniors who had a sudden change of plan. Sheetal didn't understand a word of Tamil, but the idea of being the first girl in their batch to see the latest Aishwarya Rai blockbuster appealed to her. Also, the next exam was four days away.

"Hey, did you hear that Vaibhav got tickets for *Kandukondein Kandukondein*, and Sunny took Sheetal with him?" Daisy said to Zara as they walked to the mess hall for tea. Zara didn't reply.

"Didn't Vaibhav ask you to go with him?" pressed Daisy.

"I much prefer going with the girls next weekend." Zara grabbed a glass of piping hot tea and slid onto a bench. Daisy gave her a sly look. "Did you and Vaibhav fight again?"

Zara was saved from further cross-questioning by Waheeda, who plopped down excitedly on the bench across their table. "Have I got hot news for you both!" she said, spilling tea all over the table. "Have you heard of VT, Vivek Tharakan, the second year Surgery postgrad in Gopan Sir's unit?"

"Who hasn't!" sighed Daisy. "MBBS Entrance Exam rank 8, All India Postgraduation Entrance Exam rank 15, and chocolatylick-your-lips good looking."

"He's not *that* hot," Zara said, giving her a disgusted look.

Waheeda sat cross-legged on the bench. "Mubashira Chechi is one of the house-surgeons in his unit. She heard from the boys that VT has eight goldfish, each named after a desirable Christian girl on the campus… and the two of you are in the bowl!"

"Really!" exclaimed both girls together, Daisy's tone elated and Zara's sarcastic.

The latter tone was evidently lost on Waheeda, who grinned from ear to ear. "So tell me, Zara, do you like him as a prospective groom or not?"

Zara gave her a sharp look. "Did he ask you to ask me?"

"Er, not exactly, he asked Mubashira Chechi, who asked me. You're goldfish number three!"

"What happened to goldfish one and two?"

Waheeda shrugged, "Chechi didn't say anything about that. You tell me your opinion."

Zara placed a hand on her chest. "*Dhak-dhak-dhak*, my heart is bursting with pride. I'm number three among eight, a rare honour undoubtedly."

"Don't be so arrogant! Girls are falling over themselves to catch his attention."

"My point exactly, Waheeda. If not me, there are seven others."

Waheeda was about to counter that when Sheetal burst into the mess hall looking excited.

"Hey girls," she announced, "you all should *definitely* see this latest Aishwarya Rai Tamil film – *Kundi Kandein, Kundi Kandein!*"

Zara choked and sprayed her tea over the table while the others screamed with laughter.

"What's so funny?" asked Sheetal, looking confused.

***

A Surgery Tutor emerged from the examination hall carrying a container from which Kenza and her unit mates drew lots before entering the vast hall. Twenty beds were inside, 10 on either side, each occupied by a 'case' for the practical exam. At the far end were three tables where their viva would be conducted after an hour.

Kenza proceeded to bed number seven. The man sat up hastily and flashed her a big grin. He was a frail fellow with a large neck swelling, which made him look as though he'd swallowed a cricket ball that got stuck.

"Good morning, doctor. My name is Manoharan and I'm your case today!"

Kenza almost lost her clinical demeanour at this introduction. Returning the greeting, she proceeded to jot down his complaints. Manoharan was eager to be cooperative. "I've been Gopan Sir's patient for a long time now. This neck swelling? No, no, that isn't what you need to examine, trust me. I've had it for ages, and Sir told me he could remove it. It's my legs that are important for you today; Gopan Sir told me not to forget to bring my legs when I come" – he took a moment to laugh at his joke. "My legs hurt like crazy all the time. Sir told me to quit smoking, but I still have a puff once in a while. Doctors are always saying 'Don't drink, Don't smoke', but what's life without a few pleasures, eh?"

Manoharan's monologue was very distracting during the physical examination, but Kenza reasoned it was better than coaxing details from an uncooperative patient. She wrote out her diagnosis – her patient had peripheral vascular disease (disease of the blood vessels), possibly brought on by chain smoking, and goitre (an enlarged thyroid).

"You're done?" asked Manoharan.

"Yes."

"No you're not!"

Kenza was taken aback. "What?"

"Are you *sure* you have examined me completely?"

"I… I think so." She was at a loss for words; she'd never before faced any patient this authoritative.

Manoharan spoke in a conspiratorial tone. "There is one finding you have missed. My left scrotum is enlarged. You should mention that too, or you will lose marks. It's happened before."

Kenza stared at him, wondering if this was a ruse to get her to touch his genitals. Similar incidents had occurred earlier in the OP and wards. And the eager look on Manoharan's face only heightened her doubts. But if he really did have a hydrocele or a varicocele or a hernia, and she missed it, Gopan Sir would chew her out. She would have to examine him. She donned a pair of examination gloves and led him behind a screen in the corner. He hadn't been lying. Kenza examined his varicocele and noted the findings.

"Excellent! You've done really well, doctor!" Manoharan said when he was back in his bed.

Kenza was glad he'd cooperated, but his condescending attitude was getting on her nerves. Thanking him, she moved to a table near the entrance to finish writing out the case. Luqman came over with his answer sheets.

"Was your case easy?" he began in a whisper and then stopped abruptly, staring at her chest. Instinctively, Kenza grabbed the *thalimaala* that had slipped out and stuffed it back inside her kurta. Their eyes met briefly, then Luqman quietly went back to writing.

Kenza exited the hall an hour later with mixed emotions. She was relieved that her viva with Gopan Sir had gone well, but she felt uncomfortable with his compliments for examining the patient's genitalia, which most students failed to do. She was glad Manoharan had been escorted away before Gopan Sir handed that bit of undeserved praise. Hastily, she picked up her books and bag, but someone called out her name. It was their batch representative.

"Hey, you're posted in OBG (Obstetrics and Gynaecology) now, correct? The HOD, Thressiama madam, wants to see you in her room."

"Me? Why?" Kenza asked, frowning. Had she not done well enough in her OBG practicals?

"No idea. But, er, your parents are also there."

***

The Sunday that followed was an unforgettable one for the '96 batch girls. Daisy got up early and, as was her habit, proceeded to the reading room, picked up the Malayala Manorama and inhaled the sweet, crisp smell of the fresh newspaper. She had an obsession with being the first to touch the weekend paper. She also had a fixed reading order: Horoscope-Film column-Cartoon strip-Headlines-everything else.

She started with her horoscope:

There's a sense of anticipation in the air. Certain events that went unnoticed have evolved behind the scenes and are going to be revealed shortly. But don't force the pace.

Daisy re-read it and wondered what it could mean. She certainly hadn't wilfully ignored any events. With a shrug, she proceeded through the rest of the paper, reading the film section with care and breezing through the rest. Earthquake relief news, political headlines, cricket – none of it held her attention for long.

As she folded the newspaper, her eyes fell on the notice board. The chart paper pinned there bore a blood-red smudged handprint and a message scrawled in bold black letters:

Tera kya KASOOR hai… mera kya KASOOR hai… AFTHAB is the KILLER.

Daisy's head spun. The newspaper dropped from her hands, and she screamed; an ear-splitting, glass-shattering scream.

The corridors echoed with the sounds of running feet. Daisy pointed weakly at the notice board, giving rise to shocked and angry gasps. Some didn't wait to see the chart paper, but, having heard what was happening, ran away, covering their ears and eyes.

Zara and Sheetal were among the unfortunate ones who saw the chart. "Our matinee is ruined," said a dazed Sheetal, "Who would do such a heartless thing to us?"

"Some junior, I'm sure," Zara said ruefully, "They had every reason to after that *Snegithiye* episode."

The previous year, their batch had been the first to see *Snegithiye*, a Tamil suspense movie with an all-woman cast. Afterwards, the girls had gone around the hostel dropping heavy hints about the killer's identity, much to the annoyance of the junior batch who were stuck with exams. Somebody had obviously been itching for revenge, and *Kasoor* (a Hindi remake of *Jagged Edge*) had provided the perfect opportunity.

"I had hoped to spend two hours drooling over Afthab and Lisa Ray, but now…" Zara sighed.

"You could've ripped off that paper and spared everyone else," Sheetal said bitterly as Daisy passed by.

"No way!" retorted Daisy. "Haven't you heard – misery loves company."

Eventually, some of them decided they might as well see the movie as planned, including Sheetal, Mohini and the Northie gang. Zara and Daisy declined to join, and a few hours later, they were glad for that as Waheeda arrived looking disturbed.

"Why are you here on a Sunday? Ahmed ikka off to another conference?" asked Daisy.

Waheeda appeared not to hear the question. Instead, she asked, "When was the last time Kenza stayed overnight in your room?"

"Oh it's been quite a long while," said Zara. "She came in a couple of times and put some clothes and books here, but didn't stay over. Why?"

Waheeda sighed. "She and Jayachandran have eloped, and her parents are on the warpath."

"WHAT!" said both girls together.

"It's true, but I don't know all the details," said Waheeda, "She's been lying at home about staying overnight at the hostel. Her mother called late one evening, asking if I knew where she was. She started crying and said one of the truck drivers who makes deliveries to their store had seen Kenza arm-in-arm with a man in Mukkam town. I told her I knew nothing other than that she was posted in OBG and staying at the hostel for group studies. Ahmed ikka was giving me suspicious looks. I didn't want him or my in-laws to get wind of what was happening, so I hung up quickly.

"The next day I heard from Mubashira Chechi that Kenza's parents turned up at Thressiama madam's room, accusing the teachers of matchmaking, misleading their students morally and whatnot. Madam was furious and had Kenza summoned."

"*Eeshoye*! What happened then?" asked Daisy. Zara could actually see the antennae sprouting around Daisy's head.

"Kenza's parents made such a scene that she had no choice but to leave with them. Now she's under house arrest. They think she will change her mind if she's locked up at home. My *Uppa* told them they're being unreasonable; Jayachandran can file a habeas corpus, but they're too upset to listen." Waheeda sighed heavily and shook her head. "I can't believe Kenza did this to *me*."

Zara gave her a surprised look. "Did what to you?"

"Over the years, I'd heard so many rumours about them. But I swear to Allah I believed her every single time she told me Jayachandran was only tutoring her in General Medicine." Waheeda looked so genuinely upset that Daisy and Zara burst out laughing.

"Oh Waheeda, how convenient for Kenza that you're so incurably naive!"

***

The Final MBBS University exams loomed large on the horizon, ready to descend upon the '96 batch in a matter of weeks. This was it – the make-or-break moment that separated medical students from full-fledged medical doctors.

Tensions ran high, and the air buzzed with a peculiar kind of chaos. In the clinics, students abandoned their assigned units and darted from ward to ward, hunting for *interesting cases* that were likely to be picked in the exams. For a while, the faculty remained blissfully unaware of the mayhem – until one long-suffering patient finally snapped.

She had mitral valve prolapse, and her textbook-perfect murmur made her a magnet for stethoscopes. Day after day, lines of students queued up to examine her. Fed up, she began pretending to be a bystander whenever she saw a white coat approaching.

One morning during rounds, she told Dr Gayathri, the formidable Head of Department, that she was planning to set up a ticket booth beside her bed. That afternoon, Dr Gayathri stormed into the common class and let loose a fiery tirade. She threatened to cancel two months of attendance for anyone caught outside their designated ward. Miraculously, from that day on, the cases within each ward began to seem just as exam worthy.

Meanwhile, others took a more strategic approach – cosying up to the friendlier postgrads in their unit in hopes of getting insider *tips*. After all, there was always a chance these postgrads had a clue about which long cases might show up in the exams.

And all of a sudden, the deluge was upon them. Theory exams roared by like a murderous hurricane, and after the calm of a few days, the onslaught of practical exams started.

Daisy messed up her long case in General Medicine owing to petty retribution from a certain postgrad she'd nicknamed BP (for bilateral pneumothorax) in a college skit because he always walked around with his broad chest puffed out importantly. No sooner had Daisy started examining her long case than BP got another postgrad to drop a hint that her straightforward case of malaria had an additional finding of bilateral pneumothorax. Daisy frantically knocked all over the patient's chest, and she inadvertently blurted out pneumothorax along with her diagnosis of malaria. This led to a barrage of uncomfortable questions from the miffed examiners. Only when she left the hall drenched in sweat and saw BP grinning did she realize the *tip* had been his idea of revenge.

Sheetal got into trouble in General Surgery when her clinical diagnosis was so spot-on that the examiners suspected her of receiving a *tip* when in fact she hadn't.

"Never be adamant about your clinical diagnosis when the examiners express doubts. Offer them at least one differential diagnosis to show you've considered it," suggested the Tutor who consoled Sheetal when she broke down afterwards.

Kenza managed to score extra points by discovering something that even the medicine postgraduates had missed – calcified subcutaneous nodules on the back of the thigh of her tribal patient who had been admitted with headache – a pointer towards Neurocysticercosis.

The OBG viva was not going well for Zara. She couldn't name the Babcock forceps, no matter how hard she racked her brains.

Dr Thressiama, the internal examiner and HOD of OBG, dropped a hint, "It starts with B."

Zara's heart sank. It augured a turn for the worse when the viva brought out the Scrabble enthusiast in madam.

"Er, Bains?"

"It starts with B-A-B."

"Bab… worth?"

"And ends with K."

"Bab… work?"

Dr Thressiama had *You stupid girl* written all over her face. "This is the very first time you are seeing this instrument, isn't it?" Zara flushed at the sarcasm.

"Since we've come this far, the last part rhymes with 'rock' and is the male counterpart of a hen."

"Oh, Babcock," she said in a defeated tone.

Dr Thressiama glared at Zara while the external examiner clucked 'Tsk, tsk'.

Zara walked to the side-room, demoralized and deflated. Tarachand was sitting there. "Hey, can I tell you a funny joke?"

"You can, but you may not."

"*Kya*?"

Zara grit her teeth. "I meant I'm not in the mood."

"Oh, but this will cheer you up." Tarachand pulled his chair closer to hers. "A patient says to his doctor, 'The tablets you prescribed have a funny effect on my bowels'. The doctor asks, 'Which tablets are they?' Patient replies, '*Ferocious* sulphate'!"

Zara gave him a ferocious look, and Tarachand swallowed his chuckle. His expression was so comical it felt like an apt finale to the tragedy with the Babcock forceps, and Zara started laughing. Tarachand relaxed.

"You know, Taru," she said, "I've heard seven cancer jokes today. If you tell me *tumour*, it will *benign*."

He looked at her like an adoring puppy. "What puns, Zara! Tumour – two more. Benign – be nine! Be mine…"

"What?"

"Nothing, nothing." Then he said, "What are your plans after house-surgency?"

"I haven't really given it any thought. Why?"

"I'm writing the USMLE. My chachaji is an intensivist in the USA. He's super rich and living a bindaas life. I was wondering if you too had plans of going abroad."

Zara shrugged. "I'm just living for today."

"I might make a trip to Mumbai during the two-month break before house-surgency. Can I visit you?"

"Sure, Taru, you *must* visit," Zara said warmly. "Just be sure to call before you come, okay?" *So that I can scram.*

A Tutor appeared and called them back to the exam hall. The examiners were finishing up Vaibhav's long case.

"If you suspect sepsis in your patient, what is the first thing you would look for?" asked the external examiner.

From behind the examiner, Dr Thressiama tried to give a hint by pointing her index finger into her mouth, to convey 'thermometer'.

Vaibhav blurted out, "Oral hygiene?"

The whole entourage broke into raucous laughter while the examiner 'Tsk-tsk'-ed again. That was the end of Vaibhav's case presentation, and on his way out, he mumbled, "I hope my marks are as generous as their sense of humour."

***

The exam results were announced a month after their post-exam holiday. As usual, the responsibility of spreading the news fell on the day scholars. Sunny had topped the batch – not exactly a shocker. But it was Sheetal who came in second, much to everyone's surprise, especially her own. The gossip mills went into overdrive, spinning tales of a match made in MBBS heaven.

But the only two people who had no idea if a happily-ever-after was even possible were Sheetal and Sunny themselves. Whenever Sheetal brought up Sunny at home, her parents would either pretend not to hear or swiftly change the topic. It was maddening. She vented regularly to Zara in Yahoo chat rooms – far safer than the telephone, now that her mother had taken to eavesdropping through the extension upstairs.

Sheetal: *It's all because of my horoscope* 😑

Apparently, my parents will face some 'great obstacle' before I can get married.

And guess who they've decided the obstacle is? Sunny!

So they're just… patiently waiting 🙄

Zara: *omg* 😂

Sheetal: *NOT funny*
Zara: *Okay okay sorry!* 😅
Did Sunny talk to his parents though?
Sheetal: *Yeah.*
They said I have to convert first.
Zara: *WHAAAAAT?!* 😳
Sheetal: 😭
Zara: *That's messed up.*
You don't have to convert to marry someone 😩
Look at Kenza!
Sheetal: *I know…*
What happened to her was really unfair.
Thressiama Madam totally screwed her over after that fail.

Kenza was one of the twenty-odd casualties of the finals. She was one of Sunny's rivals for the top spot until the day her parents barged into the OBG HOD's room hunting for their daughter.

Dr Thressiama had taken her parents' insults personally and refused to listen to Kenza's apologies.

"You joined a medical college to study or find a husband? Shameless girl! You will pay a heavy price for this!" Those were her parting words before Kenza was dragged away by her parents.

True to her threat, Thressiama madam had failed her in the practical exams despite the external examiner heaping praise on Kenza's clinical skills and giving her great marks.

For Kenza, her failure came at the end of a long, drawn-out, and exhausting battle to remain married to Jayachandran. Her parents had gone berserk when Jayachandran tried to get her back. When he finally filed a complaint at the police station, they threw Kenza out of the house in full view of all the neighbours. Ever since, Kenza had commuted nearly 50 kilometres to college every day from the hospital quarters in Mukkam. The weeks leading up to the finals were so physically and emotionally draining that when the exams were finally over, all she had was apathy so profound that not even the news of failure could break through it.

12. Home, 2016

23rd March, 2016
Kottayam

Every time I came back to my parents' home, something had changed. Last year, it was the kitchen renovation. This time, it was mosquito screens. I walked right into one on the main door and spilled my morning coffee.

"Vivian's kids get rashes from mosquito bites. So I had the screens put in," Papa said, without looking up from the newspaper.

I wiped up the mess, took what remained of my coffee, and stepped out into the garden. The tyre swing creaked as I lowered myself onto it – the same one that Papa had rigged up for the grandkids. From there, I had a clear view of the kitchen window, where Mama was shooting me her usual disapproving glances. Cotton shorts, apparently, were still too scandalous for the neighbours. But at least they'd stopped saying anything out loud. These days, whenever nosy relatives pestered them with the same question, "Why isn't Zara married yet?" – they simply shrugged. "Ask her."

I wondered how many times they'd used that line at Vivian's son's baptism two days ago. Vivian always had my back. "You can't blame her if she inherited Pappachen's wanderlust!" he liked to say.

Pappachen had been the original runaway. Most men in our family dropped out after school to manage the rubber and coconut plantations. But he? He took off to Bombay on a ship with just his BSc Chemistry certificate and a few rupees in his pocket.

"You either go forth in search of adventure, or you stay at home and count the coconuts," he used to say, legs propped up on the armrest of his porch chair.

He was proud that I was the only grandchild who'd inherited his spirit. When my parents lost it over my decision to take the PLAB and leave for the UK, he backed me. "Let her go. She can get married once she finds a job."

He was diagnosed with lymphoma a year after I left. Papa and Mama relocated to Kottayam to be with him during his last days.

I walked over to his portrait in the porch and touched the frame lightly. As much as I missed him, I was relieved he hadn't lived long enough to see me become a British citizen. Or, realize I had no intention of ever coming back for good.

Vivian was right – my wanderlust far exceeded Pappachen's. I'd trained in Paediatrics, switched hospitals three times, broken up with two boyfriends, and bought a house to finally 'settle down'. It almost worked, until a random conversation in the hospital cafeteria changed everything.

A nurse had just returned from Sierra Leone with MSF and was describing his work – jeep rides to remote areas, inflatable tents, field tests, malaria meds, oral rehydration sachets, food kits. I couldn't stop thinking about it.

On a whim, I applied. I wasn't expecting to get through the interview or the assessment. But a few weeks later, there it was – the acceptance email and a list of possible countries. I inky-pinky-ponkeyed my way to South Sudan.

By the time I boarded that flight, I'd bragged so much on Facebook that backing out wasn't an option.

Four months in Bentiu changed me.

The hospital was a patchwork of tin-roofed buildings that were connected by dirt walkways. OP, ICU, OT, labs, a Drug Bank – all wedged into whatever space they could find. The patient wards were *tukuls*, thatched mud huts circling the main building. We lived in tukuls too, in a compound nearby.

I'd seen poverty during my MBBS in Kerala, especially on rural postings, but this was something else entirely. The paediatric ICU was full – kids with severe malnutrition plus malaria, pneumonia, diarrhoea, and HIV. Some were in comas from cerebral malaria. We had no imaging, no blood cultures, nothing beyond basic labs.

It was just me, my clinical instincts, and the MSF guidelines. I was every kind of specialist rolled into one. And I constantly second-guessed myself. Every time a child died, I broke a little. Because in another hospital, another country, they would have survived.

But slowly, I found my footing. We saved more kids than we lost. I learned the language, taught cricket to the local children, made friends with the mothers, and even found moments to laugh. Bentiu stopped feeling foreign.

And then it was over.

I flew back to Bolton – to spring mattresses, designer shoes, and overstocked hospital wards. It felt obscene. Even my closet screamed excess.

Eventually, I made peace with the dissonance. I told myself: if I could use my privilege to keep supporting those who had nothing, I could live with the guilt.

My second mission was to Baraka in the DRC. The setup was larger; the outbreak more intense. We shared wash blocks, a rotating team, and frequent visitors from coordination teams.

One of them turned out to be Charles.

"Hey, Scopegoat! Fancy meeting you here!" he'd said, grinning. I stared at the bald head, goatee, and glasses. I wouldn't have recognized him if he hadn't spoken.

"You look the same," he joked, "except – where's the rest of your hair?"

"Got in my way," I muttered, still in disbelief.

He'd done a complete 180-degree turn – MD in Preventive Medicine, PhD in Epidemiology, working at CMC Ludhiana with his wife, Keerthi, and their three kids.

Keerthi. One of the campus heartthrobs.

Compared to that, all I had were some MSF stories and a passport full of immigration stamps.

We started spending Saturday evenings together – bar, dance floor, late-night conversations in my room.

"You had a crush on me, didn't you?" I asked once.

Charles laughed. "Ever since you roasted James with that Judas comeback during ragging. But I didn't stand a chance – what with that triangle you had going on with Vaibhav and Tarachand."

"Don't remind me," I groaned.

"They both did well, didn't they? Especially Tarachand. I'm not very active on FB, but I saw a few posts about his research work, his famous wife, the love letter to his expensive car… Rolls-Royce, was it?"

I laughed, adding: "And Vaibhav periodically writes on Facebook with these rather suspiciously progressive views on female empowerment. The instant he posts something, his followers get into a frenzy with 'likes' and comments."

"You don't believe him?" he shrugged. "People *do* change." He pointed at me. "Like you, for instance – the more we talk, the more I realize you're no longer the confused young girl I knew. I see the effort you make for these kids. Only someone with compassion would volunteer for projects like these. I think that you've, well…" he fiddled with his glasses and wiped his brow.

"I've what?"

He cleared his throat. "I think you've turned out absolutely amazing."

Our eyes locked, and there was silence.

Then came the moment. "Can I kiss you, Zara?"

I didn't stop him.

His lips were warm.

And just like that, the years collapsed between us.

The first time he said it, I was half-asleep. We were lying tangled in the sheets of my too-small bed in my too-small flat, the radiator hissing like a nosy neighbour. It was one of those rare English nights where the wind howled, and rain lashed the windows, but we were warm.

He was leaving in the morning. Back to Ludhiana. Back to Keerthi.

He brushed a strand of hair off my face, gently tracing the curve of my jaw. "I love you, Zara."

It was quiet. Barely audible. I didn't reply. Just kept my eyes closed and hoped he'd think I was asleep. But my heart was racing. Not because I didn't feel something. I did. But it wasn't love. Not the kind he meant. It was a memory. A tether to a past version of me that still believed in things like fate and forever. He pressed a kiss to my shoulder. We lay there in silence. And I thought – *what are we doing?* He had three kids. A wife. A home he claimed felt like a prison. And I had freedom. A passport with visas from war zones and refugee camps. A future I hadn't yet mapped. How could we meet in the middle?

"I love you," he repeated.

I could have lied. Said it back. Let it linger in the air like perfume.

But I didn't.

Instead, I asked, "What do we do now, Charles?"

He didn't answer. Just pulled me closer.

I felt the weight of it then – not just his body, but the inevitability of heartbreak.

***

Mama's voice broke through my reverie. "Mol, breakfast is ready." I walked into the dining room and joined them for *puttu, kadala* curry, and Bru coffee. The kind of meal that tastes like home and nostalgia, even if home no longer feels like home.

Later, I lay on my old four-poster bed, the dust shimmering in the light as I flopped down. Outside, the mango tree and the neem tree stood intertwined like lovers. Pappachen used to say they were best friends.

I picked up my phone. Another message from *The Prince*.

A location pin to a five-star hotel in Amritsar.

"It's a lovely place. When are you coming, my Queen?"

Charles still called me that. Queen Zara. He was Prince Charles. It had started as a joke in Baraka, but now… it wasn't funny anymore.

We'd had three whirlwind weeks. And then… silence, moodiness, the usual story.

We met again in Mumbai months later, at a wedding. That night, he buried his face in my neck and asked me if I would marry him. He would cut clean from Keerthi. I didn't know what to say. I didn't feel the same way.

Since then, the texts hadn't stopped. He fought with Keerthi, called her a nag, and said he missed me. I avoided his calls. I started replying like someone trapped in molasses – slow, sticky, increasingly detached. I avoided his calls. Left the blue ticks hanging like tiny accusations. Now he wanted me to come to Amritsar. And I was tempted… so tempted.

The phone pinged again. I braced myself.

It was Mohini.

"Hey, when are you going to meet Nayana?"

And just like that, everything shifted. Like a lens snapping into focus after hours of staring at the wrong thing.

13. House-Surgeons, 2001-2002

'If I ever write a book about my college days
I will title it An MBBS Mosquito'

1st April, 2001
Calicut

On the morning of 1st April 2001, 148 students slipped into their white coats with the same jittery excitement they'd felt five years earlier, back in 1996, when they first joined MBBS.

But this time, there was one crucial difference – every single one of them picked up a stethoscope and slung it proudly around their necks. They had *finally* earned the right to do so. They were no longer just students.

They were doctors. House-surgeons.

Zara hummed contentedly as she sat squashed into an autorickshaw, wedged between her suitcases, bucket, books, and a plastic bag of Maggi packets, rattling along the pothole-ridden road from the Ladies Hostel to the House-Surgeons' Quarters – HSQ for short.

The HSQ occupied one wing of the hospital block and was accessible from both inside and outside the building. Unlike the segregated hostels, the HSQ was – using Calicut lingo – a proper *'mix-ed'* setup. Boys and girls under one roof. Scandalous, yes, but sanctioned.

The autorickshaw groaned as it crawled up the steep road to the entrance, overloaded with her baggage. "Chechi, this will cost you Rupees ten extra," the driver muttered, clearly unimpressed by her optimism. On any other day, Zara would've launched into a spirited debate about metre rates and daylight robbery, but today, she was officially a doctor. She let it go.

Daisy and Waheeda were waiting at the gate to help her move in. Together, the three of them lugged her worldly possessions up to the third floor, where she was to share a room with Daisy.

The boys had taken over the ground and first floors, and both entrances to the HSQ opened into their territory. "No showman will ever trespass here," said Waheeda, "the boys are hardly ever *inside* their rooms. They will be just like security guards." Her only complaint? She'd been assigned Arundhati as a roommate. Which, in her words, meant that Anand, Arundhati's boyfriend, would always be lurking nearby.

During the HSQ room allotment, day scholars had the last pick, since they were expected to stay overnight only during duty shifts. Waheeda had missed the meeting entirely thanks to a family function, and by the time she showed up, Arundhati was the only one left.

To be fair, Arundhati hadn't been thrilled about the arrangement either.

"She doesn't seem very popular with her old roommates," Zara remarked, tucking in the edges of her threadbare mattress. "They could've gone for a triple, but they just paired off and left her out." She taped her favourite poster above the bed – a topless Salman Khan in a yellow bandana, ripped jeans, and a come-hither smile.

"I've been hearing stuff about Arundhati," Daisy said cryptically as they headed down to the mess hall for dinner. "Will update once I have confirmation."

As they ate, Zara's eyes wandered, inevitably, to Vaibhav, who was sitting in a corner with a group of boys. They weren't on speaking terms anymore, which made it extra annoying that they'd be stuck with each other in every posting. Coordination with your co-house-surgeon was *supposed* to be important. *Oh well,* she sighed internally. *At least we're in separate wards. I'll only have to see his face during rounds.*

A week into her posting in General Medicine, Daisy took her first twenty-four-hour shift on admission day. She had actually been on day shift but offered to cover night for a co-house-surgeon who fell ill. A shower and a hearty meal later, she headed back to the ward, weaving her way along the narrow corridor which was jam-packed with patients on straw mattresses. Admission day in Gen Med was always chaotic, be it in Casualty or the wards, with patients pouring in by the dozen, especially if the head of the unit was a favourite among the masses.

No sooner had Daisy reached the nurses' station and slumped down in front of a pile of case sheets that would put the Qutub Minar to shame, bystanders started gathering at the door with request forms for blood tests and investigations. She collected the forms, stuffed her coat pockets with her artillery – small penicillin bottles, needles, syringes, cotton balls, micropore tape – and entered the battlefield that was Ward No. 6.

The ward was overflowing with patients, their bystanders and visitors; it was hot, stuffy and noisy. The sole nurse on duty was pushing her cart through the crowd, alerting people to be mindful of the wheels, recording temperatures, and giving injections, all with a harried expression. There were still 20 minutes to the end of visiting time when the security guards would come around to shoo everyone out. In the meantime, Daisy had to brave curious onlookers who jostled each other to see the doctor 'in action'. Their awe was both flattering and annoying. She went from patient to patient, drawing their blood. It was the first skill she had been taught as a house-surgeon, but now it seemed as if it was the *only* skill a house-surgeon needed.

The three main duties of a house-surgeon were to:

1. Draw blood.
2. Record vital signs (and occasionally fill out the case sheets).
3. Write out discharge summaries.

Acquisition of other skills depended on how enterprising the house-surgeon was because the said three tasks – especially drawing blood—hardly left time for anything else. Daisy often wondered whether the sole purpose of the previous five years of MBBS had been to prime them to draw blood!

If I ever write a book about my college days, I will title it 'An MBBS Mosquito', she thought, searching for a vein on the arms and legs of an elderly man with diabetes and generalized oedema. The usual areas of access, like the cubital fossa, had suffered thrombosis from repeated punctures. A thin vein around the outer part of his ankle, one that looked it would collapse the moment a needle touched it, was all that was left. She would have to be super careful.

"This will hurt a bit," she warned.

"You go ahead, Sister," the old man said with a sigh. "I've become immune to pain from all the constant pricking."

Daisy wondered if the man had diabetic neuropathy. She connected the syringe to a butterfly needle and gingerly inserted it, praying the vein wouldn't collapse. It didn't.

Phew. She wiped her brow and filled two tiny bottles with blood.

"Take these to the laboratory. Go down the main corridor, past Ward Five and take the first right," she instructed the bystander, her attention diverted by a commotion near one of the beds. Ladies were wailing, and a man rushed over to her.

"Sister, sister, *Acchan* has some breathing difficulty. Can you please come?" Daisy followed the man to bed number 11, where, much to her shock, she found the patient gasping. His case sheet said he had been admitted with abdominal pain and blood in the urine, and his serum electrolytes were deranged. The clinical impression suggested some renal issue, which was followed by orders for conservative management. There was nothing in there to explain why the patient was gasping.

Panic swelled within her. What was she to do? Everyone in Casualty would be too busy to spare the time, and the sole postgrad on ward duty was unlikely to be in the duty room until late at night.

As if in response to her prayers, a postgrad appeared at the nurses' station saying, "I've come for the cross-consultation of one patient here."

In the dim overhead light, Daisy could almost see his halo and wings. "Chetta, can you please help me? It's my first night shift, and there's a patient gasping...."

He frowned. "I'm a Surgery postgrad, not Gen Med. You should call someone from Casualty."

"Please, please, Chetta, just have a look. I'll take full responsibility for anything that happens."

He hesitated, and then with a resigned nod followed her. Approaching the bed, Daisy relaxed a bit, seeing that the patient seemed to be asleep, but the postgrad rushed past her. He checked the man's breathing, put a finger to his wrist and neck for a pulse, then placed both palms one on top of the other close to the end of the patient's sternum and started chest compressions.

"Get an ambu bag, quick!" Daisy froze – the patient had not been asleep!

They took turns giving CPR (cardio-pulmonary-resuscitation) and ventilating him with the ambu bag. The ladies sobbed incessantly, and other bystanders craned their necks to get a better view. Twenty minutes into the cycle, he signalled her to stop. "Pupils are dilated and fixed; he's gone."

Daisy watched him take the male bystanders aside and talk to them firmly yet empathetically. "Write out everything as you remember it," he instructed when they returned to the nurses' station, "What time you discovered him gasping, how often you checked his pulse, blood pressure and pupils, how long you gave him CPR. Finally, write that you couldn't detect a pulse, his pupils were fully dilated and fixed, and note down the time you declared him dead. Got all that?"

She nodded, scribbling everything down.

He sat down in one of the rusted metal chairs, rubbed his eyes and yawned widely.

Maybe he was just getting off after a shift, thought Daisy, taking in his crumpled clothes, dishevelled curly hair and the mild stubble on his face. "Chetta, thanks a lot."

He gave her a piercing look. "Forget the thanks. A Surgery postgrad giving CPR in a Gen Med ward will not be taken lightly. If anyone asks, I was never here. Understood, Daisy?"

She gave a slight jolt.

Giving her the ghost of a smile, he went back into the ward for the cross-consultation.

Not that Daisy was surprised. Vivek Tharakan knew her name since she was one of the goldfish in his bowl. Naming fish after girls, as in fishing for girls? Could anything be more egotistical? At the same time, it stoked her ego to be among the eight when so many Christian girls on the campus weren't. And she did feel extremely grateful to VT for the helping hand in a moment of crisis.

***

From her first posting (Community Health) Sheetal acquired the image of a *work magnet,* attracting loads of work wherever she was posted. Sheetal agreed there was some truth to this.

While her co-house-surgeons commented on how laidback postings at PHC's were, Sheetal faced drunken brawls, cardiac arrests, stab injuries and picketing mobs. When she was posted in the Anti-Rabies Unit, a rabid dog run amok, biting close to a hundred movie-goers exiting a theatre after the midnight show. Casualty had been so full of people waiting for the anti-rabies shot that she had to send an urgent request to the HSQ for more hands. Now she was in Gen Med, and although the work was hectic, she hadn't attracted any disasters to date.

It was a dull, rainy evening, and everyone posted in Casualty was feeling a little relaxed with a lull in the flow of patients. Sheetal was hunched over an MCQ textbook, but her attention wandered to where a postgrad was regaling listeners with stories about his own house-surgency days.

"… he'd brought the dead snake, but it was so bashed up I couldn't make out if it was of the poisonous kind. Then I examined the guy, and he had two bites – one on his leg and one inside his mouth. *How did the snake bite you there*, I asked. He said in their village, there's a belief that snake poison is neutralized if you bite the snake back. When he tried that, the snake bit him."

Sheetal laughed along with the others. Deciding the stormy weather was not conducive to study, she shut her book and moved towards the group. In just two hours, her shift would end, and she could head to the auditorium to peek at the Batch Day programme of the '99 batch. Perhaps Sunny would accompany her if his work was over.

Just then, she saw the Gen Med duty MO approaching hurriedly, her brow creased. "Listen, everyone, there's news that the Kadalundi Bridge collapsed as the Chennai-Mangalore Mail was passing over it." Shocked gasps erupted. "It seems four bogies are submerged in the river."

"How many casualties?" asked a postgrad.

"No idea. But the majority will be brought here, so we need a plan of action," said the MO.

"All those who don't have emergency procedures lined up are to report to their respective duty MOs immediately. Recall everyone who's off duty or on leave, including house-surgeons." She beckoned to the postgrads. "Come, we need to set up triage areas."

Daisy stifled a yawn. It was her day off, and for want of something to do, she'd headed to the auditorium for the Batch Day of the '99 batch. But it was just about the most boring programme she'd ever attended. None of the dances or songs were as *explosive* or *breathtaking* as promised by the compere; the jokes in their skit were weaker than the rice gruel served in the HSQ mess, and the interludes were painfully long and devoid of gap fillers.

These kids are disastrously untalented, concluded Daisy as she got up to leave.

Just then, a small boy walked onto the stage with the microphone in one hand and a paper in the other. Daisy thought he might be the compere when, without any warning, he cleared his throat and started bleating into the microphone. A split second later, she realized he was singing *Harimurali*, a famous classical song by Yesudas. The boy's voice was akin to a piece of chalk being dragged across a blackboard.

For a few minutes, the whole hall was deathly silent, shocked by the massacre of such a beautiful song. Then several seniors in the front rows started bleating and braying along with him, and the hall erupted in laughter. Something whizzed right by the boy's head and splattered on the curtain. The boy turned around and, seeing it was a tomato, puffed up his chest angrily and continued bleating in an even higher pitch. The tomatoes kept flying, but the boy braved the onslaught and kept singing determinedly, covered in a pulpy mess from head to foot.

Finally, one of the senior boys jumped on stage and snatched the microphone. The boy's batch mates shouted in protest and tried to retrieve it. The senior yelled for backup, and soon a small crowd on stage was tugging and pulling the microphone.

The compere's voice boomed through the speaker, "Please be

seated, everyone, please! Then we can have the next item, which is a group dance led by Keerthi Susan Jose."

All the boys on stage froze in their tracks. They clambered back to their seats and (after the tomato mess had been cleaned up) the curtain went up. Five girls began dancing to *Ajooba Hai*, a catchy chartbuster from the movie *Jeans*, and a hush fell over the audience.

So this is Keerthi Susan Jose, goldfish no. 1 in VT's fishbowl, thought Daisy, looking at the pretty girl in the centre. The boys who'd been at each other's throats a few minutes earlier were now looking hypnotized. An image popped into Daisy's mind – the Asterix and Obelix comics where the villagers would freeze in the middle of a bash-up to stare at the lovely Panacea – and her body shook with suppressed giggles.

The song suddenly stopped. "Attention, everyone, there's an emergency. All house-surgeons and final years are wanted in Casualty," announced the compere.

The audience started mumbling, and the dancers looked at each other in confusion. The speaker crackled again, the voice more urgent, "Emergency in Casualty! There's been a train accident at Kadalundi. All house-surgeons and final years are to go to Casualty NOW!"

Daisy sprang from her seat and joined the senior students rushing down the staircase.

***

Less than an hour after they received news of the accident, the first few ambulances screeched to a stop outside Casualty. A fighting force of medical students, doctors and staff were waiting, organized into groups – to handle stretchers at the entrance, ensure availability of examination tables and beds inside the Casualty and Observation Rooms, source medical supplies as necessary, triage the patients and perform emergency procedures that may be required.

Sheetal was in the group assigned to monitor vitals and set up IV lines. Although everything went smoothly for the first 15 minutes, pandemonium soon ensued owing to the sheer number of victims, rescuers and onlookers flowing into Casualty. Several news crews and cameramen turned up, adding to the bedlam. They quickly ran out of beds, and people with less grievous injuries were laid out on sheets on the dirty, wet floor of the corridor.

Outside, the rain lashed mercilessly. Inside, Casualty was noisy, dirty, congested and as hot as a furnace. Sweat dripped down Sheetal's face and blurred her eyes as she inserted an IV line with difficulty into the vein of an unconscious man who was wheeled off to the OT. She soon lost track of time, her focus completely on running from patient to patient.

"Over here, give me a hand!" A Surgery postgrad beckoned frantically to her from where he knelt on the floor next to a moaning patient. "I'm wanted in the theatre. This guy needs to be catheterized immediately." He handed her the catheter and ran.

Sheetal looked around – no examination table was free. She would have to do the catheterization on the floor. "We need a screen for privacy. Do you have any sheets?" she asked the three men who had carried him in. They shook their heads. "Okay, then squat down around him and hold up the ends of his *lungi*…"

They did as they were told, and as Sheetal cleaned the patient with Betadine, she noticed his eyes well up.

"I understand this is a terrible ordeal for you," she said softly, "but I'm the only doctor available right now, and I'm doing the best I can." Tears slipped down his face, but he nodded.

Afterwards, Sheetal instructed the rescuers to shift the man to the outside corridor. She was searching for a postgrad to take up his case when rescuers brought in a new victim, and Sheetal was called to start an IV line. He was semi-conscious, and as she searched for a vein, he caught her hand and, through lips that were turning blue, whispered, "Sister, please give this to the police, to give to my family." He pulled a wallet and a sizeable wad of thousand-rupee notes from his shirt and thrust them at her. "Please, Sister…"

Checking her surprise, Sheetal took the items and nodded. The very next second, he collapsed, gasping. She yelled for help. One of the senior doctors and the nursing staff descended on him, starting CPR, rushing in the defibrillator, and preparing for intubation. "Why is there no IV line?" growled the doctor. "Start a goddamn IV line!"

Hands shaking, Sheetal tried inserting the needle and failed, and a nurse took over. They worked on him for over half an hour, but the man expired.

"Shit! Lost him," said the doctor, ripping off his gloves in frustration.

All of a sudden, Sheetal remembered the wad of money. *Oh no, where did it go? I've lost it!*

She had a vague memory of handing it to someone behind her when she was asked to start the IV line, but to whom? At death's door, the poor man had entrusted her with his possessions, and she had handed them over to some stranger. Sheetal's head spun, and she felt nauseous.

A gentle hand fell on her shoulder, and she looked up into Sunny's face. "Come Sheets, let's catch some fresh air." She followed him outside mechanically. The heavy rain had eased into a light drizzle, and the cool night air helped clear her head. By the entrance to Casualty, a group of third-year students were busy sorting through a massive pile of medical supplies – donations from nearby pharmacies. Across the street, auto drivers were helping policemen manage traffic at the junction, making way for incoming rescue vehicles. The crowd had thinned out, but the sense of urgency hadn't faded. In times of humanitarian crisis, everyone was pitching in, finding a way to help. Sheetal glanced at her watch. It was 2 a.m.

"Are you okay? You looked a bit sick back there," said Sunny as they sipped coffee at the Milma booth. Sheetal told him what had happened.

"Really unfortunate," he said, "but you were trying to help the man. Don't blame yourself."

When they returned to Casualty, the MO announced that those who had come in earlier were being relieved of duty as the inflow of victims had dwindled significantly. Sheetal trundled back to the HSQ along with several others, dragged herself up the stairs to her room, peeled her sweaty clothes off and fell on the bed. She was out in a second.

***

The alarm woke her up at 7 a.m. as usual. Freshening up, she went to the TV room where everyone was gathered around the newspapers. Around 42 people had died, and 230 were injured. The Navy had deployed close to 50 swimmers for the rescue. Experts were divided on the actual cause of the accident; some blamed the bridge, which was one hundred and forty years old and built during British rule. They thought a pillar of the bridge had sunk into the river, causing an uneven kink in the track that snapped when the train hit it. Others claimed the train coaches that had derailed were faulty as they fell on both sides of the track. The opposition accused the government of inefficiency, and the government reproached the media for their frenetic reporting.

"Enough fodder to make headlines for several months to come," remarked Daisy, retaining the entertainment page and handing the rest of the newspaper to Sheetal, who quickly scanned the obituary – nothing about the man who had died on her, or about a good Samaritan handing over a bundle of money.

She sat quietly, her mind blank, and then went off to start another regular day.

***

From: zaraZAM96@rediffmail.com
To: eipekutty2000@rediffmail.com
Subject: Thank you!!!
Dear Pappachen,
Thank you SO MUCH for the mobile phone! It's the best-est birthday present ever! I'm one of a handful in my batch that owns a mobile, and I flash my Nokia quite frequently to bask in the envious stares. The only problem now is finding the money to make calls – I mean, at Rs 3 for outgoing and Rs 1.50 for incoming, my stipend won't last very long if I decide to use the mobile! I think it's better if we stick to using a landline to call each other, and I'll use the mobile for sending you SMS.
I'm off duty today, so I have the time to email you. It's a little over three months now, and I'm already dead tired. House-

surgency is so entirely different that I might as well be doing a separate course. The worst part is that there are no guidelines or rules on how to tackle any situation. We don't receive any orientation at the start of a posting, and yet we're expected to somehow know how to manage patients all by ourselves.

Our only 'orientation' comes from hand-me-down wisdom. Which is, whatever the previous batch remembers and decides to pass on. It's like playing Chinese Whispers, except the stakes are actual human lives. Sometimes, if we're lucky, a postgraduate takes pity and gives us a ten-minute crash course before vanishing into the mist.

Just yesterday, the ICU postgrad handed over his chair and said, "Just cover for half an hour. I'll be back soon."

"Don't worry," he added. "They're all stable."

Famous last words.

The ICU looked like a horror movie set. Five patients, all hooked up to beeping machines in a tiny, airless room. I sat perched on the edge of a plastic chair like I was expecting it to explode. Every time a monitor beeped a little faster, so did my heart.

Mercifully, nobody died in those 30 minutes.

For a while, I assumed all this incompetence was my fault. That maybe if I'd studied a little harder, I'd feel less like a fraud in a white coat. But then I saw Sunny – yes, BuJi Sunny, who sleeps in the library – completely lost in the Emergency Room. That's when I realized: it's not just me. We're all winging it. Together.

I live in constant fear of actually killing someone. Not through some grand mistake, but through sheer, banal ignorance.

I've got used to the deaths now, though. I'm no longer the traumatic mess I was after my first night duty when three patients passed away, and I stood around feeling like a useless lump. There wasn't a postgrad or knowledgeable senior around, and the Assistant Professor I hesitantly dialled as a last resort lambasted me for calling at that unearthly hour and told me to go find a postgrad. I sat in the duty room and cried.

What I've come to understand is that house-surgeons are nothing more than cheap labour – to draw blood, write out case sheets and play traffic police during admission day. The only posting where we have some importance is in the Labour Room, because who else is going to handle the great volume of normal deliveries?

And soon after breaking our backs doing all this cheap, unskilled work, we have to face the next entrance exam for postgraduate courses.

Pappachen, I know this is an upsetting read when you still haven't finished distributing kaju katlis to celebrate the first doctor among your grandchildren. Worse – I don't know if you will believe all that I'm saying. Papa and Mama certainly don't; they tell me to count my blessings because I got into MBBS when thousands didn't, including them.

While that is true, it doesn't change the fact that I'm living someone else's dreams. Charles is right to call me a scopegoat.

Write to you later.

Love,

Zara

It was *Uthradom*, the first of the four Onam holidays, and the HSQ was unusually quiet as almost everyone had gone home, leaving only those who were either on call duty or had homes too far away. The OP departments and wards wore a deserted look, and only the occasional emergency case showed up in Casualty.

Sheetal was alone in her room, reading a Tom Clancy paperback after lunch, when there was a knock on the door. "Ay Sheets! How're ya doin?" Zara walked in with a silly grin. Daisy leaned on her, giggling.

Sheetal frowned. "What's wrong with you both?"

"Ohhhhhh, we're just celebrating," said Zara, "Daisy's now an aunty, you know. She brought wine when she came from home. Since we didn't have anything to do today, we opened the bottle."

Daisy started weeping. "My parents flew to America to see the baby. Zara's Pappachen has gone to Mumbai. We're both orphans in this great big HSQ."

"You're both drunk. Go sleep it off," said Sheetal, trying to close the door, but Zara held it open.

"Hey, wait, we want a favour. We want you to test us, to see who can hold their drink best."

"Oh? What test?"

The two girls barged into the room and sat down on the bed.

Sighing, Sheetal put her paperback away. "What should I do to get rid of you?"

"Standard neurological clinical examination – first the finger-nose test, then the tandem walking test. Ready?"

Sheetal held out her index finger at a short distance. The girls had to touch the tips of their own noses with their index fingers and then quickly touch the tip of Sheetal's finger. If coordination were lost, they wouldn't be able to do this. Sheetal kept challenging them by changing the position of her finger, but both Zara and Daisy passed the test with the ease of seasoned alcoholics.

"I'm impressed," admitted Sheetal.

The trio moved into the corridor for the tandem walking test. They had to walk heel to toe, that is, placing one foot in front of the other such that the heel of the front foot touched the toes of the other. Zara walked the length with ease, but Daisy started to tip over halfway through.

"Sorry, Daisy, you lose. Zara won that test. Zara? Zara?" She had vanished.

Sheetal looked inside her room, and then, on a hunch, ran down to the boys' floor. Sure enough, Zara was there, in front of Vaibhav's room, shouting expletives and trying to kick his door down.

"Stop it, you idiot! He's gone home." Sheetal pulled her away.

"*Ye Zara ko kya hua*?" asked Tarachand, poking his head outside his door.

"*Kuch nai, thabiyath thoda kharab hai.*" She pushed Zara up the stairs.

Back in the room, Sheetal collapsed on the bed while Zara continued swearing at Vaibhav.

"*Ayye*, why is a nice *Nasrani* girl like you, hic, still after that stupid fellow?" asked Daisy. "Why don't you take VT's offer, goldfish number three?"

Zara giggled, glassy-eyed. Making a 'V' sign with her index and middle fingers, she hollered, "VT! VEEE TEEE! WE TWOOO!" and sprawled on the bed, unconscious.

"She's deaaaad!" wailed Daisy.

"Oh shut up! She's just passed out," said Sheetal. "Do you have any limes in your room? My grandmother used to say the best method to revive someone who's passed out is to squirt lime juice in the eye." Daisy walked unsteadily back to her room and took the key from her *kurta* pocket, but the lock was missing! *Some idiot has stolen our lock*; she started giggling.

She pushed the door, but it didn't budge. *Jammed as usual*, she thought, pressing her shoulder against the door. The rusted bolt gave way, and the door slammed inwards, sending Daisy crashing over a small chair piled high with clothes and trinkets. She staggered to her feet and jumped out of her skin. A huge gorilla was lying on top of a naked girl on the bed. The girl squealed and the gorilla quickly rolled off her, pulling the sheet over them.

Daisy bolted down the corridor yelling – "King-Kong! King-Kong! King-Kong!" – burst into Sheetal's room and toppled over the chair there.

"What happened? Are you hurt?" Sheetal helped her get up.

"I entered Arundhati's room by mistake. King-Kong was in bed with Arundhati!"

"What rubbish! That wine is making you hallucinate. Maybe it was Anand."

"Nooooo. It *was* King-Kong! No one else is that big and hairy!" Daisy shivered.

Sheetal gave her a disbelieving look. "You've both had enough excitement for one day. Time to leave!"

The two girls hauled Zara to her feet, and the three of them staggered down and across the hall.

"Our lock is not stolen after all!" Daisy said with a giggle as she inserted the key and swung the door open.

A caterpillar crawled along Daisy's back, and when it reached her neck, it made a fist with one of its feet and knocked sharply on her head. *Knock! Knock! Knock!*

Daisy awoke with a start and scrambled frantically to remove the creature that had gotten inside her *kurta.* Her hand closed around it, and in one swift movement, she flung it on the ground. Except it wasn't a caterpillar or any bug. It lay long on the floor, glinting in the pale moonlight that peeked through the gaps in the curtains.

Daisy was about to pick it up when someone knocked on the door again. *Knock! Knock! Knock!* Bleary-eyed, she peeked through a chink in the door … and caught her breath. A man was standing outside! But she couldn't see him clearly in the dim corridor light. Was it an intruder in the HSQ?

"Get up! Get up!" she whispered, giving Zara a rough shake. "Some guy is knocking on our door. Maybe a thief or a molester."

Zara was instantly awake. Jumping off the bed, she seized a small, lightweight frying pan from the shelf and stood on the side of the door. On her signal, Daisy quickly pulled the door open, and as the man entered, Zara swung the pan and connected with the side of his head. The man fell like an axed tree and stayed still.

Turning the light on, the girls got the shock of their lives – it was Tarachand! The parcel he held had spilled its contents – paracetamol tablets, candy and ice packs.

"I think he was just checking on us," said Zara, kneeling by his side. She patted his face, and when he didn't wake up, she made a cursory examination of his pulse and breathing.

"We didn't kill him, did we?" whispered Daisy, turning pale.

Zara shook her head. "Knocked out properly." They rolled him straight, and Zara held one of the icepacks against the angry lump forming on his head.

Daisy snapped her fingers. "I know – Sheetal told me that squirting a lime in the eye wakes up anyone who's passed out." She rushed to the shelves.

Tarachand stirred and turned his head. Seeing Zara bent over him with an anxious expression, he gave a loopy grin and sang in a whisper, "*Chaudhvi ka chand ho… yaa afthab ho…*"

Daisy appeared with the lime and squirted it right into his eyes before Zara could stop her.

Tarachand screamed in agony, scrambled to his feet and dashed out of the room, howling:

"*Koi mujhe in paagal ladkiyon se bachao*!"

The following day was *Thiruvonam,* and there was a sumptuous *Onasadya* lunch in the HSQ mess hall. Sheetal had started eating when Zara and Daisy traipsed in. "Didn't see you two for breakfast. Hangover *khatam*?" she whispered as they slid next to her on the bench.

Daisy elbowed Zara and signalled to a corner of the mess hall where Tarachand ate alone, wearing an oversized cap. He pretended not to see them.

"Sheetal, meeting in our room after lunch," declared Daisy.

"Why? If you plan to repeat yesterday's antics, the answer is No."

"It's something else," Daisy said with a mysterious air and refused to explain anything further.

Once they were back in the room, Daisy picked up something from the table and dangled it in front of Sheetal. Her mouth fell open – it was the charm bracelet her *Didi* had gifted her; the one that had gone missing during their second year. "How did you… where did you find it?"

"Inside my *kurta*."

"*Kya*?"

Daisy sat down on the bed. "Yesterday, when I accidentally barged into Arundhati's room, I crashed into a chair that had a lot of random stuff on it. Afterwards, in my sleep, I felt something inside my top and pulled it out. It must have stuck to me when I fell on the floor. Which means" – Daisy paused dramatically – "Arundhati is our thief!"

Sheetal's mouth remained open. "But why would she steal…? Her family is well off."

Zara suddenly recalled the incident in the Casualty side-room.

"You never told me about the blue crystal pendant!" Daisy said with an accusatory expression. "We could have cornered her two years ago!"

"What if I was wrong? I couldn't be sure it was the stolen one. Anyway, it seems Arundhati is a kleptomaniac."

Daisy snorted. "If you ask me, she's more than one type of maniac! I've been hearing rumours about her cheating on Anand, but I thought it was with some postgrad. Let's pay her a visit."

Arundhati's eyes opened wide on seeing the three girls and their grave expressions.

"Hi, are we disturbing you and King-Kong?" Daisy gave her a wink.

"Don't think for a second you can blackmail me!" she retorted viciously, "I'll tell everyone you were so drunk you broke my door."

Daisy shrugged. "Big deal. The boys are always boozing on the HSQ terrace, and half the doors are already rotting. We came across something else, which is better discussed inside."

There was a moment's hesitation before Arundhati stepped aside to let them enter.

Daisy held up the bracelet. "This travelled outside your room, stuck to my *kurta*. It belongs to Sheetal. Where's the remaining stuff you've stolen over the years?"

Arundhati's distraught expression was all the confession they needed. Nevertheless, she tried a weak defence. "You can't pin the thefts on me. You can't prove that it came from my room."

"That's true," said Daisy, "but if you tell us the truth, *we* won't tell anyone about you two-timing Anand."

Zara gave Daisy a suspicious look for making a deal she wouldn't keep, but she crossed her arms in a show of solidarity.

The beautiful face crumbled, and Arundhati fell on her bed, sobbing uncontrollably. "I admit it. I took all those things. I didn't mean to hurt anyone. I can't help it… I just can't."

The girls looked at each other, dumbstruck; this wasn't the reaction they had expected. Arundhati's anguish was so genuine that Zara found her anger ebbing away. She sat on the bed and put her arms around Arundhati.

"I think you really need to get psychiatric help," Zara said, stroking her hair.

That night, Sheetal lay in bed swamped by a deluge of memories in which she was constantly accusing Mala of theft. Arundhati had laid open a small suitcase stuffed with all the things she had stolen over the years. Most of it was worthless – safety pins, glass bangles, ball pens, hair ties – but there were a few valuable items as well. Daisy's suggestion that Arundhati should return these if the owners were still around had driven her into such hysteria that the girls feared she would harm herself. Finally, they decided to secretly drop off the items themselves, in or around their owners' rooms.

From the suitcase, Daisy recovered her miniature Jesus statue and Waheeda's Sheaffer pen, while Zara found an HMT wrist watch that belonged to Nayana.

Sheetal stiffened; it was a long time since she had thought of Nayana, the other person she had wronged. A lump formed in her throat.

If I tell Zara what really happened just before Nayana's accident, will she show me the same understanding and forgiveness as she showed Arundhati, wondered Sheetal. Then she decided against it.

Trust had died the day she moved out after Daisy levelled accusations at her of going through everyone's bags. After that incident, she and Zara had fallen apart, maintaining a semblance of friendship just to keep the peace.

Shortly after the *Onam* holidays, Kenza began her house-surgency. To her great joy, Mala had cleared the finals, and they were posted together in General Surgery. As she was five months behind the regular batch, Kenza's postings were with other batchmates, not her unit mates of the past five years. So Mala's presence provided the comfort of a familiar face.

Into her second (and last) month, Kenza's previous unit mates started their posting in General Surgery, leading to a bit of awkwardness on both sides (especially when Luqman was posted in her ward), and she stuck to Mala's side all the more.

"What are your plans after house-surgency?" asked Mala as they sat in the nurses' station writing out discharge sheets. "Will you be shifting to Jayachandran's hometown?"

"Don't think so. He's thinking of accepting a job offer in Abu Dhabi."

"Wow! You're going abroad."

Kenza nodded absently. She had planned to write the postgraduate entrance exams after house-surgency but Jayachandran convinced her that some time away would help to dampen tensions in both their families. Besides, it was a very lucrative offer, and she couldn't deny she was excited; she'd never flown on a plane before.

There was a knock on the door of the nurses' station, and Chekku, the bystander of a patient named Kurumban, poked his head in timidly. "Sister, Chettan's dressings have not been changed in two days. His bandages are completely soaked and leaking."

"I'm not in charge of Kurumban anymore," said Kenza, "Please inform the new doctor who's assigned to his bed."

"I did, but he shouted at me and left."

Kenza sighed. "All right, bring him to the side-room."

A month earlier, Kurumban arrived in Casualty one evening, bringing with him the most horrific stench. "Fournier's gangrene," said the Surgery postgrad to Kenza, who was assisting him.

There was a huge ulcer on Kurumban's scrotum, and the skin over his genitals and lower abdomen was an angry, dusky blue-black-red. "It can result from diabetes, abscesses, intestinal surgery, but from Kurumban's history, I assume it's idiopathic," explained the postgrad as he cut off masses of dead skin and tissue with a surgical blade. He doused the entire raw area with Betadine and wiped him using gauze pads. "See? He needs to be cleaned like this every day. Don't allow slough to form. When the wound starts healing, we'll do a skin graft."

His specific instructions had given Kenza an inkling that Kurumban would be allotted to her care, and she'd been right. For the remainder of the month, she changed his dressings daily in a laborious ritual that took nearly two hours and kept her in the ward long after her co-house-surgeons had left.

When her previous unit mates arrived in the second month, the beds were re-allotted, and Kurumban became Latheef's responsibility. She'd been relieved to have Kurumban off her hands, but now he had bounced back.

In the side-room, Kenza peeled off the layers of wet gauze and inspected Kurumban's wounds.

"We were very happy under your care, Sister," said Chekku. "Big sir told us Kurumban needs to be cleaned daily, but the new doctor cleans only once every three days."

"Why don't you inform the Unit Chief about what's happening?"

Chekku's timid look returned. "If I complain, the new doctor may get angry and stop looking after Kurumban altogether. Sister, can you tell the new doctor?"

The next afternoon, Kenza cornered Latheef in the side-room just as he was leaving after his shift. Her query quickly escalated into a heated argument, and a senior postgrad was brought in to mediate.

Kenza turned to the postgrad. "Chetta, I've spent so much time and effort on Kurumban's care; all that will go to waste because of this fellow's laziness."

Latheef sneered, "Who asked you to spend so much time on him? Is he your father or what?"

The postgrad gave him a furious look. "I'm doing you a favour by not dragging you to the Unit Chief. Don't make me change my mind!" Latheef lost his smirk. "From now on, you are to change Kurumban's dressings every day, and I will be checking with the patient. Any lapses and I will promptly inform the Unit Chief, understood? Now get back to work, all of you!"

The postgrad left the side-room followed by the house-surgeons. Latheef blocked Kenza at the doorway. "You think you're very smart? You think you've won?"

Kenza glared at him. "This isn't about winning. It's about a patient's life…"

"Don't preach to me, you two-faced *kafir*," he spat angrily, stepping close to her. "Bullshit!"

"Shut up, you asshole!" Luqman shoved him away.

Giving him a dirty look, Latheef left the room.

"Don't mind what he said, okay?" Luqman said. "He's always been a bloody idiot."

Kenza nodded, grateful to Luqman for his support, even though her insides were still shaking.

***

The Infectious Diseases ward had been busy during the day, but at 11 p.m., calm prevailed. Zara was on night duty and curled up on the creaky hospital bed in the side-room, reading *Love in the Time of Cholera*. She felt the title was apt for her current posting.

The nurse on duty was efficient and promised to keep calls to a minimum. Owing to fewer patients, the nurse-to-patient ratio was better than elsewhere, and consequently the nurses were cooperative and polite, unlike in the bustling Gen Med wards, where the nurses were always stressed out, irritable and rude.

The downside to being posted in the Infectious Diseases ward was the risk of catching some bug. The previous year, the ward had been shut down following an outbreak of chickenpox originating from a patient who died of chickenpox-induced pneumonia.

Zara was nodding over her book when there was a knock on the door. She jumped off the bed, thinking it must be the nurse, but to her utter astonishment it was Vaibhav.

"Hi. Can I come in?"

You can, but you may not! She switched off the voice inside her head and let him enter. Ever since Vaibhav confessed to the Nayana-Vagina episode, they had avoided each other even when posted in the same ward.

He stood before her, unsure of what to say, until Zara broke the silence. "It's nearly 12. I'm tired."

He nodded, then blurted out, "I'm sorry I was such a jerk…" Zara crossed her arms,

"…and I'm sorry we broke up so badly." He looked straight into her eyes.

Zara didn't feel the butterflies in her stomach as before, because it was no longer the question of a future with him that bothered her. "What about Nayana?"

"What about her?"

"You know what."

Seeing his shoulders slump she knew she had hit the target. "That too," he mumbled, eyes averted.

Zara's heart melted a little. "Maybe we should have just remained friends instead of complicating everything."

He nodded slowly.

Tensions eased after that, and they talked about random things – their postings, taskmaster Unit Chiefs, funny incidents at work, the Kadalundi Bridge accident. He told her how impressed he'd been with how she handled the children rescued from the train accident.

"You should specialize in Paediatrics."

"No way! I've never really been bothered much about children."

"Why? Don't you like kids?"

She shrugged.

Vaibhav threw her a googly. "Zara, tell me honestly – on a scale of one to ten, what are your feelings for me now?"

Caught off guard, she blinked. She wasn't sure. But as they had just patched up, she decided to play along and pretended to think deeply about it.

"A five maybe," she said, opting for the middle ground.

"Wow, really? I was expecting a zero or a one. And your feelings… are they love, or are they lust?" Not understanding what he was getting at, she took the middle ground again. "A bit of both, maybe."

Vaibhav looked embarrassed at the reply, and Zara wondered if she had put her foot in her mouth. "As part of coming clean, I have a confession to make," he said. "When we were avoiding each other, I was so curious about what you were up to that I tried to hack your email address. I tried guessing your password, then I wondered if I should just select the *Forgot my password* option and set a new one. But then you wouldn't be able to access your own account. So I didn't."

Zara felt a spark of anger but controlled herself; he was making a confession after all. "Vaibhav, my password is a combination of our names."

"Really?" He looked pleased. "Well, if I had hacked into your email, was there anything you might not have wanted me to read?"

"Not really." Then she remembered something. "Well, there is an email from a guy, a stranger I met in a chat room. He seemed depressed and kept talking about his dead sister. Now he keeps pestering me to send him my pic."

"Oh, there's an easy solution to that," he said. "Send him a photo of a toothless, wizened grandma."

Zara laughed at this outlandish suggestion. Vaibhav stepped forward, cupped her face with his hands and kissed her hard. The feel of his lips, his hands and the smell of coffee on his breath – it was all so wonderfully familiar.

Before she could wrap her head around what had just happened, he flashed a shy smile, said *Goodnight* and left.

The following day, as she passed the TV room on her way back after duty, their eyes locked. He left the football match he was watching to walk with her. They talked of inane topics like his dream of specializing in Orthopaedics, her interest in Psychiatry and his new Alcatel mobile phone.

"Any plans for this evening?" he asked when she stopped at the staircase.

"Not really. Daisy is on night duty, so I thought I'd do some ironing."

"Shall we meet then?"

"Sure. Where? Coffee House?"

He looked pointedly at her. "Shall I come to your room?"

It was quite common in the HSQ for guys or girls to drop into each other's rooms for a friendly chat. But this was different, and Zara knew it. This was going to be more than just a kiss…

Yet she found herself nodding.

"I'll be there at nine," he said and went back to the TV room.

As soon as Daisy left at 7 p.m., Zara set about tidying the room. As she dusted and mopped, voices inside her head kept chanting *Virginity, Chastity, Purity* over and over again.

In between, her Mama's voice interrupted to quote from the Bible – *Flee from sexual immorality. Every other sin a person commits is outside his body, but the sexually immoral person sins against his own body. Corinthians 6:18-20.*

Zara flipped open the lid of the dustbin, dumped the trash and went for a bath.

As she stood under the cold shower, she thought hard about why she'd agreed to this clandestine affair. One, she missed him and didn't want to break up again after he'd apologized; and two, being on talking terms freed her from the strain she felt as his colleague.

But were these the only reasons? She remembered all those times she'd sneaked glances at his dimpled smile, his tousled hair, his coffee brown eyes… and the question he asked last night came back to her – Is it lust?

When she returned from the bathroom, the clock showed 8.15 p.m. Their room looked acceptably neat except for Daisy's bed, which was piled high with dirty laundry, washed clothes, her iron, her trinkets and her bags. Daisy was so lazy that at night she just spread a sheet on the floor or used Zara's bed if she was on night duty.

Zara had no inclination to tackle that mess, so she covered it with the sheet Daisy slept on. Then she lay down on her bed and closed her eyes, trying to ignore the voices in her head. She found herself standing on the pitch of a gigantic cricket stadium nestled amongst acres of lush green fields. The wickets were in place, and on the ground lay a brand new, shiny red cricket ball. She picked it up, admiring the fine red leather held in place by six rows of neat seams. The spectator stalls were completely empty except for a large white cockatoo seated in the VIP box. It flew over to her and, in a voice that sounded eerily like Mama's, said, "I was waiting for you, *mol*. We need to have a little chat."

"Where am I?" she asked the bird.

There was a rustling sound, and a twenty-foot black serpent glided over the grass to her, hissing, "I'm surprised you can't recognize this place, Zara! This is the Eden Gardens of Kolkata, one of the biggest cricket stadiums in the world."

The cockatoo and the serpent stood on either side of her while she fiddled nervously with the ball. "I'd like to leave, please."

The cockatoo made a clicking sound. "Not until you tell us what your decision is. Are you going to let him in tonight?"

"I… I think so."

"Are you mad? Giving up your virginity? I forbid it!" the cockatoo screeched, its black, shiny eyes bulging.

Before Zara could respond, the serpent spat, "Stupid bird! You dare to suggest that her worth lies in her vagina!"

"Listen to me, *mol* – if wealth is lost, nothing is lost; if health is lost, something is lost; if character is lost, everything is lost. EVERYTHING!"

The serpent looked bored. "This foolish bird just parrots what it's been taught by society."

"Are you calling me a parrot?" screeched the cockatoo.

"Didn't I tell you this bird is stupid?" The serpent laughed heartily. "Virginity is a construct of society to devalue females and treat them like commodities, to make them ashamed of their sexuality."

The cockatoo flapped around her, screeching *No, No, No* as Zara stared mesmerized into the emerald green eyes of the huge snake. "Can anyone change your identity in one night? Are you just a receptacle for the *right man* that society chooses for you?"

"Of course not!" gasped Zara.

The cockatoo grew increasingly agitated. "Don't listen to that evil snake! Everything will be lost."

"Nothing will be lost!" hissed the serpent.

"Everythingggggg!"

"Nothinggggg!"

"Everythingggg!"

Thump! Thump! Thump! Zara woke with a start. Someone was pounding on the door. She looked at the clock, and her eyes popped – 10 p.m.

Opening the door, she found a fuming Vaibhav standing there. "I have been knocking for one hour! What the hell were you doing?"

Feeling mortified, Zara babbled something about a headache.

"Well, let's not waste any more time," he said, closing the door behind him and removing his shirt. Zara's heart pounded like crazy as he pulled her into his arms and kissed her. He undid the knot at the side of her kaftan nightgown, put one hand inside and ran his fingers over her bare back. Goosebumps erupted, and Zara shivered.

Vaibhav kept kissing her, holding her close with one hand, his other hand caressing her back and waist, but every time he approached the curve of her breasts, she pushed his hand away. He changed his approach, moving his hand upwards to undo her brassiere, but the steel clasp was old and twisted out of shape. He tried to open it using both his hands, giving a quizzical look at her lack of cooperation, but she just couldn't bring herself to do it.

Finally, he lost his temper. "I was going to watch a blue film with the guys, but changed my plan to be with you. Then I spent close to an hour knocking on your door. If you weren't interested, why did you say 'Yes' to me?" With that outburst, he put on his shirt and walked out of her room.

Over the next few days, Zara tried her best to patch things up with Vaibhav. She tried talking to him during work, when she met him in the HSQ corridors or the mess hall, but he ignored her completely. A week into this pitiful existence, Zara woke up one morning to find a sheet of white paper pushed under her door. On it was one sentence in Vaibhav's handwriting: *Stop pestering me, you filthy slut.*

The final embers of her affinity for Vaibhav died instantly. She never looked at his face again.

***

Kenza rushed to the bathroom in the women's duty room and threw up. When she returned to the Second Stage of the Labour Room, Mala was stitching up the episiotomy of her patient. "I thought I'd take over in case you needed to rest. Are you okay?"

Kenza nodded.

"I think it's better if you avoid the Second Stage for the rest of the day. I'll cover for you," offered Mala. Croaking a *Thank you* at her, Kenza walked off to the reception area, but the rush there was no better, and she started feeling sick again. She headed back to the duty room and lay down. *What an inconvenient time to be pregnant*, she thought bitterly. It had come as a shock to both of them, especially as Jayachandran was about to fly abroad. With no family to support her, Kenza moved into Waheeda's room in the HSQ, which had an empty bed following Arundhati's departure.

"No idea what got into Arundhati," Waheeda said. "She left a few days after *Onam*. Just packed up and tore off. Plenty of rumours are flying around – that she's in a live-in relationship with someone, that Anand slapped her when she broke up with him, and that she got secretly married. Only *Allah* knows what the truth is. She's still coming for duty, though."

Waheeda had moved into the HSQ, but for different reasons. "Ahmed *ikka*'s mother is going around whispering to relatives that there's something wrong with me because I've not conceived after two years of marriage." She dabbed her eyes with the end of her headscarf and sniffed.

"Why not see a gynaecologist?" asked Kenza.

"We did. I'm not the one with the problem. But *ikka* is too embarrassed to tell his parents the truth, even though he knows his mother is taking her anger out on me. One day, she accused me of secretly taking contraceptive pills, and I broke down. That's when *ikka* suggested I move to the HSQ." Waheeda wiped the tears from her cheeks. "He's searching for a job elsewhere, far from home, so there will be a valid reason to move out."

Kenza knew Waheeda was too conservative to opt for contraceptives. But it boggled her mind that using contraceptives had never occurred to *her*, especially when she had the wherewithal of a medic. She could have avoided her present situation had she prioritized herself before her job or academics; a sentiment echoed by Dr Thressiama when she requested a change of posting from Labour Room to Gynaec as she had hyperemesis.

"If you were smart, you'd have waited until house-surgency was over. Besides, pregnancy is a physiological process; there's no need to make a big deal of it. I won't allow you to use pregnancy as an excuse for laziness."

Fortunately for Kenza, other faculty members and her co-house-surgeons were quite supportive. (Much later, Kenza heard from an Assistant Professor that Dr Thressiama had taken six months leave to care for her own pregnant daughter).

Mala entered the duty room and lay down next to Kenza. "All quiet for now. You rest. Just wake me up if it gets busy." She was asleep the moment her head touched the mattress.

The number of *trolley* calls increased all too soon, but Kenza didn't have the heart to wake an exhausted Mala. She left the room, donned personal protective equipment, and followed a patient being wheeled into Second Stage. The case sheet said her name was Udayabindu, and this was her second pregnancy.

Kenza went about the procedure mechanically – she injected local anaesthetic into the vaginal wall, made the episiotomy incision, extracted the screaming baby and dashed off with it to the neonatal room. When she returned to remove the placenta, Udayabindu had a sudden attack of diarrhoea and emptied her bowels all over the Second Stage floor. Simultaneously, the umbilical cord lengthened, indicating the placenta was separating. Kenza called urgently for an attender and stepped carefully around the mess on the floor to tug on the cord. She eased the placenta into a kidney dish and examined it closely for defects.

An attender turned up and got to work cleaning up the floor. Kenza turned her attention to the episiotomy wound that she had to close and the mess covering it. Not even her mask could fend off the nauseating smell of poop mixed with blood, which threatened to overwhelm Kenza in her delicate state.

The patient started weeping. "Sorry doctor… sorry Chechi… I couldn't control it."

"Don't be upset, *Mol*," said the attender, "it happens all the time. Isn't that right, doctor?"

"What? Oh yes, all the time."

Kenza's heart went out to the exhausted woman crying in embarrassment. "You know, I'm pregnant too, and I get nauseous all the time, so I understand how you feel."

"Really, doctor?" said Udayabindu, wiping her eyes. "How many months are you?"

Her attention shifted to questioning Kenza about her family

history, marital history, menstrual history and antenatal care history.

She's better at case-taking than I am! Kenza bit back a smile as she sutured the episiotomy, trying to ignore the smell and her urge to vomit. By the time she was done, Kenza was well informed about Udayabindu's family and extended family members, and received a detailed recipe for an antiemetic using ginger, *tulsi* and a bunch of other herbs.

Checking the last of the stitches, Kenza said, "Okay, you're all done. The attendant will move you out and bring your baby shortly."

Udayabindu's eyes welled up. Bringing her palms together, she said, "Thank you, doctor."

Kenza smiled, surprised to hear a word not uttered often in the hospital. It was the first time she had been thanked by a patient.

"You're welcome. Take care, okay?"

In all of Kenza's later years as a practising gynaecologist, no *Thank You* felt as profound as the one she received in the labour room from Udayabindu.

***

The medicine speciality postings were a combination of either Psychiatry and Gastroenterology, or Neurology and Cardiology, and were allotted at random. Daisy had been hoping for the former combination because, one, she was a Sigmund Freud fan, and two, both postings were not too hectic. But to her dismay, she received the latter combination, and no one was willing to exchange.

The two weeks in Cardiology had been super busy, and now she was eager to get through Neurology. Her last night's duty in the department seemed to be a test of her patience with patients. She'd gone to bed around 11 p.m., dead tired, when there was a knock on the door.

"Hello Sister…," began the patient.

"I've told you before – I'm the doctor. What do you want?"

"Er… Doctor, I can't sleep."

Daisy stared at him. "What were you doing all morning?"

"Sleeping."

"And in the noon after lunch?"

"Er… sleeping."

"Then how do you possibly expect to feel sleepy now?"

Not liking the look on Daisy's face, the patient slunk away mumbling something about trying warm milk. She went back to bed and had hardly dozed off when another knock sounded on the door. This time it was a bystander. "Doctor, do you know at what time the first bus to Wayanad leaves in the morning?"

"My dear Chetta, I am from Ernakulam, so pardon me for not memorizing the bus timings for Wayanad."

"Oh, too bad. I'll ask one of the security staff then."

Jesus, where do these characters even come from? Lying down, she shut her eyes… and another knock sounded on the door!

Daisy jumped out of bed, breathing fire. But this time it was the nurse. "Doctor, Govindankutty's wife is asking if you can look at him." She went over to the patient's bed. "He is shaking more than usual," his wife said, wringing her hands. Daisy thumbed through the case sheet – it said he suffered from Parkinson-plus syndrome. She had no idea what the management was.

"I'll call the postgrad."

"He got called to Casualty an hour ago and is not back yet," said the nurse.

Daisy rushed down two flights of stairs and the winding corridors to the Casualty block in search of the Neurology postgrad. But he was nowhere to be seen. On the way back to the ward, she ran into Madhu Mohan.

"Hey Madhu, did you have a posting in Neurology?"

"No. Why?"

She explained her predicament. "It might be a seizure," suggested Madhu Mohan, "I've seen patients like him being given IV Diazepam in Casualty. Maybe you should try that."

Daisy thanked him, headed back to the duty room, consulted her SIMS handbook for dosage and gave orders to the nurse. "Don't worry, Amma, he'll be alright soon," she consoled the wife.

Barely half an hour later, she was woken up by frenzied knocking. "Doctor, come quickly!"

This time, Govindankutty was lying as still as an axed tree. No tremors and no movements.

The wife wailed and beat her chest. "Doctor, doctor, what did you do to him? Oh God! He's never ever been *this* still before!"

Other bystanders strolled over to enquire what the fuss was.

Daisy was shocked – surely the patient hadn't died from a dose of Diazepam! Examining him, she was relieved to find a normal pulse and blood pressure. His systemic examination was also normal. But why was he this calm all of a sudden? Was he only sedated or comatose? What was she to do next?

"Don't worry, Amma, he's absolutely fine. Just, er, relaxing." The wife didn't look reassured, but she stopped making a ruckus.

Daisy lost all sleep after that, getting up every half hour to check his vitals. Towards the crack of dawn, the nurse informed her that Govindankutty's tremors had returned.

"He's back to normal, doctor!" said the wife, beaming at her husband, who was shaking with as much intensity as before.

Daisy wondered why the wife had even complained to begin with! Lying down, she fell into a deep sleep until she was woken up later for the morning rounds.

Following Neurology, Daisy had two months of General Surgery. But before that, she went home for a *pennu kaanal* function. She returned the following day in an utterly foul mood. The prospective groom was neither a doctor nor an engineer, and she fought with her parents when they asked her to consent to the proposal. With their house and most of their fortune given away as dowry to Rose, Daisy's options dwindled drastically, because in arranged marriages, a woman's desirability is directly proportional to her parents' wealth.

But she didn't blame her parents. Arm-twisting for additional dowry after the engagement was common practice. So, Rose had an ostentatious wedding and, like clockwork, popped out her first child before their first wedding anniversary. All expenses related to the birth of the first child were, by custom, borne by the wife's side, which led to a further drain on Daisy's family's resources. The long and short of all this was that Daisy couldn't even dream of proposals from doctors or engineers because her parents couldn't afford them.

It was in the midst of these gloomy thoughts that Daisy recalled that Vivek Tharakan was posted in her Surgery Unit. *The nutcase with the goldfish bowl* – was how she used to think of him. But in the current circumstances, her perspective shifted. VT was a good-looking guy from a respectable Christian family, and a final year postgrad. Suddenly, being one of his goldfish seemed like a golden opportunity, for in a love marriage, the groom's family did not demand much dowry.

But was being ranked fifth among the goldfish enough? Was there a way to eliminate the competition? She found it difficult to get close to VT. He was friendly but extremely busy and focused on academics. One day, the opportunity came; Daisy found him in the side-room scribbling notes from patient files. He told her it was for his thesis, but tabulating the data of so many patients was boring him to tears. Daisy offered to do it for him.

"But why?" he asked, astounded. "It's the laboratory data of five hundred patients, a herculean task."

She gave an innocent smile. "It's just to familiarize myself with the manner of research."

"Really? I didn't know you were so interested in research."

Even I didn't know till now, mister. She hoped he wouldn't cotton to the elaborate web she was spinning.

A week later, the painstaking tabulation was done. It was literally a labour of love.

"Wow, Daisy, thanks! Let me at least take you out to dinner. I'll come to the HSQ by seven, okay?"

Daisy was beyond ecstatic. She picked out a black silk *salwar kameez* that had a slimming effect on her chubby frame, matched the outfit with an intense blue, mirror-worked dupatta and black metal chandelier earrings. She blow-dried her curls to frame her round face, inspected her *kajal* and maroon lipstick in the mirror, and slipped into platform heels with matching blue straps.

Zara did a double-take when they met on the staircase. "Wowee! Where are you off to looking like that?"

"A treat."

"With whom – Salman Khan?"

"For you, it's *always* Salman Khan. There are better guys, you know."

"Okay, then tell me who."

"Someone you don't give a shit about."

Zara laughed. "That covers almost all the guys on campus." She mimicked the *tut-tut-tut* of a machine gun. "If looks could kill, you'd make a great assassin." Daisy ignored her.

VT was waiting at the HSQ gates in his Maruti 800. He looked nice in a pale green T-shirt and stonewashed jeans. Getting into the passenger seat, Daisy was nearly knocked out by the strong scent of aftershave. They drove to New Pops restaurant, a favourite haunt of medical students. Luckily, there was no one there that Daisy knew.

VT seemed a bit tongue-tied, so Daisy chattered away on the one topic she was an authority on – campus gossip. He listened politely, looking rather bored, until she told of her disappointment in not getting a Psychiatry posting.

"You know, Daisy, I initially joined Psychiatry, but my parents were appalled their son had chosen to be a *brandhanmarude* doctor. They forced me to change during the second round of counselling. I'm okay with Surgery, but Psychiatry is still my first love."

From then on VT was unstoppable. "Did you know Freud was the person who revolutionized dentistry?"

"Dentistry?" All that Daisy had learned from Freud was how to interpret the advances of the opposite sex.

"Yes! Freud discovered the anaesthetic properties of cocaine and found out that drugs like lignocaine are chicane compounds. He dosed his patients liberally with cocaine, and the disappearance of their symptoms made him think it was a cure. All his patients developed withdrawal symptoms or became addicts. So today, if we *smile* while our teeth are being drilled, it's thanks to him."

Daisy toyed with the fork on her plate. "I've never had to visit a dentist to date. My elder sister wasn't so lucky."

"Never been to a dentist?" VT asked, surprised, "A good part of my childhood was spent in the dentist's chair." From then on Daisy had the distinct feeling that VT paid extra attention to her pearly whites.

When they left the restaurant at nine, Daisy was nowhere near executing her original plan. They drove up to the HSQ in silence. When he said *Goodnight*, she gathered her courage and blurted out, "I think I'm in love with you."

VT was speechless with surprise. Not getting a reply, Daisy said nervously, "Can I kiss you on the cheek?"

His whole face turned red, but he leaned over, and she pecked his cheek. Then Daisy got out of the car and raced upstairs to her room. Zara was not around, much to her relief.

What were you thinking, she chided herself. It was the most impulsive and stupid thing she'd ever done. Feeling ashamed of her recklessness, she spent a sleepless night worrying about how to face VT the following day. Thankfully, they had Major OT, and he was busy.

The day after, Daisy avoided him in the wards as much as she could. Around noon, he came up to her. "Hey Daisy, join me for lunch?" She walked beside him in a trance all the way to the Coffee House. They ate quietly until, without any warning, VT blurted out, "Why don't we get married?"

Daisy choked on her food and had a coughing fit.

"Sorry," he said, looking sheepish. "That night at the restaurant, I was totally stunned that a girl could propose to a guy. It's quite unorthodox, isn't it? I've always imagined doing the proposing."

Daisy secretly pinched her inner arm. *Ouch!* She wasn't dreaming! "So, are we a 'line' now?"

VT shook his head solemnly. "No 'line-wine' business. I'll ask my parents to meet yours, and they can fix our engagement date."

In everyone's eyes, it was the most natural thing to happen – a postgraduate proposing to a desirable house-surgeon posted in his unit. Nobody, not even Daisy's closest friends, ever came to know that *she* had proposed to VT, the goldfish bowl guy.

It was the one secret that the 'BBC of the '96 batch' kept to herself!

***

On 20 April 2002, the batch of 1996 celebrated their convocation; the culmination of six years that had been a mad jumble of gruelling exams, endless academics, batch programmes, hostel life, broken hearts and lasting friendships.

Only two months of house-surgency remained after which they would disperse in different directions, perhaps meeting again for an occasional reunion, perhaps not. There was much banter and laughter as the young doctors, dressed in their finest, gathered outside the college building for a batch photograph. At 5 p.m., they donned flowing black graduation robes and caps and, preceded by the Chief Guest and other faculty members, walked down in two rows to the front of the stage that was erected erected in the college garden to seat themselves on the marked chairs. There were several speeches and toasts followed by the Hippocratic Oath recital and the scroll ceremony. Pappachen was so overwhelmed to see Zara accepting her scroll from the Chief Guest that he burst into tears. Vaibhav's family had also come, but Zara ignored him completely, even refusing to point him out when asked, much to her mother's delight.

Sunny was their best outgoing student and received a special award. Later in the evening, Sheetal and Sunny introduced their parents to each other, leading to awkwardness on both sides.

Kenza was by herself as Jayachandran hadn't been able to fly down from Abu Dhabi. She hung around Waheeda until the end of the scroll ceremony, when families gathered together for photographs. She then switched to sticking with the few Northies (Tarachand included) who had no family members attending.

Mala's entire extended family had come for the convocation. Her father, brothers, aunts, uncles and cousins had pride writ large on their faces. Madhu Mohan was polite enough to stay for introductions, but evaded Mala later.

The trio of King-Kong Kamaraj, James and Charles also participated in the convocation.

Arundhati did not attend.

During the dinner buffet afterwards, Zara and Pappachen bumped into Charles at the *vellappam* counter. "I still remember you as a small boy riding on your grandfather's shoulders," Pappachen reminisced, misty-eyed, "You look a bit like him too, especially the ears!"

Charles was at his charming best, impressing Pappachen with his Bible quotes. After he left, Pappachen said, "Such a nice, well-mannered boy, don't you think?"

Zara quickly lied that he had a girlfriend.

Many families left soon after dinner, not waiting for the cultural programme that started at nine. Daisy tried her best to convince her fiancé's parents to leave along with hers, but when they didn't, she panicked and pulled VT aside.

"What!" VT's eyes bulged on hearing that Daisy was participating in a mock striptease group dance. "How could you decide something like that without asking me first? I absolutely forbid it!"

"It was Zara's idea, *Achachan,* but I can't back out at the last moment. Besides, it isn't a *real* striptease… we just throw off our hats, jackets and ties. That's it."

"You're still undressing in public, aren't you? It seems this Zara is a bad influence on you!"

VT breathed fire, but seeing Daisy close to tears, he packed his protesting parents back to their hotel room.

As she swayed onstage to *Yeh Raat*, the slow seductive number from the movie *Aks*, and the partly inebriated crowd showered them with hoots and catcalls, Daisy saw VT's face pass through several deepening shades of red. For the moment, however, she cast aside the gnawing feeling that this episode was a prelude to her future after marriage.

The event wound up around four in the morning. Only those who didn't have to report early for duty remained, and the small group ambled sleepily back to the HSQ.

"Joined anywhere for postgrad entrance coaching yet? Decided what you want to specialize in?" asked Charles as he walked alongside Zara.

She yawned and shrugged. "After one year of rotating through all the departments, I've decided I don't like anything."

Charles laughed heartily. “Spoken like a true scopegoat!”

They reached the staircase leading to the girls’ floor and stopped. “Well, Scopegoat, I think this is where we say goodbye. See you again, someday, somewhere. Try not to miss me too much till then, okay.”

Giving her a wink, Charles walked off down the HSQ corridor whistling loudly.

Zara climbed the stairs, thinking, *Try not to miss him too much?* She was quite certain he was the last person she wanted to see again.

14. Zara, 2016

25th March, 2016
Kochi

Finding the Nrityakala Academy for Bharatanatyam at Kadavanthra, Kochi, wasn't difficult at all. It was just half an hour from the railway station, and every auto driver knew where it was. What *was* difficult to nearly impossible was accepting that the exotic creature who stepped into the reception of the renovated old house to greet me was the same Nayana I'd once known in college.

"Zara, Zara, Zara!"

Nayana enveloped me in a tight embrace, then ran a manicured hand through her tumbling mane of reddish-brown hennaed hair. She wore a pristine white chikankari kurta-pyjama, a double-layered feroza and pearl necklace, dramatic eye makeup, bright red lipstick, and an assortment of nose rings and ear piercings. The soft strains of classical music playing through the overhead speakers and the sweet smell of incense heightened the almost mystical aura around her. "I was wondering when you'd come… in fact I was hoping and praying you would…"

"Glad to see you too, Nayana."

"Shush! Shush!" She flapped her hands at me. "It's Devangana, Devangana Priyadarshini. But you can call me Devu."

I nodded. "Sorry."

It was still hard to wrap my head around this new Nayana. Was she genuine or just playing a part? Mohini had warned me what to expect when she'd called me in January. I'd been in the thick of work then, juggling a packed schedule, relentless video calls from Charles, and threatening texts from Vivian if I dared to miss his son's baptism. When Mohini's name popped up, I'd sighed in relief, thinking it would be a lazy chat and some good gossip.

"Arre Zara, I didn't call to chit chat. There's some unbelievable news you need to hear!"

"Okay, tell me."

"I've told you before how my husband is obsessed with crazy

artsy stuff, right? Anyway, he decided we would spend our wedding anniversary (just the two of us) at Bolgatty Palace and visit the Muziris Biennale. I think you know what that is?"

I said I'd heard of it.

"So I'm tagging along behind him, and we visit David Hall in Fort Kochi, where a Bharatanatyam dancer is giving an interview about her dance installation. At first, I wasn't listening, but then she said something about the influence of Kathakali in her childhood and renouncing a career in medicine for dance. And suddenly I thought, could this be Nayana? And you know what, it *was* her!"

"WHAT!" I nearly dropped my phone.

"Yes! At the end of the interview, I went up to her. She looked so different I couldn't be sure at all, but the moment I asked, her whole body language changed. I *knew* it was her."

"Did she recognize you?"

Mohini giggled. "Not even my parents can at the moment! I'm into my third trimester and totally oedematous. When I told her who I was, she became all emotional. My God, Zara, can you believe it? Running into Nayana after not having a clue about her for 20 years!"

I'd gone silent then. So, Nayana was in Kochi. Had she been there all these years or only moved recently? That one time I'd phoned her, she was in Thodupuzha. Had they moved around a lot after that?

But Mohini had already answered that question. "Nayana seemed genuinely interested in hearing about my life, but she just nodded vacantly when I mentioned other batchmates. And when we said goodbye, she remarked how overjoyed she was we'd met, even though she preferred to keep the past in the past."

"*Mathlab*?"

"I presume she doesn't want to reconnect with anyone. She didn't even ask for my mobile number. When I asked for hers, she gave me the brochure of her dance school with the office number." She paused. "If you want, I can send you photos of the brochure."

After we'd hung up, I went through the pictures of Nrityakala Academy for Bharatanatyam, founded by Dr Devangana

Priyadarshini, who posed elegantly on the front page in a rust and peacock-blue costume, exquisite jewellery and heavy makeup.

'Yes, that's Nayana's name now!' read Mohini's message below the images.

Devangana Priyadarshini.

The name struck a familiar chord.

Where had I heard it before?

It swirled in my mind until one day, while clearing out my mobile gallery, I came across the photos and videos I'd saved from Onam 2015, organized by the LIKA (Liverpool Keralites Association). And then it clicked. Devangana Priyadarshini had been one of the names in the artist lineup.

I quickly scrolled through the videos and found the one with Chenda Melam. The camera zoomed to a troupe of dancers on stage, and there she was! Nayana Krishnakumar! Completely transformed in her Bharatanatyam attire.

It was surreal. We'd been in the same hall, so close, and hadn't known it! Or… had she known and chosen not to acknowledge me, just as she'd done years ago on the phone?

That's when I booked my tickets to Kerala. I let Vivian know I'd be coming for the baptism.

***

The Nrityakala Academy was a two-storeyed old house painted in bright colours. The reception walls were crowded with framed photographs of Nayana receiving awards and posing with celebrities. She led me around, animatedly explaining how she'd founded the school.

"Now that the annual school vacation has started, the number of students is higher," she explained. "We also have adult students; most of them come in the early morning or late evening."

An attendant brought us tea, and Nayana led me into a small garden beside the house. We sat in lacquered wicker chairs under a mango tree, its leaves rustling in the breeze.

"You know," I said, "I was at the Fernsby Leisure Centre in Liverpool last September. I saw your performance. I only realized it was you when I saw your name in the school brochure."

"Is this actually true?" She clasped her hands in surprise. "Oh, what a loss we couldn't meet up then!"

"And your dance, I've never seen Bharatanatyam that is so contemporary, so modern. You were simply brilliant."

"Thank you, sweetie," she beamed.

"But why Bharatanatyam? You used to say you wanted to be a Kathakali artist like your father."

Her smile dimmed, and she changed the subject. "Tell me about yourself – are you working in Liverpool? Do you have a family?"

"Not in Liverpool; I'd just come for the show that day. I'm a Paediatrician in Bolton. And I'm still single."

"Oh, a lonesome rose like me!" she gasped. "Come here, sweetie, we need to hug." She opened her arms wide.

I hesitated, then set down my teacup and clasped my hands together. "When Mohini urged me to visit you, I was in two minds. Especially after our last phone conversation… when you told me never to contact you again. But I decided you owe me an explanation."

Her smile faded; her shoulders drooped. She sat back in her chair, expressionless. "What do you want me to explain?"

"Everything. What happened after you fell off the hostel roof? Your disappearance. Why did you cut me off after I tried so hard to find you? Honestly, there's not a day I don't think about what happened to my best friend."

Her eyebrows shot up. "Best friend?" She threw her head back and laughed, loud and theatrical.

"What's so funny?"

She straightened and tossed her hair. "I hate digging into the past. Let's end this conversation."

"No, let's not."

Our eyes locked in silence until she broke it. "Were you ever my best friend, Zara? You knew that stupid boy, Vaibhav, was after me, didn't you? You knew he kept calling me at the hostel, pressuring me to be his 'line' because of some stupid bet. But you kept quiet because you were besotted with him. Even when he humiliated me publicly, you made excuses for him. And Daisy – she said I was a psychiatric patient because she saw my OP ticket. But you never stopped her. And Sheetal, you knew how horrible she was to me, but you ignored it because you didn't want to lose either of us. It didn't matter to you whether your 'best friends' clashed, as long as your world stayed untouched."

She paused for breath and then laughed again. "*Eeshwara*, I'm ranting like a bloody teenager!"

I sat there, stunned. "Wow. For someone who's trying to forget the past, you really remember a lot of it."

She shrugged. "We never forget those who hung us out to dry, do we?" She ran a hand through her curls. "I suppose Sheetal told you how she discovered my secrets through my diary?"

I nearly gasped, but caught myself and lied quickly, "Er, yes, she did."

All this time, I'd believed only Kenza and I knew about Nayana's past. Sheetal had *never* hinted she did too. The fire in Nayana's eyes gave way to sorrow.

"What a shock it was for my sixteen-year-old self to realize I couldn't be my parents' biological child," she began, forming dance poses with each word, "An inadvertent discovery during a class on Mendelian genetics! I asked if an A-positive father and an O-positive mother could have a B-Positive child. The teacher said it was impossible."

I was spellbound. She narrated her story like a performance, emoting every word with grace and pain.

"Frightened. Confused. Depressed. The demons were born. They whispered constantly… of my parents' disproportionate affection for their younger daughter; the one who looked like them, their real daughter. I had breakdowns, I started sleepwalking," her expression turned defiant, "yet I refused to believe… There had to be another explanation. I bottled up my demons and channelled my efforts into fulfilling my parents' dreams. Thinking they might love me more if I became a doctor as they wished."

I watched breathlessly, bewitched by Nayana's emoting, which was as arresting, as powerful and as exquisite as her performance had been at Liverpool. I was now the sole audience to a very private storytelling, the painful climax of which was already known to me.

Nayana's face was grief-stricken. "But the demons soon returned. I took to scribbling my woes in a diary. I built a mental wall around my doubts. But one ill-fated day, it became clear to me that Sheetal knew my secrets, my demons."

"She confessed that she knew?"

Nayana stared at me and then smirked. "I see that Sheetal conveniently left *that* part of the story out." She sat down again. "Sheetal was furious with me because I'd unwittingly revealed her rare blood group to our senior (some bossy girl, I can't remember her name). At the blood bank, Sheetal asked this senior girl a question about the very same combination of blood groups between a child and its parents, and she looked straight at me. Then I knew that she knew. I guessed she'd gone through my diary because there was no other way for her to have known. The shock of having it thrown in my face by someone I detested was too much to bear."

"And you sleepwalked off the roof," I whispered. "What happened afterwards?"

"The afterwards is all a big blur now." Nayana got up and started her slow dance again. "Of fury and sadness and smashed plates and swear words; of changing homes frequently to avoid attention from the neighbours; rage against the parents who refused to reveal my background; insane jealousy of the sister; lots and lots of pills; sleep, sweet sleep…" Nayana made a pillow with her hands and put her head on it. "I wished to sleep forever and ever, but I woke up eventually, changed, as a jigsaw puzzle pieced together incorrectly to form a new picture with gaps and ragged edges. Nayana disappeared forever. It was around that time you called asking for her."

I felt a lump in my throat. "So, you were Devangana by then."

"I had to fight for that, too. The parents refused to accept my new identity or my decision to be a dancer. All they cared about was me going back to medical college as soon as I was on my feet!" Laughing scornfully, she broke into a frenzied dance, moving so rapidly that I felt dizzy. "You see, dance helped me to recover, it gave me a purpose."

"But why Bharatanatyam and not Kathakali?"

She stopped with a twirl. "I'd already trained in Bharatanatyam in school. And Kathakali is the father's passion, Devangana doesn't aim to please him."

"But they did treat you like their own daughter, didn't they? They gave you everything."

"No, not everything!" Nayana cut in, her eyes blazing. "They withheld the one thing that I deserved most from them – honesty. It's what you denied me, too."

I felt my face flush.

She sighed, sat down, and closed her eyes. "Thinking back, our hostel room was toxic. I should've moved out, but I dreaded the gossip. Inaction has consequences, Zara. I nearly paid with my life. But I learnt. When my parents pressured me to go back to medicine, I fought for *my* life."

"Did they ever tell you how they adopted you?"

She nodded slowly. "Nothing dramatic. They adopted me from an orphanage in Madras when they thought the mother couldn't conceive. Later, the sister came along unexpectedly. They feared the truth would ruin our bond. So they chose silence."

We fell quiet.

A small black bug crawled over the teapot. A leaf floated into my empty teacup. Music drifted from the house, and I heard Nayana hum along softly. I wanted to stand up and say something—anything, but I stayed seated. Around us, the rustle of the mango leaves had softened. A stillness settled, the kind that comes not from peace but from exhaustion.

Nayana was humming, her eyes were closed, her face composed, as if the long and winding monologue hadn't peeled off old wounds and laid them bare in the sunlight.

I didn't know what to say. Part of me wanted to reach out, to apologize—not just for what I did or didn't do, but for not knowing better, not being better. And yet, another part bristled at the coldness in her words, the way she spoke as if I were only a bystander in the past and not a participant.

Now, I understood why she'd vanished. Why she'd built a

fortress around herself with anklets and eyeliner, swirling in rhythm and silence. She didn't need our version of the truth anymore. She had crafted her own. She was now Devangana – daughter of the Gods.

We were all a bit immature during our college years. I knew that. And maybe some of us, me included, were a little self-centred too. Still, I never hurt anyone on purpose. I looked at Nayana—Devangana now and said as gently as I could, "Would you accept my apology now?"

There was a moment of silence. Then she cackled, full of mockery and bitterness.

"You came looking for me, thinking I owed you an explanation for the past. But now you realize the past actually caught up with you! The past always catches up with everyone one way or another, doesn't it?" She laughed again, sharp and triumphant. "But what good is your apology, sweetie? Devangana Priyadarshini has no use for it. You're looking for Nayana Krishnakumar, but she died a long time ago. Your regret has come too late. This is what I told Vaibhav as well."

I blinked, caught off guard. "Who?"

"Vaibhav Reghuthaman. We met once, several years ago. He was the first one to offer an apology to a non-existent Nayana."

***

The train ride back to Kottayam was a blur of rain and wind, but I noticed none of it. Torrential rain battered the windows, coconut trees bent under the force of the wind, and paddy fields looked like waves of green under siege. But all I could see was Nayana-Devangana, and everything she'd said.

And suddenly, Vaibhav's cryptic public apology on Facebook made sense.

"It was pure coincidence," she had said. "I was attending a marriage function with my parents, and there he was, sitting in the row across. He looked just the same as I remembered, and I must have as well, for he recognized me and came over. He tried to make small talk; he said he was doing postgraduation somewhere and was engaged to be married. I kept quiet mostly. Then, out of the blue, he said how sorry he was for who he'd been during his undergrad days and for how he treated me. His face fell when I told him I was Devangana, and he was too late to apologize to Nayana."

I'd later scrolled down his post, reading that line over and over again:

'... But for many years, I was a coward. It's only now, close to my forties, that I've found the courage to do the right thing ...'

It seemed clear now – he'd realized too late that the girl he'd wronged was beyond apology. Guilt had gnawed at him long enough to drive him into that public confession. The past had caught up with Vaibhav.

But had it caught up with me, too?

Surely, I hadn't been as selfish as she had made me out to be? Surely her memory was coloured by her own pain?

But the memories stirred inside me, refusing to be soothed. I remembered sitting in the back row, laughing with Vaibhav, fully aware that his eyes were trained on Nayana in the front. I remembered the hot satisfaction I'd felt whenever she fumed after another prank call from the Men's Hostel. And yes, I remembered thinking – quietly, guiltily – that if Vaibhav ever accepted her rejection, maybe he'd turn to me.

As for Sheetal and Daisy, was it really my fault Nayana hadn't gotten along with them?

But then, other fragments surfaced. I saw Daisy's conspiratorial whispers spreading Mala's secrets around the hostel like wildfire. I saw Sheetal flinging accusations at Mala, her voice shrill with suspicion. Sheetal's paintings with the doors. She was always the last to sleep. Did she bolt the terrace door behind Nayana the night she fell? I couldn't bring myself to ask her.

Nayana had accused me of dishonesty, of not taking a stand. And maybe she was right.

If I had intervened back then, would it have changed anything?

Probably not. But I would've been the friend I always claimed to be.

Instead, I'd watched things fall apart from a safe distance, always hoping things would fix themselves without my interference. I hated conflict. I always waited for things to settle on their own, just so I could stay on good terms with everyone.

At least, that's what I'd told myself.

I opened my phone and stared at the photos Mohini had sent me – the dance school brochure, the cover photo of a woman in full Bharatanatyam costume. That woman. That stranger.

For 20 years, I'd wondered what had become of Nayana. But I'd only seen her through the rose-tinted memories of college camaraderie. I'd never seen her pain, her isolation, her transformation.

Now I knew. I hadn't lost her now. I'd lost her long ago – back in those hostel rooms and lecture halls when I'd chosen silence.

I sighed and leaned back. Then, with a quiet sense of finality, I selected all the photos of her dance school and deleted them.

It was around 9:30 p.m. when the autorickshaw dropped me off at my parents' house in Kottayam. They were early sleepers, so I let myself in with the spare key and crept upstairs.

I changed into my pyjamas, sat cross-legged on the bed and opened up my laptop.

To: Sheetal

Subject: Nothing Urgent

I stared at the blinking cursor. Then started.

Hey,

It's been raining in Kottayam. You'd like it here – low skies, howling wind, that scent of wet jasmine after dusk.

I met someone today. Someone I hadn't seen since medical college.

She said I betrayed her.

Maybe she's right. Maybe that's the thing about our twenties, we're all so desperate to belong, we abandon the ones who make us uncomfortable.

Sheetal, I know the answer, but I need to ask you this...

I stopped. Deleted the last line. Closed the email without sending.

Sheetal didn't need this.

I didn't need this.

And yet, the words lingered, heavy like unshed rain.

A minute later, my phone buzzed in my tote. Unknown number.

Probably another telemarketer, I thought.

"Hello, is this Zara Ann Mathew?"

A woman's voice.

"Yeah. Who's this?"

"It's Keerthi Susan Jose from the '99 batch. I'm sure you remember me."

My fingers froze around the phone. The tote slipped off my bed and hit the floor.

"Hi Keerthi," I said slowly. "How did you get my number?"

"From my husband's phone, unfortunately." Her voice was tightly controlled, but the edge was unmistakable.

There was a long pause before she said, "Listen, we need to talk."

I sank onto the bed, phone still pressed to my ear.

The past wasn't done with me yet.

15. Zara, 2016

18th August, 2016
Bolton

At 11 that morning, I was vacuuming the house and so almost missed the doorbell. I turned off the machine just in time to see the delivery boy standing there, holding a bouquet of red roses. For a moment, I thought he'd got the wrong house. But no – the flowers were for me. Nestled among them was a card that said, 'Happy Birthday, my Z-weetheart! I'll be at The Four Hounds at 3 p.m. as planned.'

I arranged the roses in the chipped vase I'd picked up at a Bolton charity shop, my mind whirring. Flowers – and not just any flowers, these were *red* roses. It was so unlike him. I had no idea how to interpret this gesture.

The rest of the day passed in a blur, and by quarter to three, I found myself seated at my favourite pub. I was scrolling through my Facebook page, flooded with birthday wishes, sending out obligatory heart emojis.

Then I saw it.

Vaibhav.

He had liked my post. And wished me. The same Vaibhav who had ghosted me since the house-surgency. The same Vaibhav who once weaponized silence with the precision of a neurosurgeon.

I scrolled back to the post I thought might have triggered this return-from-the-dead moment. It was the one I'd written on a late night of moral clarity.

People hurt other people. It's inevitable. Sometimes it's unintentional. People can wound others out of sheer ignorance. But once you realize your mistake, what's the next step? I think the answer is obvious – you apologize.

Like my batchmate did a few months ago. An open apology to all the girls he'd tormented inside and outside the college.

This was the boy who once said of a raped and pregnant twenty-

year-old girl who died of sepsis in our labour room, 'Aanungalodu kalichaal ingane irikkum' (This is what happens to females who think they can mess with men).' The boys around him had laughed.

All the while, my only thought was that these boys would one day be treating patients, many of whom would be women.

It's been close to six months since that apology went up on Facebook, and my batchmate still hasn't taken it down, despite the brickbats. Two of the boys who laughed back then even dropped by in the comments section with weak jokes. I guess it's too much to hope that every boy would change.

But I'm glad my batchmate has. A genuine apology is the first step towards healing – for both sides.

Over a thousand Likes. One of them, his.

So, it *had* struck a chord with him.

I had written it on a whim, in a reflective mood. If his apology was sincere, maybe it deserved acknowledgement. Not that I *had* to respond – but I didn't want to keep sitting on the fence anymore.

Daisy's birthday wish was just above my post. I noticed, mildly surprised, that she had reverted to her maiden name. I wondered what had prompted that sudden burst of self-assertion. Her message made me chuckle: *'Happy birthday Zara kutty! May you find The Prince and become his Princess.'* Trust Daisy to sneak in a matchmaking jab even during casual conversations. She was still hot on the trail of 'The Prince' and showed no signs of giving up.

That was one secret I wasn't planning to divulge to anyone – especially not now, when it seemed Charles and Keerthi had seemingly patched things up.

That was a rabbit hole I should've avoided. I tapped over to Charles' Facebook page. His new cover photo showed him, Keerthi, and the kids, all grinning in front of a water theme park – the perfect family portrait. I clicked on Keerthi's name; her cover picture was the same.

I thought back to that night, months ago, at my parents' home, when Keerthi had unleashed her fury on me – a litany of cuss words in Malayalam I hadn't even known existed, followed by tears and sobs. I had listened in silence because I deserved it. In the end,

I apologized and promised never to contact Charles again. And I kept my word.

Charles hadn't contacted me either after Keerthi's meltdown. Sometimes I wondered what had happened between them afterwards — had Keerthi threatened to leave him? Had their families been dragged into it, with accusations flying back and forth? I had no way of knowing. I imagined the worst.

Weeks later, they began posting couple photos. Little displays of unity. It was comical in a way, but also clear that they were trying to fix their marriage. By the time I flew back to the UK and rejoined my hospital in Bolton, I realized just how much I missed Charles. His texts and late-night calls had been the highlight of my hectic days. Yet, part of me was relieved it hadn't ended in a bigger disaster.

Sometimes, late at night, I would ask myself – if Charles had left Keerthi for me, would I have agreed to be with him? Deep down, I knew the answer. I valued my freedom too much to be tied down to domesticity. Maybe part of Charles' appeal had been the *impossibility* of him – the knowledge that he wouldn't always be completely available. Maybe, deep down, I wasn't looking for security at all. Maybe it was the thrill of spontaneity. The promise of adventure.

So yes, Bolton was back to being Bolton. Grey skies. Grey mood. NHS cafeteria food with the consistency of a damp towel.

Then out of the blue, my phone buzzed.

"Hi Z-weetheart! How are you? Have I got some great news for you!"

"Let me guess," I said, yawning. "You found a new girlfriend during your Kenyan safari."

"Arre yaar, that safari was last year! After that, I toured the Andamans, remember? I sent you pics."

"Ah, yes," I laughed. "You send me so many pictures that I mix up your timelines. So, what's the great news?"

"I'm in Manchester."

"What? Like... right now?"

He laughed. "Yes! Landed five days ago. Joined a college here for a course in film editing."

"Film editing? But aren't you a chef?"

"Yes! But now I want to shoot food. Not just eat it."

Of course he did.

He reminded me of one of those TED Talks where someone reinvents themselves every six months to keep from imploding. But that was Rishab Manchandani. Restless, spontaneous, and dangerously charming.

"Two decades since school and we're both in the UK," he said. "What are the odds?"

"Yeah," I said softly. "Who would have guessed?"

At 3 p.m., Rishab walked into *The Four Hounds* like he owned it. Like he was expecting a standing ovation. Maybe a slow clap. Definitely eye contact.

In the back of my mind, I could hear Mama's voice – like a Nokia ringtone that had somehow survived every software update since 1996.

Orthodox. Syrian Christian. Ancient Family.

Each word enunciated like a courtroom verdict. It came layered with judgement and the faint rustle of a starched cotton sari.

And there he was. Rishab. Time had barely touched him. A few strategic grey hairs, salt and pepper stubble that probably wasn't intentional, and that same grin. The one that made you feel seen. And slightly manipulated.

I hated how familiar it all felt. Like muscle memory. Like an old injury that only flares up in the rain. Now that he was settled at the University, we were back to *ghoomna-phirna* on weekends. We'd gone hiking around Manchester the week before last. This weekend, I planned to show him around Bolton.

"Happy birthday, Zeeeeeeeeee," he announced, dropping his rucksack with a theatrical thud, like he'd just returned from war. He folded me into one of those hugs that made it hard to breathe and kissed my cheek.

"Did you get the flowers?" he asked, like he was checking off an item on a very specific to-do list.

"I did. Thank you. I'm... honestly surprised you remembered."

He gave me a look – part eye-roll, part mock-offence. "Seriously?

I'm surprised you forgot that I've never forgotten. Like, ever. I have a flawless birthday memory. It's my only superpower."

I blinked. He wasn't wrong. And somehow, that made it worse.

"I realized something recently – I've been to a lot of places ... met a lot of people ... faces come and go. But, truthfully, if there's one person I can never forget, it's you, Zee. You are home to me," Rishab said softly. "Because you're just another version of me. Don't you know that by now?"

He reached over and held my hand, and we sat in silence looking at each other.

It was a moment of pure epiphany – if there was anyone truly like me in this world, it *was* him.

And, somehow, I felt like I was finally at home.